DARK GUARDIAN CRAVED

THE CHILDREN OF THE GODS BOOK 12

I. T. LUCAS

THE CHILDREN OF THE GODS

TRY THE SERIES ON

AUDIBLE

2 FREE audiobooks with your new Audible subscription!

CHAPTER 1: WILLIAM

*A*s he scrolled through the day's mediocre gaming results, William lifted his glasses over his head and pinched his eyebrows between two fingers. Admitting failure was difficult, but to keep hoping for a pleasant surprise every time he opened the portal was irrational. The idea that had seemed so promising was good for producing profits but not for discovering Dormants.

At first he thought he'd made the game too difficult, but he was starting to realize that precognition, the only thing his game was designed to test, was just too rare of a talent.

With a sigh, William powered down his desktop. It was after midnight, and staring at the screen wasn't going to change the numbers. It was time to call it a day.

The sound of a phone ringing in his quiet apartment startled him. Who could be calling now? It wasn't as if people had tech emergencies that couldn't wait for normal business hours. Unless it was Kian. On occasion, when the guy was on the phone with someone in a different time zone, a tech question would come up.

But when William looked at the screen, it was Anandur's smiling face that stared back at him and not Kian's.

"Is everything all right?"

"Could you do me a favor and come stay with Fernando tonight? Nathalie's water just broke, and Andrew took her to Bridget's. I can't stay, and Bhathian will want to be with his daughter."

"Sure. I'll be there in a couple of minutes." William disconnected the call.

What exciting news.

With most of the clan's expectant mothers traveling to Annani's retreat to deliver their babies, Nathalie and Andrew's would be the first baby born in the keep.

Laptop tucked under his arm, William headed out and almost tripped over the wires strewn over the living room floor. Carefully, he maneuvered around them to reach the door. One of these days he'd have to organize his equipment better so he could vacuum the floor. The dust bunnies coating the wires were getting bigger by the day.

When he got to Andrew and Nathalie's place, Anandur was waiting for him with the door open. "Thanks, man. I really appreciate it." He clapped William on the shoulder and headed out. "I'm late for my rounds."

"No problem." William didn't mind helping out with the old man. Fernando was good company. Loony at times, but that was entertaining as well. Certainly beat spending entire days alone.

Making himself comfortable on the couch, William flipped open his laptop. But he wasn't in the mood for looking over more uninspiring reports.

Instead, he leaned his back against the couch's soft pillows and closed his eyes. Nathalie's mother was probably on her way as well. They would need to be careful about keeping Fernando from bumping into her in the morning.

To see his ex-wife after so long, looking even younger than when he'd met her over thirty years ago, would freak him out. Dementia made Fernando forget many things, but not Eva. He still talked about her as if they were together.

Fascinating story. Statistically, Eva's activation by an unknown immortal was impossible. As was the probability of there being unknown immortals at all. If only there were a way to find them.

But if there was, he couldn't think of one. Embarrassing for a guy who was supposed to be a genius and have a solution for every problem.

With a shrug, William picked up one of the throw pillows and put it on his thighs, then put the laptop on top of it. Better ergonomics. Navigating to one of his favorite news apps, he started scrolling through the articles in search of something new and interesting to read.

One piece caught his attention. It was about a new information-sharing agreement the US was trying to broker with other countries. Specifically their facial recognition databases.

If that happened, it could prove problematic. Clan members' fake documents had to be redone every fifteen years or so. If countries started running passports through facial recognition software and looking for matching pictures on documents belonging to different people, it would make travel abroad complicated. After all, if Mr. John Doe's picture from twenty years ago looked exactly like Mr. John Smith's picture today, someone would start asking questions.

Wait a minute, how the hell didn't I think of it?

If Andrew could get him access to that database, William could run it through his own facial recognition program and look for those alleged immortals.

I should start working on it right away.

3

Snapping his laptop closed, William tucked it under his arm and got up. Only when he was at the door, he remembered why he was there.

Damn.

With a sigh, he went back to the couch. There wasn't much he could accomplish with the help of his laptop, for that he needed the heavy lifting equipment in his lab, but he could start organizing his thoughts.

CHAPTER 2: EVA

*E*va put her hand on Bhathian's thigh, taking comfort in the connection as her feelings kept swinging between excitement and apprehension.

This late at night the roads were practically deserted, which was good since he was driving as if his heavy sport-utility vehicle was a race car, speeding and taking sharp turns —screeching tires and all. The way his powerful hands were gripping the steering wheel, it was a wonder the thing hadn't disintegrated under the pressure.

"Slow down, Bhathian, we don't want to get into an accident."

"We won't. My reflexes are fast enough to avoid collision."

"There is no reason to hurry. This is Nathalie's first delivery, and it's not going to happen for a while. We have hours of waiting ahead of us."

Bhathian lifted his foot off the accelerator an infinitesimal fraction. "I worry about her. The baby is big."

Eva patted his shoulder. "Nathalie was big too, eight and a half pounds, and her birth wasn't particularly difficult."

He cast her a sidelong glance. "You were an immortal

when you had her. Your body would've fixed any internal bleeding and whatever other possible complications that could've happened before any of the doctors or nurses became aware of them. Nathalie is still a human."

He was right. As her gut did the flip and sink thing, Eva ran a shaky hand through her hair.

No, he wasn't right.

She shouldn't let Bhathian stress her out like that. He was overreacting. Women gave birth to big babies every day, and most of them survived. Especially in a well-equipped hospital with a well-trained staff assisting in the delivery.

Crossing her arms over her chest, Eva turned to Bhathian. "I don't like it that your in-house doctor is taking care of Nathalie. If you're really that concerned about your daughter, you should insist that she be moved to a hospital with a proper labor and delivery department."

Bhathian nodded. "Nathalie is human, and she should be in a human hospital. Bridget is a good doctor, but her experience is mostly with immortals." Finally slowing down, he turned into the entrance of the parking garage. A few moments later they stood in front of the bank of elevators. He pressed the down button.

"The clinic is in the basement?" Eva asked.

"Not exactly. I wouldn't call the underground complex a basement. It's several stories deep and sprawls under several buildings."

"For safety?"

"Yes. There are exit and entry points in several of the neighboring buildings."

As the elevator doors opened at the clinic's level, the sound of multiple voices indicated that they were not the first to arrive. "Who else is down here?"

He shrugged. "Probably half the immortal population of the keep. Everyone loves Nathalie."

The hallway outside the clinic was teeming with immortals. Some were standing and talking, while others were sitting on the carpeted floor and leaning against the concrete-block walls.

Clasping her hand as he strode briskly through the crowd, Bhathian only nodded in greeting to the people as they moved aside to let Eva and him pass.

He knocked on the clinic's entry door and opened the way. The doctor's office was to the right of the reception area, and since her door was open, they walked right in.

"Where is Nathalie?" Bhathian asked.

"Over there." Bridget pointed as she pushed to her feet. "Let me check if she is okay with you coming in." The petite redhead ducked into the adjacent room and closed the door behind her.

"How come we don't hear anything?" Eva still remembered Nathalie's birth, and it hadn't been a quiet and peaceful affair. The grunting, and in the end screaming, could not have been silenced by a wall and a closed door. Especially when those on the other side had immortal hearing.

Was Nathalie sleeping? Not likely if she was having contractions.

"The soundproofing here is done with immortals in mind. Unless the door is open, we won't hear a thing."

Bridget opened the door wide and stepped out. "Go ahead."

"Hi, guys." Nathalie looked lovely and still smiling. The doctor must've given her something for the pain.

"You got here fast." Andrew stood up and offered Eva his seat, then sat down next to Nathalie on the hospital bed.

Eva ignored the offer and walked over to Nathalie's other side. "How are you feeling, sweetie?" She clasped her daughter's hand.

"As well as can be expected." Nathalie grimaced. "The

7

contractions are coming every three minutes. I didn't know they would hurt like that."

Eva glanced at the various wires connecting Nathalie to the monitoring equipment. No wonder her daughter was in pain. She wasn't hooked up to an IV drip yet. "Why no pain medication?"

"Too early. Bridget wants me to walk around a little before she hooks me up. Only after my cervix dilates to four centimeters, she's going to give me an epidural."

Just then another contraction gripped Nathalie. Her pretty face twisting in pain, she rose up and clutched Andrew's hand on one side, and Eva's on the other, breathing in and out until it passed.

"God, I hate this." She collapsed back on the bed.

"About that," Bhathian said, his raspy voice drawing Eva's attention to his face. The poor guy looked green. "I think you should go to a human hospital."

Nathalie arched a brow. "Why?"

"Bridget is only one person. What if you need a cesarean? Who is going to assist her? And what about complications? She has no experience with human mothers."

Bridget entered through the door which had remained open. "I assure you I can handle it. If I couldn't, I would've been the first to suggest moving Nathalie to a hospital."

"And what about a cesarean? You can't do everything yourself."

"I have two nurses to assist me. They are on their way."

A tight squeeze on her hand alerted Eva a moment before another contraction rolled over Nathalie. Stronger and longer than the previous one. A quick glance at the screen confirmed it. The spike was higher.

"I need to check how Nathalie is progressing." Bridget walked over to the sink and washed her hands, then pulled a pair of surgical gloves from a dispenser. "You should leave." She snapped the gloves on.

Eva pushed a strand of sweat-soaked hair off Nathalie's forehead. "We will be right outside if you need us."

Nathalie managed a weak smile. "It's getting worse. I don't think I want anyone other than Andrew to see me like this. After all, it's his fault, so he should suffer along with me."

Andrew paled and swallowed.

"It was a joke, Andrew!" Nathalie slapped his bicep.

Before the next contraction had a chance to roll out, Eva grabbed Bhathian's hand. "Let's go. We're not helping Nathalie by being here."

"One moment." He pulled his hand out of Eva's grip and walked over to Nathalie. "We are here for you. Anything you need. If you decide you want to go to a hospital after all, I'll take you. I'd like to see anyone try to stop me." He smoothed his hand over her hair and bent down, planting a quick kiss on her cheek.

"I'll be fine. Don't worry about me."

He nodded, but the worry lines on his face didn't fade.

"Come on." Eva hooked her arm through his and dragged him out.

"I'm walking. You don't need to pull me." Bhathian pushed the door closed behind them.

"I know. But I didn't want Nathalie to suffer through another contraction with us there. The sooner Bridget checks her, the sooner she is going to give Nathalie pain relief."

Outside the clinic, it looked as if Nathalie's café had been moved to the hallway. Robert was pushing a rolling cart similar to those Eva had used while working for the airline. A big carafe with coffee and another one with tea were on top; wrapped sandwiches and cold drinks were on the

9

bottom. Carol handed out the sandwiches, while Robert served the drinks.

Nice fellow, Eva thought. He was helping Carol despite the dismissive way she treated him. Most guys wouldn't have given her the time of day. Living in such a close-knit community, the odd couple was the main subject of gossip. Even Eva, who was still an outsider and hadn't visited the keep often, had heard the whole story.

It was a shame he couldn't leave the keep. Sharon would've liked him. A quiet, hard-working guy, who also happened to be tall and handsome, was exactly her type.

CHAPTER 3: ANDREW

The Demerol drip was doing nothing for Nathalie. She seemed to be in as much pain as before, just lacking the energy to do anything other than whimper.

It was killing him. Every contraction, every grimace, every whimper was tearing him to shreds.

"I'm so sorry, baby." He kissed her hand, which hadn't left his since her ordeal had started. He was dying to take a piss but refused to leave her side even for a moment. It would have to wait. As long as she suffered, so would he.

"Nothing to be sorry about," she whispered. "Not your fault. I was joking before."

"I know. But I can't watch you suffer like this. I wish I could bear the pain for you."

Nathalie closed her eyes. "Can you ask Bridget to come and check if I'm ready?"

The doctor had done it less than twenty minutes ago, and there was little chance Nathalie had dilated enough since, but he was going to ask anyway. He'd do anything so Nathalie didn't have to suffer a moment longer than necessary.

Andrew pressed the button, and a few seconds later Bridget walked in.

"I know." She lifted her hand, forestalling his arguments. "Let's check again. The contractions are getting stronger and closer. You may be ready, Nathalie." She snapped a new pair of gloves on.

As Bridget lifted the thin blanket covering his wife, Andrew pushed to his feet and turned around, giving her a measure of privacy. No one wanted to be watched at moments like that. Not even by their spouse.

"You're good to go," Bridget announced.

Thank God. Both he and Nathalie sighed in relief. Salvation was near.

Bridget opened the door and called for her nurse. "Hildegard, I need you in here." She then turned to Andrew. "You have to leave. I'll call you once the epidural is in."

"Why?"

"It's okay, Andrew. Go grab something to eat and drink. There isn't enough room in here. You'll just be in their way."

The women looked at him impatiently. He hated to leave, but it seemed no one wanted him to be there during the procedure.

"Fine, I'm going." Andrew kissed Nathalie's forehead and made himself scarce, so she could get what she needed as soon as possible.

"What's going on in there?" Bhathian grabbed Andrew's arm.

"Bridget is giving Nathalie an epidural. Let go. I need to take a piss. I've been holding it in for hours."

Bhathian nodded, and his hand dropped away.

When Andrew returned, he was in a better state to notice what was happening in the corridor outside the clinic. Guardians and civilians were everywhere, talking, eating...

"Where did everyone get the food?" he asked Syssi.

"Carol is making rounds. She went to the kitchen to make another batch. I think I hear her cart rolling back." She looked behind his back.

"Okay, gang. I made more!" Carol called out before noticing Andrew.

"Hey. How are things going? Is Nathalie okay?"

"So far so good. She is so brave."

Carol pulled out a sandwich and handed it to him. "Yeah. I never want to be where she is now. I'm going to come play with your baby, but I don't want any of my own."

Andrew unwrapped the napkin and peeled away the top slice to see what was inside. "Lots of meat. Just as I like it."

"Enjoy. Coffee?"

"Yes, please."

Robert poured some into a paper cup. "Milk? Sugar?"

"No, thanks. I take it black."

"Here you go." The guy handed Andrew the cup.

The two continued down the hallway, with Robert pushing the cart and Carol handing out stuff. Nice collaboration. Maybe their lack of compatibility wasn't a forgone conclusion.

Andrew was on his last bite when Bridget came out. "You can come back in."

"Dispose of it for me, will you?" Handing Bhathian the wrapper and empty cup, Andrew rushed in.

Inside, he found a different woman than the one he'd left only moments before.

Nathalie's face was relaxed, and she smiled as soon as he came in. "This is amazing, Andrew. No pain. None at all. The only way I know I'm having a contraction is a slight rolling sensation, or seeing that graph spike." She pointed at the monitor.

The relief was so tremendous Andrew had to sit down. "You have no idea how happy it makes me."

"Oh, yes I do. But not as happy as me."

He chuckled. "True."

Bridget came in and dimmed the lights. "Try and get some sleep while you can, Nathalie. Andrew, do you want me to get you a cot?"

"No, I'm fine on the chair."

"As you wish." Bridget backed out of the room and closed the door.

"I think I'm going to listen to the doctor." Nathalie closed her eyes and a moment later began to snore lightly.

Excellent. She needed as much rest as she could get.

Following Nathalie's example, Andrew let his eyelids drop. The next time he cracked them open was when Bridget came in to check on her patient.

"I'm sorry to wake you guys up, but I have to check Nathalie's progress. Andrew, do you mind?" She started lifting the blanket.

He turned away and looked at the monitors. The big spikes were getting closer. Their daughter was almost ready to come out.

"We have an eight. It won't be long now," Bridget confirmed his uneducated guess.

But an hour later the opening was only eight and a half.

Bridget pulled the surgical gloves off and sighed. "I'm afraid we will have to do a cesarean. The baby is big, and she is stuck in the birth canal. I don't want to wait any longer and risk her going into distress."

Nathalie and Andrew exchanged glances. Bhathian had talked with Nathalie about a cesarean, but she'd dismissed him. For some reason, neither had considered that it might be a real possibility.

"I've always been told that I have childbearing hips. You want to tell me that they are good for nothing except making shopping for clothes a nightmare?"

Bridget smiled. "That's an old wives' tale. How you're shaped on the outside has nothing to do with how you're shaped on the inside. Let me call Gertrude. We need to wheel you out to the operating room."

"I can do it." Andrew stood up.

"Sorry, buddy. Medical staff only."

"Please don't tell me that I'm not allowed in the operating room. I need to be there for Nathalie." And to witness the birth of his daughter. Andrew wasn't going to miss that for the world.

"You can follow behind. Hildegard will give you scrubs to change into and show you how to properly clean up before entering the OR."

Pressing the button that lifted the back of her bed, Nathalie asked, "Are you sure there is no other way?"

"Theoretically, we can wait and see. Maybe a miracle will happen, and you will dilate fully. But I don't advise it. It's safer for the baby if we act now."

"Okay." Nathalie looked deflated.

Bridget patted her hand. "Don't look so glum. The way she is born is not important, only that she's healthy and thriving. Most mothers expect to have a vaginal delivery, and yet around one-third of births end up being cesarean. And if you're worrying about the big, ugly scar, don't. After the transition, there will be no trace of it."

"I know. It's just that I've never considered it, and I wasn't mentally prepared. I was so sure I'd be in the two-thirds that have a normal, vaginal delivery."

Bridget patted Nathalie's hand again, then turned to Gertrude. "Let's get this party moving."

"Yes, Doctor."

CHAPTER 4: BHATHIAN

*W*hen the door opened and Bridget stepped out, Bhathian's gut clenched with worry. The doctor didn't come out unless there was trouble.

"Talk to me," he barked.

"Calm down, Bhathian, everything is alright. You're getting your wish granted. Nathalie is going for a cesarean."

Eva walked up to Bridget. "Why, are there any complications?"

"The baby is stuck in the birth canal."

That didn't sound good. Bhathian didn't remember reading about it. "Is Nathalie or the baby in danger?"

Bridget shook her head. "It's nothing out of the ordinary. A common problem and a common procedure. I'm going back to get ready."

"Wait, can we see her before she goes in?"

"Sorry, but no. By the way, there is a waiting area next to the operating room. It's two doors down. You'll be much more comfortable there."

Eva tugged on his arm. "Let's go. I prefer sitting in a chair to standing or sitting on the floor."

He nodded. "Anyone else want to join us?" he addressed Syssi and Amanda who were standing right next to Eva and him. Not that he really wanted company, but it would've been impolite not to offer.

"Sure. Do you know if there is enough room?"

"How should I know? I've never been there."

The four of them proceeded down the hallway and found the waiting room. The place was utilitarian but cozy. Its six chairs were divided into two rows of three, one on each side of the room. A square wooden coffee table, topped with stacks of old magazines, was part of each row, tucked between the second and third chair, and there was a slim fridge next to the door.

Opening the thing, he was surprised to find it stocked with soft drinks. Bhathian wondered how long they had been there. Probably years, unless the room was a late addition to Bridget's sprawling underground empire. He couldn't remember anyone using or even mentioning this room before. "Anyone want a Coke or a Sprite?"

"Is it Coke or Pepsi?" Eva asked.

"Coke."

"Then I want one."

Bhathian smiled and tossed her a can, then pulled out one for himself. "I don't like Pepsi either." He loved to discover another thing he and Eva had in common.

Syssi clicked on the television that was mounted above the fridge and started flipping channels, then clicked it off. "There is nothing on."

Amanda picked up a magazine then dropped it back on the table and picked another one. A moment later she dropped it too. "The stress is killing me."

"Where is Kian?" Bhathian asked Syssi, just to start a conversation and lower the stress level in the room.

"In his office."

"This late at night?"

"Sari called. Over there it's the middle of the day. Something about a car manufacturing facility that came up for sale on her side of the Pond."

That piqued Amanda's interest. "Cars? That's new."

"Not just any cars. Flying ones. They think there is a market for them in Alaska."

"What about California?"

Syssi chuckled. "Maybe in rural areas. I can't see flying cars in the city."

"Bummer." Amanda lost interest and picked up another magazine.

Eva shifted in her chair. "Have any of you heard about a club named Allure?"

Amanda shook her head. "I know of a cruise ship by that name. But I'm not up to date on clubs. That chapter of my life is closed. I'm happily mated now."

Syssi cast her a sidelong glance. "Do you miss it? You used to love the club scene."

"Not at all. I'm a home body now. Spending time with Dalhu or with you guys is all I want to do."

Syssi shook her head in mock despair. "How the mighty have fallen."

Amanda lifted a finger. "Not fallen, risen. No one compares to Dalhu."

Eva seemed fascinated by the exchange. "I haven't met your husband yet. And after all that praise I'm curious."

"Dalhu is not my husband. Mated is not the same as married."

"How so?"

"Mated means that he is the one and only for me, and I am for him. We don't need a big party or a piece of paper to sanction our union."

"Are you saying that it's for life?"

"Of course. And a very long life at that."

"So you guys stay together no matter what? What about cheating, or discord?"

"There is none."

"How is it possible?"

Amanda put down her magazine and crossed her legs. "I don't know if Bhathian explained it to you, but we have a concept of fated mates. It doesn't mean that everyone finds one. Even in the old days, when there were plenty of potential mates to choose from, only a few were lucky enough to find their one and only."

Eva frowned. "How do you know, though? How does a fated mate differ from a non-fated one?"

Amanda pinned Eva with her blue stare. "When no other man would do. When being away from him means agony, and being with him is the only thing that feels right even if your mind tells you that it's all wrong."

Next to her Syssi nodded. "Exactly. I couldn't have said it better."

Eva turned to Bhathian and regarded him as if seeing him in a completely different light. "Is it true? Is that how you feel?"

He grabbed her hand and clasped it. "I'm not as eloquent and concise as Amanda, but I told you the same thing once or twice." He lifted her hand and kissed it.

On the other side of Eva, Syssi cleared her throat. "Amanda, are you up for another cup of coffee? Carol said she used the commercial coffee maker in the basement kitchen and made enough to last everyone the entire night."

"Sure, why not?"

"You don't have to go." Eva lifted a hand to stop them. "I promise not to embarrass you guys again."

Amanda's brows lifted, making her expression seem

condescending. "I'm not embarrassed. It would take much more than a little love talk to achieve that."

"I don't think an orgy would." Syssi snorted. "Amanda thrives on scandalizing people. Especially me."

"That's because you blush so prettily. You make it far too easy."

"You know I can't help it."

"I know." Amanda leaned over and kissed Syssi's cheek. "I love you just the way you are."

Watching Eva listen to the friendly exchange, Bhathian was surprised to see a look of longing on her face. Was she envious of Amanda and Syssi's close relationship? Did she lack female companionship?

"You seem really close." The tone of her voice more than the words themselves confirmed his assumption.

"We are. As soon as Syssi walked into my lab, I knew she was the one for my brother. I fell in love with her first."

Syssi blushed and leaned her head on Amanda's shoulder. "I love you too."

Eva cast Amanda a curious look. "How did he feel about your matchmaking? From the little I've seen of him, Kian doesn't strike me as a man who would let anyone interfere in his life."

"The old goat fought me every step of the way. But then fate intervened and he had to come to my lab. It was a done deal the moment he laid eyes on her."

"How about you, Syssi, was it a done deal for you too?"

Eva's questions gave Bhathian hope. Perhaps she was finally ready to accept that they were meant for each other.

Syssi nodded. "I wanted Kian like I've never wanted any man before, but I thought it was just an infatuation. Someone as incredibly handsome as Kian would make any woman weak at the knees. I tried to shield my heart and not fall for him because I was sure he was going to chew me up and spit me out. But it was futile. There was no fighting this thing between us. And mind you, I was still human back then, and although Amanda believed I was a Dormant, Kian didn't. We both thought our relationship was doomed, and yet we couldn't help the incredible pull. Luckily for us, I transitioned and the impossible dream became a reality."

There was a suspicious shine in Eva's eyes. Was his tough-as-nails mate a closet romantic?

"Unlike Amanda and her mate, you guys got married, though, right?"

"We did. Since it was the first the clan ever had, Kian wanted a huge wedding. I was terrified. An introvert like me hates big crowds in general, and especially when all the attention is on me. But I did it for Kian and for the clan. The funny thing was that I ended up enjoying our wedding tremendously, which proves that sometimes we need to step outside our comfort zone to find out what makes us happy."

CHAPTER 5: NATHALIE

"*C*an you feel it?" Bridget pricked Nathalie's belly again.

After the fourth or fifth prick, when Nathalie kept insisting she could still feel the needle—which meant that she wasn't numb yet—Bridget began looking doubtful.

It was the scariest thing. What if the doctor started cutting her open before she got numb?

With the previous one, Nathalie wasn't sure if she felt the prick or just the pressure. But this time she'd hardly even felt the needle touch her belly. It was time to get on with it.

"No, I didn't feel it this time."

"Good. Let's do it," Bridget said.

Nathalie squeezed Andrew's hand, and he squeezed back.

Neither them could see what the doctor was doing behind the screen Gertrude had hung just below Nathalie's chest. Which was good. This was scary enough without watching her stomach getting split open.

"I'm in," Bridget said.

Nathalie hadn't felt a thing.

"You're going to feel pressure as we push on your belly and massage the baby out."

Weird. The cutting hadn't registered at all, but the pushing did.

A few moments later Nathalie heard the best sound in the world: A soft baby cry. But why so quiet? A big baby should have a mighty cry, not a little whimper.

"Is she okay?" she asked.

"She's perfect. Gertrude will clean her up a little and then hand her over to Daddy, and then Daddy will hold baby for Mommy to see."

Daddy.

Tears misted Nathalie's eyes. "You're a daddy, Andrew."

"And you're a mommy." He lifted her hand and kissed the back of it.

As Bridget and Hildegard got busy putting Nathalie back together, Gertrude handed Andrew a tiny bundle wrapped in a pink blanket. "You can lay her on Nathalie's chest," the nurse said. "But hold on to the baby."

There were tears in Andrew's eyes as he kissed their daughter and then gently lowered her to Nathalie's face, so her soft tiny cheek touched Nathalie's. "Say hello to Mommy, precious little one."

CHAPTER 6: SYSSI

*A*s Bridget opened the door to the waiting room, Syssi loosened a breath. The doctor's scent told her all she needed to know. Bridget was happy.

"Congratulations to Grandma and Grandpa and aunties. Phoenix weighs a healthy ten pounds and two ounces."

"Can we see her?" Eva made a move to step through the door to the operating room area.

Bridget stopped her. "Andrew will bring the baby out in a moment. Mommy is resting in the recovery room and shouldn't be disturbed."

Eva looked like she was about to argue, but Bhathian put a hand on her shoulder. "We'll wait for when the doctor says it's okay."

It wasn't long after Bridget had returned to her patient that Andrew opened the door, holding his bundle of joy close to his heart with the other. "Bridget said to make it brief."

"How is Nathalie doing?" Eva asked.

"She's good, sleeping."

Eva came closer to take a peek. "Oh, my goodness, look at

this little beauty. She looks exactly like her mama did when she was born. Can I hold her?"

"Only for a few moments." With utmost care, Andrew transferred his baby to her grandmother.

As Eva cooed to the baby, Kian came rushing in. "What did I miss?"

Syssi wrapped her arm around his waist. "Nothing. Andrew just came out to show us his daughter."

"Where?"

Syssi pointed at Eva.

"Oh." He craned his neck to look over Eva's shoulder. "So tiny."

"Actually, Phoenix is huge for a newborn. Ten pounds and two ounces," Andrew said proudly.

"Congratulations, man." Kian offered his hand and pulled Andrew into a bro hug.

Bhathian went next, clapping Andrew's back so hard that the baby started fussing.

"Shh... little one, Nana is going to rock you back to sleep." Eva started swaying gently on her feet and humming a tune.

With a heart that was aching with the need to hold the baby, Syssi waited impatiently for Eva to be done, but it didn't look as if Grandma was going to relinquish her treasure any time soon.

Not unless Syssi asked. Shifting from foot to foot, she waited another moment or two until she could wait no more and blurted, "May I?"

Eva kissed the baby's forehead. "Here you go, little beauty. Your aunt wants her turn."

With slightly trembling hands, Syssi cradled her niece and brought her close to her chest. "She is beautiful, Andrew. Phoenix doesn't look like a newborn. She looks like a three-month-old baby. Smooth skin, clear features, and a headful of hair." Wispy dark brown strands. A couple of shades lighter than her mother's, but it would get darker as she got older.

Amanda pushed to her feet and leaned over Syssi's shoulder to take a look. "I think she looks like you, Andrew. She has Nathalie's coloring but your face."

"I think she looks like her mommy. Don't you, sweet pea?" Andrew took his daughter from Syssi, holding her in the crook of his arm as if he'd been holding babies his entire life.

But then he had, hadn't he?

Andrew had taken care of Syssi and their younger brother Jacob when they were babies. At fourteen, he'd assumed the role of a third parent in the household, not an older brother. And with their parents' busy schedules, he'd often been the only one she and Jacob could turn to.

Syssi rubbed at her chest. Jacob's loss was still as painful as hell. The sharpness of it had dulled a little over the years—she no longer cried her eyes out every time she thought about him—but it would never go away. She wouldn't let it. If Andrew had a second child, a boy, she would ask him to name him after the brother they'd lost. But the problem was that after Nathalie's transition, her chances of conceiving would become just as nonexistent as Syssi's.

God, how she wanted a baby of her own.

"Go home, people. I'm going to stay here overnight with Nathalie and Phoenix."

"Nice name. I like it," Syssi said. "Any symbolism behind it?" She suspected that there was.

"Yeah, there is. Good night, everyone." Andrew left without offering an explanation.

Tight-lipped as always.

Amanda stretched and yawned. "Well, I'm going to bed."

Syssi gave her a hug goodbye. "See you tomorrow at the lab."

Plopping onto a chair next to Kian, she put her head on his shoulder, drawing comfort from his closeness.

He wrapped his arms around her. "What's the matter?"

"Nothing."

"Oh no you don't. Nothing, my ass. When you say nothing, I know a shit storm is coming my way. What did I do this time?"

She kissed his cheek. "Not everything is about you, Kian."

Bhathian chuckled. "I thought you two lived in perfect harmony."

"We do," Kian said.

Syssi cast him an incredulous glance. "Kian is delusional. Perfect harmony doesn't exist. Every couple has their spats."

"And here I thought that fated mates lived blissfully in love ever after." Eva's tone was laced with sarcasm.

Kian lifted Syssi and repositioned her on his lap. "That's right. In love forever. Besides, with no fights, there would be no make-up sex. A terrible loss." He kissed Syssi's neck. "I'm hungry."

She wasn't sure which hunger he was referring to.

"Me too," Bhathian said. "Maybe Carol left some sandwiches in the kitchen."

As they headed over there, Syssi glanced at Eva. She seemed preoccupied. Syssi looked away, leaving the woman to her thoughts. Emotional drain affected immortals the same as it did humans, and it had been an eventful night.

Eva must've sensed her eyes on her and turned with a faint smile ghosting over her lips. "Can I ask you a question?"

"Sure." Syssi expected more inquiries about matehood. The subject seemed to fascinate Eva even though it was obvious she thought it was bullshit.

"How did Amanda know you were a Dormant?"

That was a subject Syssi loved talking about, but seldom did outside the lab. "Her hypothesis was that Dormant humans exhibit paranormal abilities, and she tested it in her lab at the university. I was very good at predicting things."

"You said her hypothesis was. That's no longer the case?"

How very perceptive. But then Eva was a detective. She focused on those little things that gave people away. When she listened, it was with a different ear than an untrained civilian.

"Amanda was lucky to find two. Me, and Michael who is a strong telepath. But we've found no one since, even after doubling and tripling our efforts. One problem is that we can test only a narrow spectrum of paranormal abilities, and the other is that most immortals have no special talents other than thralling. And if they do it's weak. Nothing our test would deem significant. Reluctantly, we were forced to accept that fate is a major player in this. Not an easy thing for a scientist to do."

As they reached the kitchen, the guys zeroed in immediately on the tray of sandwiches Carol had left. Syssi had had two of those during the long wait, which was one too many. But coffee was always a good idea. "Coffee?" she asked Eva.

"Sure."

She turned to ask the guys, but Bhathian had already pulled two beers out of the fridge and was handing one to Kian.

Syssi poured two cups and joined Eva at the counter.

"Thanks." Eva took a sip. "So what now? You're just giving up?"

"Not yet. I had another theory we decided to check out. I think Dormants and immortals feel an affinity toward each other, as do immortals to other immortals. Like recognizes like. The tricky part is how to get them together. We came up with the idea of having immortals volunteer at the lab, exposing the potential Dormants to more of us."

Eva nodded. "I get what you're saying. I have just one little trick up my sleeve, but it's nothing you guys would be impressed with."

"What is it?"

"You're going to laugh."

"No, I'm not."

"Okay. So I know what you mean when you talk about affinity. I sense it as well. When I meet someone that I feel is different, a misfit as I call them, I ask one question. What makes you special? And everyone I've ever asked answered truthfully. I know because some people told me very private things. I tried it with other questions, but regrettably it didn't work with anything else. Considering what I do for a living, it could've been very helpful."

That was fascinating, and maybe could even prove useful to their research in some way. "I bet. Did you find anyone special?"

Eva lifted three fingers. "My crew. Sharon can predict what people will say next, and she knows who is good and who is bad. Nick has a way with technology that seems magical. Tessa swears she has nothing special, but I think she hasn't discovered it yet. She is the youngest of the three."

"Hm…" Syssi drummed her fingers on the stainless steel counter. "We could test the new theory on your crew. Get them to mingle with some of the immortals and then question the two groups, each one separately, of course, to see how they react to each other."

"I can arrange a housewarming party," Eva suggested. "And invite Bhathian and some of the extended family."

"That would be fantastic. I'll talk to Amanda tomorrow

morning and see what she thinks about it. After all, she is the professor, and I'm just the research assistant."

Eva regarded Syssi with her brows arched high. "Just a lowly assistant, huh? One who happens to see the future and come up with new theories when the old ones don't work?"

Well... when you put it that way...

CHAPTER 7: AMANDA

"Where are you going?" Syssi asked when Amanda passed their onramp and continued driving straight.

"I want to buy flowers for Nathalie."

"Good idea. I'll buy some too. How about a present for the baby, though? Do you think it's okay now?"

Following some silly superstition, Nathalie had refused a baby shower and any gifts prior to the delivery.

"I promised her I wouldn't buy anything before, but I think it safe to unleash my super shopping power and make sure that this baby is the best dressed little girl in town."

"Department stores or catalogs?"

"Internet. I don't have the patience for store-hopping the way I used to. But I like to browse in Dalhu's studio while he paints. That way we both get to do what we like and be together at the same time."

"Do you mind if I join you? You can help me choose cute stuff."

Amanda put a hand on Syssi's arm. "I would love to. We

can invite a few girls and have a baby shower of our own, ordering shitloads of the most adorable baby girl clothes."

"And not invite Nathalie?"

"Yeah, I see your point. But it will be some time before she can socialize, and the baby needs clothes. The silly woman didn't buy anything. Not even diapers or bottles or blankets. Nothing."

"I'm sure Eva and Bhathian took care of it by now."

"I hope so." Amanda slipped her Porsche into a parking spot right in front of the flower shop.

Syssi unbuckled and stepped out. "How did you find this place?"

"Remember the flowers I got Hannah for her one-year anniversary at the lab?"

"Yeah, they were gorgeous."

"I got them here. I searched for a flower shop in Google Maps, and this was the closest one. Come on, I want you to meet Melissa, the owner."

Syssi cast her a sidelong glance. "Why? Anything special about her?"

Amanda nodded. "I want a second opinion. It's not so much about the woman herself as her plants. Talk about a green thumb. Everything thrives. I haven't seen green this vivid since I returned from Hawaii."

"Could that be a paranormal talent? Coaxing plants to grow?"

Amanda locked her car. "Who knows?"

Syssi opened the door and held it for Amanda. There was a guy in front of them in the line, standing at the counter and tapping his foot impatiently while waiting for Melissa to be done with the elderly couple she was helping in the back of the shop.

Syssi closed her eyes and inhaled. "It's so peaceful in here."

"I know, right? Let's take a look around. Which kind of flowers do you think Nathalie likes?" With so many beauties it was hard to choose.

"I think it's best to let the expert recommend a bouquet."

As they strolled down the narrow aisles between potted plants and buckets of cut flowers, Amanda was soothed by the smells and vibrant colors. Soft classical music was playing in the background, but she couldn't make out the composer. Was she getting rusty? Usually, a few notes were enough for Amanda to recognize a classical piece and its creator. Maybe this was written by a lesser known one.

"Amanda, good to see you again." Melissa offered her hand.

Good memory. Amanda wondered whether Melissa remembered the names of all her customers or just those she felt an affinity with.

"You too, Melissa. This is my sister-in-law, Syssi."

The two shook hands.

"How can I help you, ladies?" Melissa asked.

"We need a bouquet for a new mother."

"Do you have a budget in mind?"

"Unlimited. Make the best one you can."

A corner of Melissa's mouth lifted in a smile. "I remember you saying the same thing the other time."

"Hannah loved the arrangement you made for her. It was worth the money."

"I'm glad. Would you like to take a seat while I work on it?" She pointed to a bench.

That was a nice surprise. "You are going to make it right now?" The other time Amanda had to come back for the flowers.

"I have time. It's a quiet evening. No big orders to fill out today." Melissa started collecting flowers from various buckets. "When I have an order for an event, it's a madhouse in here."

"Do you have someone to help you?" Syssi asked.

"I call the lady who sold me the place. She is always happy to get back to work, even though it's painful for her with her arthritic hands. Sometimes, when there is a really big order, she brings her daughter along." Melissa spread what she'd collected over a wooden work table and started weaving her magic.

"What do you think?" Amanda whispered in Syssi's ear.

"You're right. There is something about her. But it's nothing like what I felt for you, or for Nathalie, or any of the others. It's not like it's a particular sort of feeling that I recognize. It's a fleeting sense that she's okay and maybe we can be friends and find out more about each other. Am I making any sense?"

"I know what you mean. I was trying to figure out what it was too. Every person is unique. The only commonality I found was that in each case I was intrigued and wanted to find out more."

Syssi nodded. "Yeah, something like that. Also, I feel like I want to stay. But that might be because it's so peaceful in here, relaxing. I wish she had a hammock somewhere so I could lie down. Do you think it's her? It might be the effect of all the plant life."

Amanda shrugged. "I wish I knew. That's why I wanted your opinion."

Syssi crossed her legs at the ankles and leaned back. "Next time, we need to bring a guy with us. Maybe the males have a better sense about the opposite sex."

"That's a possibility. Any suggestions?"

"I'll think about it. For now, I just want to close my eyes and relax."

CHAPTER 8: CAROL

*C*arol put down a cup of coffee in front of Robert and sat next to him to drink hers. "I don't know what the big fuss is. Sure, the baby is cute, but come on, all she does is eat and poop and eat and poop, and cry in between."

Robert palmed his cup and took a sip. "Did you get to hold her?"

Carol shook her head. "I'm afraid I'll break something. Her head just flops around like it's hanging from a noodle." She demonstrated. "Did you?"

"I didn't even get to see her yet."

"Do you want to?"

Robert shrugged. "Not really. I'd have to stand in line behind all the females. That's all they've been talking about lately."

With a sigh, Carol slumped in her chair. "Am I weird? Am I the only one who doesn't get it?"

"I can't answer that."

"Can't, or won't?"

"Can't. I'm a guy, what do I know about maternal instincts?"

"That's true."

Talking about the baby filled up about two minutes, and now that it was done, Carol struggled to come up with what else to say. She and Robert had gotten a little closer since the night of the delivery. They had made a good team, working together as they had.

If only it could've translated to the rest of their relationship.

Robert could've made a great business partner if Carol ever decided to open her own restaurant. He was hard working and organized, two qualities which she lacked.

"After Nathalie comes back to work, I'm thinking about going to culinary school." Maybe that topic would fill a few more minutes.

"Instead of interning with your cousin?"

"Yeah. I kind of scrapped that idea. Gerard is a prick."

Robert took another sip and stretched out his legs. "What's involved? Is it long?"

"There are all kinds of courses—as short as six months and as long as a four-year degree. I would rather take a short one, but I need to find out if it's enough to teach me what I need to know."

"And that's what?"

Carol shrugged. "For starters, I want to learn how to cook large quantities. But who knows, maybe one day I'll decide to open my own place."

Robert chuckled. "I think that before you decide, you should swallow your pride and work in Gerard's kitchen for a few days. You may change your mind about how wonderful running a restaurant is."

"You're probably right. Though if I ever decide to open my own place, I would do it with a partner. Someone who is good under pressure and hard-working." She smiled suggestively, letting Robert know she was thinking of him.

"I would love to. But unless you want to open it right here in the keep and become Nathalie's competitor, you'll need to find someone else. Kian is not going to let me out of here."

"He can't keep you locked up forever. Eventually he will have to trust you."

"Do you want to suggest it to him?"

Carol smiled and reached for Robert's hand. "Let's not put the carriage before the horse."

Robert scrunched his forehead. "What does a carriage have to do with anything?"

Poor guy. With his flawless English, it was easy to forget that Robert wasn't a native and had never learned the many idioms which were a big part of the language.

"Darling, if you ever want to fit in, you should start dedicating some time to reading, or at least watching television. Things like this give you away."

His cheeks reddening, Robert shifted in his seat. "Tell me what to read and what to watch, and I'll do it."

A man who was willing to listen and learn wasn't a lost cause. "I'll make you a list."

"It would be greatly appreciated. Thank you."

CHAPTER 9: EVA

"*W*here do you want me to put it?" Bhathian adjusted the large box of beers under his arm. Snake's Venom, naturally. The immortals considered other brands no better than piss water.

"We set up the bar over there." Eva pointed to the patio.

Everything was ready for the "housewarming party." Their living room was too small even for the limited number of people invited, but although their back yard was barely the size of a patio, they'd managed to squeeze in two folding tables with six chairs each, and another long table to serve as a bar. The food had been ordered from Fernando's Café, the tables and chairs had been rented, and the paper and plastic serve ware had been bought at the local supermarket.

Not exactly a high-class affair, but then Eva had no such aspirations. It wasn't necessary. Her idea of a good time was a simple, friendly get together, with plenty of good food and quality booze. She could still remember the barbecues at her parents' modest house. Food wise there had been nothing fancier than hamburgers and Budweisers, but her mother had put colorful tablecloths over the folding tables, topping them with fresh flowers from her garden and setting the table with precision. She'd managed to make it look festive without breaking the bank. Everyone had always had a great time.

Eva had a feeling that Syssi would approve, but she wasn't so sure about Amanda, especially given the woman's fancy designer clothes and larger-than-life attitude. Not that Eva cared one way or another. This was her house, and she didn't feel the need to impress anyone. If Amanda wanted something fancier, she could plan a party of her own.

Bhathian came back inside. "There is no more room in the cooler. Do you have another one?"

"No. But you can put the rest in the fridge, and we can refill the cooler later."

"Good deal." He carried the box with the remaining beers into the kitchen.

"Thank you for inviting Jackson and the guys," Tessa said.

Eva smiled. "They are bringing in the food. I don't think it counts as an invitation."

A pink hue crept up Tessa's cheeks. "I hope they will have some free time to enjoy the party."

"They sure will. Not much to do after the food is served."

"I was thinking about taking Jackson down to the beach."

"After the desserts."

"Okay." Tessa glanced out at the patio, then back at Eva. "We've never had guests over before."

"No, we have not."

"It feels weird. It was always just the four of us, and you specifically forbade bringing anyone over, not that any of us wanted to, but still."

Eva put a hand on Tessa's narrow shoulder. "Is it stressing you out?"

The girl shook her head. "No. I like Bhathian, and if the rest of his family is as nice as he is, then it should be fun."

"I'm sure they are. I wish Nathalie could come, but she doesn't want to take the baby out of the house yet. It has been only ten days."

Bhathian wrapped his arm around Eva's waist. "She is the cutest little girl ever. Do you want to see pictures?"

Tessa's eyes sparkled. "Yes. I would love to."

Bhathian whipped out his phone and handed it to Tessa. "There are a lot of them. Just scroll down."

"She is adorable!" Tessa squeaked. "Such huge eyes, and all that hair. It's hard to believe she is a newborn." She scrolled through a few pictures. "And Nathalie looks so happy. Is that her husband?" She lifted the phone, showing a picture of Andrew holding Phoenix.

"Yes. That's Andrew."

"He looks so in love with his tiny daughter," Tessa whispered. "She is a lucky baby to have adoring parents like them."

"She is." Bhathian took his phone back. "And grandparents."

"Do you have pictures of them too?"

Bhathian's expression was priceless. "No, I don't." He stuffed the phone into his back pocket.

"Oh." Tessa sounded disappointed.

"I think there is someone at the front door," Eva said. "Tessa, could you see who it is?"

"Sure." The girl hurried away.

Bhathian let out a breath. "That was a close one."

"You should watch yourself."

"I know, and I usually do, but Tessa feels so much like family that I sometimes forget she is not one of us."

Eva kissed his cheek. "Maybe she is. And the way you feel about her might be a clue."

"Did you talk to Jackson?"

"About our experiment?"

"Yes."

"Not yet. I didn't have a chance. I'm going to tell him when he comes in. But we can't count him as an objective tester. He has feelings for her."

A smirk tugged on Bhathian's lips. "But that's the thing. I know that boy. He is a chick magnet. Until he met Tessa, he had no qualms about using his charms to get in as many pairs of girls' panties as he could. He was a player."

"What if he still is?"

Bhathian shook his head. "Not with her. He is different with Tessa."

"You're such a romantic. Jackson is just a boy. Today he is infatuated with Tessa and tomorrow it will be with someone else."

"Maybe, and maybe not. Should we bet on it?"

Gordon walked in with a stack of aluminum foil containers. "Hi, where do you want these?"

"On the kitchen counter." Eva pointed.

"No problem."

Vlad was next.

Closing the procession, Jackson sauntered in. His stack of trays tilting precariously, he bent sideways to plant a quick kiss on Tessa's cheek and then followed his friends to the kitchen.

Eva grimaced. The girl looked too happy. She'd be crushed when Jackson moved on. "I need to talk to that boy." She pulled away from Bhathian.

He tugged her back. "No need to unsheathe those claws, lady cougar, he has done nothing wrong."

"Not yet."

"You don't know that he will, but you know what they say about assumption—it's the mother of all fuckups."

Eva pinned Bhathian with a hard stare. "What are you willing to bet on?"

"You choose."

Oh, that was good. He was going to regret he'd ever made that wager. "Loser does the dishes for the next three months."

A toothy grin split Bhathian's face as he lifted her hand to his lips. "That's harsh, love." Teasingly, he brushed them over the back of her hand. "Those latex gloves of yours will come in handy."

The man was tangling with the wrong woman. "I don't think my gloves will fit you, big guy. You should stop by Walgreens and get your own."

Shaking a finger at her, he laughed. "You're good."

Eva had to give it to her man. He was a good sport. "Thank you." She inclined her head in a mock bow. "As much as I would like to stay for more compliments, I'd better get Jackson and tell him the score before the party starts."

"Don't worry, you'll get them after it ends." Bhathian winked.

In the kitchen, Tessa was helping the guys organize the trays on the counter, so pulling Jackson aside required a small lie.

"Jackson, I need your help with something." Eva waved her hand toward the patio.

"Yes, ma'am."

"Follow me." She headed out, with Jackson following behind.

She took him to the furthest corner of the small patio. "I need to talk to you."

"I figured."

"First of all." She pointed a finger at him. "If you break that girl's heart, I'm going to make you regret it for the rest of your extremely long life."

"I won't break Tessa's heart."

"You're an eighteen-year-old boy. Today you may think

she is your one and only, but tomorrow it will be someone else."

"For now, we are just friends, Eva. Tessa is not ready for anything else."

That was a relief. "Keep it that way."

Jackson smiled, and it was clear why females were drawn to him like flies to honey. The boy oozed charm and confidence. "I'm not the one running the show. Tessa is. Whatever she is comfortable with, I'm there for her. I want her to feel free to explore and experiment with no pressure whatsoever coming from me. She needs it."

It sounded so altruistic and noble, but could he handle it? From what she'd learned about immortals, males and females alike, they weren't known for their restraint. It wasn't going to work unless Jackson was having sex with others while he was "friends" with Tessa.

"I hope you're releasing steam elsewhere. It's not going to work otherwise."

Jackson's smile melted away. He looked as if she'd insulted his mother and his entire family. "With all due respect, my sex life is none of your business."

"You're right. I apologize."

He nodded. "Apology accepted. I know you love Tessa and want what's best for her, but putting her inside a protective bubble is not the solution."

With a sigh, Eva pulled Jackson into a quick hug. "I can't help it."

The boy pulled away as quickly as he could. "Are you trying to get me killed?"

She narrowed her eyes. "What are you talking about?"

He pointed behind her.

Eva turned her head and stifled a chuckle, finally understanding how her handsome guy earned himself the unflattering nickname ogre. Standing just outside the patio doors, his bulging arms crossed over his massive chest, he was glaring daggers at Jackson.

She walked over and patted his arm. "Calm down, big guy. This was just a motherly hug."

He snorted. "Motherly my ass. You're too hot for motherly."

"That's so sweet." She wrapped an arm around his waist and stretched to kiss his cheek. "I need to tell Jackson about our experiment. Can you keep Tessa busy in the kitchen?"

"What experiment?" Jackson asked.

Bhathian uncrossed his arms. "Fine. But no more hugging or touching. Motherly or otherwise."

She saluted. "Yes, sir."

"Phew." Jackson wiped invisible sweat from his brow.

"Are all immortals so jealous and possessive?"

Jackson winked. "Just those who are in love with their mates."

Was Bhathian in love with her?

Was she in love with him?

Eva had no clue. What was the difference between just loving someone and being in love?

Rainbows and butterflies?

She shook her head. "I'd better get to the real reason I dragged you out here. Amanda and Syssi have a new theory about Dormants. They think immortals feel a special affinity toward Dormants and vice versa. That's the reason behind this housewarming party. We suspect Tessa, Sharon, and Nick might be Dormants. After mingling with them, the immortals are going to report their reactions."

It seemed Jackson heard only the part about Tessa. "Tessa is a Dormant?"

"She might be. I felt something special for each of them when I met them, and it could be the affinity Amanda and Syssi are talking about. Nick and Sharon have unique abilities. Tessa doesn't. But I think that whatever her special talent is, it's just stunted."

Jackson opened his mouth, then shut it, then opened it again, and closed it again. The poor guy looked like a fish out of water. It was the only time Eva had seen his self-assured countenance waver.

She clapped him on the back. "Breathe, Jackson."

"It explains so much. Why I feel the way I do about her. I think she's my destined mate."

Eva rolled her eyes. "Dramatic, much? You like the girl, and she likes you back. That doesn't make you destined mates. Use your head, Jackson, and don't let your heart hijack your brain. I know it's difficult at your age, but you're a smart guy. You can do it."

He nodded, but from the glazed look in his eyes, she knew her words had fallen on deaf ears. Perhaps she'd gotten it all wrong, and it wouldn't be Tessa's heart that was going to get broken. It would be Jackson's.

CHAPTER 10: JACKSON

*A*s he was making rounds with plates of small sandwiches, Jackson was hardly paying attention to the other immortals at the party. Eva hadn't asked him to do it, but he needed something to keep him busy. It helped muffle the buzzing in his head. Going on autopilot, he fell back on the skills he'd honed running the café, smiling and joking with everyone while pretending nothing had changed, and his world hadn't tilted sideways, and the ground hadn't slipped from under his feet.

Tessa was a Dormant. There was no maybe in his mind. All the pieces had aligned, and the puzzle was solved. She was the one and only for him.

But she was broken.

What if she never healed? What if she could never suffer his touch?

It would kill him.

Jackson wasn't as obsessed as some of the other immortal males who had fewer generations separating them from the original gods and their insatiable appetites, but he was a highly sexual creature nonetheless.

Since he'd reached puberty, Jackson declared himself a lover. Giving pleasure was more important and more satisfying to him than receiving it. He could never be happy with a woman who could barely tolerate his touch. He needed his woman to crave him, to blissfully fall apart in his arms.

Hell, he wasn't sure he could even climax unless she did so first. Given the effects of the venom, there was no chance she wouldn't reach her peak. But that was cheating. A chemically induced orgasm didn't count. Not in his book.

"Hey, Jackson. Shouldn't you refill the platter?" Anandur jerked him out of his thoughts.

Damn it. Apparently, he'd been offering people an empty tray. "I'll be right back." He scurried inside with Anandur's laughter following him to the kitchen where Vlad was making more bite-sized sandwiches.

Fucking immortals and their big appetites.

He lowered his platter to the counter and sat down on a stool. "How long?"

"Two minutes," Vlad said.

Gordon handed Vlad another pack of cold cuts then turned to Jackson. "How come you're not hanging out with Tessa?"

"I don't want to monopolize her time. She's finally meeting new people and having fun." It was partially true, and maybe there was no harm in telling the guys what was going on, but not yet. They might talk, and news would spread through the immortal community before Tessa was even told. Besides, he was in no mood to deal with their questions and their excitement. For the time being he'd keep the news to himself.

Wrapping his head around the possibility that he'd found his one and only at eighteen wasn't easy. He needed time to think.

"I'm going out for a few minutes." Jackson pushed to his

feet and headed out the front door. With his long legs eating up the distance, he soon found himself on the beach and broke into a sprint on the sand.

His mate had been harmed, maybe irreversibly, and there was nothing he could do about it. Jackson funneled the rage into his legs, pumping his arms and running at a speed that was sure to raise a few human eyebrows, but he didn't care.

Tessa should be avenged, but he wasn't stupid enough to think that he could go after the monsters by himself. With no training and no connections, he had no way of even finding them, let alone meting out justice.

Kian.

He should approach the regent and ask for his help.

Kian had what it took. The question was whether he would be willing to do anything about it. Perhaps with Tessa being a potential Dormant, not just a human girl who'd been hurt, Kian would consider allotting resources to avenge her.

Fuck. It wouldn't be right to share Tessa's story with Kian without asking her permission first. Would she grant it?

Later, when everyone finally went home, he would ask her. Turning around, Jackson sprinted back to the house.

"Vlad has more ready for you." Gordon handed Jackson a loaded plate as soon as he entered the kitchen.

His friends were awesome. There was no way they hadn't noticed that he was acting strange, Vlad and Gordon knew him too well to be fooled by his fake smile and well-practiced swagger, and yet they let him be.

Not Tessa, though.

Her big eyes full of concern, she stopped him and took a tiny sandwich off his tray. "What's going on? You look troubled," she whispered.

Futile given the company but she didn't know that.

He faked a grin. "Just waiting for everyone to go home so I can be alone with you."

He heard Kri snicker, and then Michael shush her.

Tessa blushed. "What do you want to do?"

"How about a walk on the beach?"

She sighed. "That would be lovely."

Kri must've spread the word because half an hour later people started saying their goodbyes.

Bhathian caught him by the elbow. "Way to clear the party."

"It wasn't me. The food is gone." Which was true. Jackson and Eva had underestimated the quantities.

Bhathian waved a finger at him. "You're one lucky bastard to find a good excuse."

"Yeah. Lucky is my middle name." The sarcasm dripped from every word.

"Jackson, my man, you don't know shit. Take it from someone who's learned it the hard way. Today's troubles might bring tomorrow's joys and the other way around. The bloody Fates are fickle and love tangling things up for us." He squeezed Jackson's shoulder and leaned to whisper in his ear, "Besides, you've done me a favor. I wanted everyone gone too. Any chance you can get Eva's crew out as well?"

Jackson eyed the guy. "No, I can't. And why did you give me grief about it when you wanted the same thing?"

"For shits and giggles. You're taking yourself too seriously."

Easy for him to talk. He hadn't found his mate and discovered she might never be his...

Fuck, he had, hadn't he?

Bhathian had found Eva thirty some years ago, had her for one night just to get a taste of how good it could be, and then lost her. The lonely years of searching for his one-true-love mate must've been torture.

How had he survived?

"I'm glad you and Eva found each other again."

"Me too. But if you think this is the happy ending, you're wrong. Everything worth having in life takes a lot of work. And there is nothing more worthwhile than your mate."

"Amen to that." Jackson glanced around, looking for Tessa and finding her hauling a big trash bag.

"What are you doing with that?" He ran up to her and snatched the bag from her hands. "This thing is almost as big as you." He lifted the bag and strode outside to the trash bin, depositing it on top of a couple of others.

"Any more trash?" he asked as he got back inside.

"That was the last one."

A mop in one hand and a bucket in the other, Sharon shooed them away. "I need you guys out of the living room. And don't come back until the floor is dry. I'm not mopping it again."

Perfect excuse to grab Tessa and go. "My lady?" He offered her his arm. "The beach awaits."

She threaded her arm through his.

"Leave your shoes outside when you come back. Whoever drags sand into the house does the floors from now on." She pointed at them with the mop. "Don't tell me I didn't warn you!"

"Bossy, that Sharon," he said after closing the front door behind him.

The sun had set already, but Venice's streets were well illuminated, and so was the boardwalk. The crazies that loved hanging out there at night might scare Tessa, but they were harmless. Besides, with him at her side, she had nothing to fear.

Tessa shrugged. "Sharon hates everything to do with housekeeping. She took the floor mopping because it needs to be done only once a week."

"So everyone has chores?"

"Yes. Mine are dusting every day and cleaning the fridge

once a week. Nick takes out the garbage and takes care of whatever needs to be done with the cars. We take turns washing dishes and cleaning the kitchen, and everyone does their own laundry and cleans their own room and bathroom."

"What about Eva?"

"Eva is working her butt off to pay for everything, but she still takes turns in the kitchen and cleans her own room. Sometimes she is so overworked that I sneak in and do it for her. She pretends to be mad about it, but I know she appreciates the help."

"You love her."

"I do. I owe her my life. If not for Eva, I would be dead, or wish I was."

Jackson spotted a vacant bench and steered Tessa toward it. "I like sitting here and watching the waves," he said.

She sat down beside him, close, her thigh touching his. "I love the sound of the ocean."

Tentatively, he wrapped his arm around her. When she stayed within his loose embrace, her body not tensing and her breathing even, Jackson closed his eyes and offered a quick thanks to the Fates. In the short time they'd known each other, Tessa had made tremendous progress. He was well aware that the road to recovery was still long and full of potholes, but this gave him hope.

In a moment like that, bringing up her past was the last thing Jackson wanted to do, but he felt he had to. Waiting for a better opportunity was a luxury he couldn't afford. As long as those monsters were out there with no one doing anything to stop them, more kids were going to suffer just as Tessa had.

"I want to ask your permission for something."

Tessa tensed and the sweet moment was lost. "To do what?"

"I have a cousin who is a big shot with lots of resources and connections. Last year our cousin Carol was kidnapped, and he mobilized an army to rescue her."

"Did he succeed?"

Jackson chuckled. "He was too late. She had someone from the inside help her escape. But he freed a lot of other girls who were held against their will."

Tessa shivered. "Slavers?"

"In a way. They kidnapped girls for their own use, not to sell. But it's just as bad."

"What did your cousin do to the kidnappers?"

"Some were killed, others imprisoned."

"How come it didn't make the news?"

Damn, him and his big flapping mouth. Now he needed to lie to her. "That's the thing. It was a private operation, and no police were involved."

"Why are you telling me this?"

"Because I want to talk to him about your case. I want to go after those monsters who hurt you and take them out, but I can't do it on my own. Hell, I wouldn't know where to start."

She turned sideways and looked into his eyes. "I don't want you going anywhere near them, Jackson."

He took her hand and kissed it back. "I'm not a warrior. As much as I would've loved to put my hands on the scum, I know that others are much better at this than I could ever be. I would only get in their way. Maybe if I start training now, I could be of some marginal help in ten years or so."

Tessa tilted her head and brought her palm to his forehead. "Are you feverish? You're talking nonsense. Ten years to train? Not that I want you to train at all, but even elite commandos don't take so long."

He was such an idiot. "I meant ten months. I heard that SEAL's training takes that long."

Tessa relaxed. "That sounds more reasonable."

"So how about it? Can I tell Kian? I don't need to get into the specifics, or even mention your name. I just want him to get involved." With only two new potential Dormants, Sharon and Tessa, Kian was going to figure it out in a nanosecond.

Twisting the bottom of her shirt between her fingers, Tessa dropped her head, her hair falling forward and obscuring her face. "I don't know why your big shot cousin would want to get involved in this. Those are dangerous people. And even if he finds a reason to do it, I don't think he can make a difference. People don't realize how widespread this evil is. If he takes one organization out, two will sprout to take its place."

"It needs to start somewhere, and Kian is the only one I know who can make it happen."

She shook her head, her brown wavy hair swaying with the movement. "I can't say no. Even if one girl is saved, it's worth it. But I don't want your family to feel sorry for me, to look at me as if I'm damaged goods."

Jackson squeezed her hand lightly. "I will talk to him in private. He will not tell anyone if I ask him not to." Tessa was willing to cooperate. Maybe he could convince her to take it one step further. "To spur him into action, I need to make him angry, furious, and I'm starting to think that a diluted version about some hypothetical girl is not going to do it."

When Tessa lifted her head and looked at him, he didn't see the tears he'd been expecting. What he saw in her eyes was the need for vengeance. "Do you want me to come with you and tell him myself?"

Jackson shook his head. As it was, getting a private meeting with Kian was going to be tricky. The clan's regent wouldn't want to waste his time on a teenager. Bringing a human along, even a potential Dormant, guaranteed that he'd be refused audience.

"I don't think it will be needed. You know how convincing I can be."

Tessa chuckled. "With women. I don't think your charm would work on your big boss cousin."

She had a point.

CHAPTER 11: BHATHIAN

*D*one with the living room, Sharon entered the kitchen with an annoyed expression on her face. Eva and Bhathian were in her way. She wanted them gone.

Eva chuckled. "Let's get out of here before Sharon chases us away with her mop." Grabbing the last bottle of Snake's Venom from the counter, she took hold of Bhathian's hand and pulled him toward the stairs.

Casting a grateful smile at Sharon, he followed Eva. The girl had provided them with the perfect excuse to continue the party in the privacy of Eva's room. Just the two of them. Throughout the afternoon, as he'd watched Eva schmoozing, looking so sexy and sophisticated, he'd fantasized about throwing her over his shoulder and carrying her to the nearest bed, caveman style.

Bhathian loved that she was a lady outside the bedroom and a wild tigress inside it. Even more, he loved being the only one who got to see that other side of her. With him, Eva shed her civilized façade and let her inner immortal female out.

He couldn't wait to get her alone and make her scream his

name as she came. Good thing her crew was human, for now, because he was planning on making lots of noise.

Climbing the stairs behind her, he was transfixed by her magnificent ass swaying from side to side. Eva looked good enough to eat in her tight black leggings and white button up shirt that was too sheer for his taste. It was fine for him to ogle the curve of her breasts encased in one of her designer bras, but not for anyone else.

Once he was sure no one could see them, he palmed both of Eva's butt cheeks and squeezed.

She turned around with a smirk.

"With you dangling that ass of yours in front of me, I can't help myself."

"I like your hands on me." Laughing, she let him push her up by the ass all the way to her room. "You can let go now."

"I don't want to."

"Yes, you do if you want me to peel off these leggings."

"I can do it." He hooked his thumbs in the elastic band and pushed down, getting on his knees to pull them off all the way. Eva kicked off her shoes and lifted one leg at a time, helping him do it faster.

His woman was just as impatient as he was.

Praising the inventor of the thong, Bhathian palmed Eva's butt cheeks. Firm but pliable, her heart-shaped ass fit perfectly in his large hands. He pulled her closer, nuzzling her cleft through the tiny white panties and inhaling her unique musk.

The heat radiating from her center called him home.

She rubbed against his nose, and he rewarded her with a long lick on her pantie-covered slit. The fabric was so thin and sheer that it felt as if she was wearing nothing at all.

"Take them off." Her whisper was husky with desire.

He did, slowly, only pulling them down to her lower

thighs. It was enough, and he couldn't wait to bury his tongue inside her.

As Eva's fingers burrowed into his cropped hair, Bhathian wished it was longer so she'd have something to hold on to. But she managed just fine, clasping his head and grinding herself against him.

"That's so good, Bhathian."

It was, but he could do so much more with her lying on the bed, spread out for him. Besides, she was still wearing too many clothes. Wrapping his arms around her thighs, he lifted her as he pushed to his feet and carried her to the bed.

"I love how strong you are."

"Lift your arms for me, love," he instructed.

Eva obeyed, kneeling on the bed and letting him pull the shirt over her head. He tossed it on the floor, then climbed on the bed and knelt in front of his woman, so close their chests were almost touching. The only remaining article of clothing was the designer bra. It was a sexy number, the shiny white fabric contrasting with Eva's tanned skin, but it had to go as well. Naked was better.

He palmed her breasts and brought his mouth to hers. She cupped his head, holding him close as she kissed him, her tongue bold and demanding like its mistress.

There was no one like Eva.

Sometimes she liked to submit and let him dominate her from the start, other times she liked to fight him for dominance, and from time to time she wanted to be in charge and tell him what to do.

He loved it all even though it was clear to him that no matter what game they played, Eva was the one making all the rules and he was her obedient servant. There was no chance in hell that he would ever get bored with his mate, and guessing what she was in the mood for was part of the fun.

Tonight it seemed that she wanted to fight for it.

The first few times Eva had made it obvious that she wanted him to fight her, he'd held back because he'd been afraid of hurting her. She hadn't been pleased. Not at all. And he'd learned that she didn't want gentle and careful, or need it.

Maybe it was her training, or maybe her confidence, but he was damn sure that none of the other immortal females could've gotten free from his hold. Even Kri struggled, and she had decades of training. Eva was almost as fast and as devious as Kri, even though the woman had never been to a gym, and the last time she'd gotten any training was thirty something years ago—assuming DEA agents trained to maintain their skills the same way as Guardians. If they didn't, Eva's last session was when she'd graduated from the academy. About fifty years ago.

Superior genes. Had to be.

When Eva was in the mood for a fight, she didn't give up until she was convinced that there was no way out.

He broke up the kiss. "Get on your hands and knees."

Her pupils dilated, only a thin band of amber remaining around the black. "Make me."

Game on.

He'd guessed right.

Lifting Eva up, he twisted her around before the last syllable left her mouth. His hand on her nape, he pushed her down, so her face was on the bed and her ass high in the air. She tried to get up, but he'd known she would and held her head pinned to the duvet-covered mattress, delivering a hard smack to her upturned behind at the same time. A couple of weeks ago, he would have cringed at the red hand imprint he'd left on her skin. But he'd learned that she wouldn't have been happy with anything less.

Straightening her legs, Eva flattened herself on the

mattress and twisted sideways. He had to let go or risk injuring her neck.

The damn woman had known that and used it to her advantage. A triumphant smile illuminated her face as she waited for his next move. He reached for her, but she twisted away again.

It was like trying to capture an eel.

Slippery buggers.

Bhathian had two options—either pounce on Eva and pin her down, using his arms and his thighs, or get undressed and taunt her with his body. He chose the second one. After all, wrestling Eva with his pants on defeated the purpose of their little game.

Her brows lifted in surprise as he got off the bed, her eyes narrowing as he started his slow striptease. Very, very slow.

"Not fair. That's cheating," she said.

He shrugged and let his T-shirt drop to the floor.

Eva licked her lips as he unbuckled his belt and popped the first button on his jeans, then the next one, and the next one, until all that hid his shaft from her eyes were his boxer briefs. Stretchy and white, they didn't leave much to the imagination.

Mesmerized, she watched as he pushed his jeans down, a groan escaping her throat as he folded them neatly and put them on top of the dresser. With a smirk, he hooked his thumbs in the elastic band of his boxer shorts and pushed them down in increments of half an inch at a time.

With her eyes glued to his crotch, a low growl started in Eva's throat as he taunted her with the excruciatingly slow reveal. But getting naked was just the first part of his plan. There were a number of ways to make her do what he wanted.

Out of his boxer shorts, Bhathian fisted his cock. "You want this?" He ran his hand up and down the hard length.

"Yes."

"What are you willing to do for it?"

She narrowed her eyes. "What do you want?"

"Get on your arms and knees."

"No."

With a smirk, he continued the slow up and down movement. "Then you're not getting this."

Eva's eyes were shooting daggers at him, and her growls were getting louder and throatier.

"You can keep growling and hissing as much as you want, but if you want this, you'll do as I say."

With a look that would've petrified a lesser man, Eva flopped to her belly and then pushed up to her knees and forearms.

"Good girl." He climbed on the bed and knelt behind her. With each caress of his hand on her beautiful ass and her bowed back, he felt the tension leave her muscles, and when he cupped her moist center, she let out a moan and rested her cheek on the duvet.

"I still need to punish you for before." He penetrated her with one finger.

"Aha…" she breathed.

What was she thinking? That this was the punishment?

The hard smack he delivered to her left butt cheek and another one to its twin dissuaded any such illusion.

She didn't fight him when he delivered two more, which deserved a reward. Bending down, he extended his tongue and gave her wet slit a long lick. "Delicious." He smacked his lips before diving for more.

CHAPTER 12: EVA

*T*here was something deliciously wicked about getting tongue fucked from behind. Very unladylike.

Who cares.

Not Eva. She was spiraling toward an orgasm in record time, powerless to stop that tsunami from hitting fast and hard even though she would've loved to prolong the sweet agony for a few more minutes.

But it was all good. There were many more where where that one was coming from.

With the last vestiges of reason, she grabbed a pillow to scream into when she lost the battle and could hold back no more.

As she collapsed to the side, boneless, Bhathian curled behind her, spooning her and wrapping an arm around her. Any other man would have just speared inside her, but he knew she needed a few moments to come down from the high.

Eva had never been in a relationship where she felt

comfortable enough to engage in the kinds of sex games she was playing with Bhathian.

It was fun, liberating.

There was no pretense between them, and no secrets. She could be herself with him, but didn't have to. Sometimes she wanted to spice things up and pretend to be someone else. For his pleasure and hers.

The problem was, acting had become such an integral part of her life that it wasn't easy to stop even when she wanted to. After doing it for so long, it felt as if there were several personalities sharing her brain, ready to be called upon when needed. But outside of sex, Bhathian didn't allow it. Every time she'd inadvertently slipped into one of the many roles she used to play, he called her on it.

It was a process, a journey of discovery, and Eva was glad to have Bhathian along for the ride.

He was her compass, her sounding board, the one person whom she'd dared to confide in and show her ugly side. Her demons didn't repel him. His acceptance was priceless to her. A boon.

Was that love? Eva wasn't sure. But even if it wasn't, it was good enough. What she had with Bhathian was more than she'd ever expected to have. And the guy was one hell of a lover. Attuned to every little nuance, he knew how to please her well. Which given her shifting moods wasn't an easy feat. And yet, aside from the clumsy beginning, he'd never erred.

A warm palm closed around her breast, a thumb lazily circling her nipple. "Are you ready for more?"

She turned around and plastered herself against his warmth and his strength. "Thank you."

"You're welcome. And my tongue thanks you for giving him the opportunity to serve." He kissed her nose.

"It's not only for the tongue. It's for everything."

His eyes softened. "Oh, love, you've seen nothing yet. I have one mission in life, and it's to make you happy."

"An ambitious goal. I'm not a cheerful kind of person, and neither are you."

"That doesn't mean we can't be happy. I'm happy now."

"Me too."

Surprisingly, she realized it was true. Life didn't get much better than that. She had her daughter back, a sweet baby grandchild, a man who cared about her, a thriving business, and a fascinating hobby...

They should make a reality show about her.

Damn. She'd better get her head back into the sex before her thoughts wandered into dark places that didn't belong in her bed. "Make love to me, big guy."

"With pleasure."

He entered her in one smooth thrust, his shaft sliding home with ease. A perfect fit. Kissing her deeply, he went slow and steady, his body communicating his love better than any spoken words.

That was her Bhathian. Not a big talker, but a mighty doer.

This time the climax came more like a wave than a tsunami, swelling gently and then cresting in an easy flow rather than crashing to shore. She turned her head, inviting his bite. Bhathian's soft lips made contact first, then his tongue, and lastly his fangs, piercing her skin just as gently as his lovemaking.

Eva sighed, letting the euphoria wash over her and carry her on its wings to a place of bliss where nothing negative existed. Was that what heaven was like? A place of bliss?

Unfortunately, the effect was temporary. A reprieve that lasted somewhere between a few minutes and a few hours depending on how long ago the last time had been. Frequency diluted the effect.

"It's like alcohol," she murmured.

"What is?"

"The venom. If you drink only once in a while, you get drunk faster and easier than if you do it every day. Same with the venom-induced euphoria. It doesn't last as long now."

"What troubles you, love?"

She smiled, cuddled closer and kissed his lips. "What makes you think I'm troubled?"

"You would not have been bemoaning the loss of the euphoric cloud otherwise."

"You know me so well, it's scary."

He frowned. "Why scary?"

She kissed the crease between his bushy eyebrows. "It's just an expression."

"You want to talk about it?"

"After we shower. We still have that one bottle of Snake's Venom, but I draw the line at drinking in bed."

They made love again in the shower. Twice. Fortunately, the house came with a tankless instant water heater. The old fashioned type would've run out of hot water a long time before they had finally gotten clean.

Dressed in the matching bathrobes she'd bought for them on her last out of town trip, they sat on the sofa in her bedroom's sitting area. Bhathian popped the beer open, and they took turns drinking straight from the bottle.

Neither wanted to go downstairs for glasses.

Eva took another sip and handed the bottle to Bhathian. "We are two lazy immortals."

He chuckled. "Not lazy, exhausted."

Exhausted wasn't the right term. Eva wasn't tired. It was just the general languid feeling of a sated body.

Leaning against the plush sofa pillows, she didn't bother crossing her legs and let the bathrobe gape. Her mother, bless her soul, would've been appalled at such a lewd display. Eva doubted the woman had ever let her husband see her naked. Her parents had probably made love only in the dark.

She was so bad for letting thoughts like that go through her head. Shame on her.

"What got you upset now?"

"It's nothing."

He looked offended.

"Look, those were just some stupid random thoughts about things I shouldn't be thinking about. It has nothing to do with you." Did he expect her to share everything with him? Some things were just not worth sharing.

"How about the thing you wanted to tell me about before?"

Yeah. That was a much better subject for conversation. More interesting, that was for sure.

"The night I took out that guy I told you about, I saw someone who looked a lot like the guy who had turned me."

Bhathian's back went rigid. "Could it have been him?"

"No. He had the same build, same coloring, but the eyes were different. My guy had blue smiling eyes and an easy-going disposition. The man in the club had dark brown eyes, almost black. Piercing. Scary." Eva shivered. "There was something sinister about him. I rarely meet anyone I'm afraid of. But I wanted to get as far away as quickly as I could from that man." She reached for the bottle and took a small sip. There wasn't much left. "He wasn't physically intimidating, or even angry looking. He was cordial and seemed cultured, and yet I couldn't help thinking that this guy was the closest I've been to the devil."

Bhathian chuckled and pulled her close. "Let me warm you up. You have goosebumps on your arms."

"I'm not cold. It's that guy. Creepy as hell."

"Where did you see him? Maybe we can snoop around."

Bhathian was going to freak out about her picking up her target in a sex club. "Do you remember when I asked if anyone had heard about a club called Allure?"

"What about it?"

"That was where I picked up my target, and where I saw that guy. It's a fancy members-only sex club."

Yep. Just as she'd expected Bhathian's eyes began glowing, and his fangs punched over his bottom lip. "You went to a sex club?"

She patted his thigh. "Calm down, big guy. I went on a tour as a prospective member. I didn't participate in anything other than smoking a cigar in the cigar lounge. It's not like people are screwing everywhere. There is a big room with a bar just for mingling, and the lounge is outside on a covered patio. Very high class. The sex happens in closed-off areas."

Bhathian's eyes were still glowing, but his fangs shrunk back to their normal size. "Did you go into any of those areas?"

"I had to as part of the tour. But I only saw the most mundane stuff, nothing extreme. The furthest I went was into a room dedicated to those who get off on doing it with an audience. I told my guide I wasn't comfortable with seeing anything more."

That seemed to mollify him. "Where did you find your mark?"

"In the cigar lounge. He was a guest of a member. No doubt trying to sell him something." She grimaced. "Or someone."

"And the one who creeped you out?"

"Like me, he was taking a tour. I saw him only for a few moments. He thanked his guide and left."

"Maybe he bought a membership? I can go and check it out."

At the thought of going back to that club, a shiver ran down Eva's back. It was a bad idea regardless of whether the scary guy was there or not. "I don't want you there."

A satisfied smirk brightened Bhathian's face. "Afraid I'll see something I like?"

Did he think she was jealous? Men and their egos. Eva crossed her arms over her chest. "It's not about that. You can watch the live porn for all I care."

"How about we go together?"

"I can't. You're allowed up to two visits as a prospective member. After that, the only way in is to buy the membership or to get invited by a member."

"I don't see what the problem is. You have one more free visit. We can say that you brought me along because I'm also interested in a membership. Bringing a new prospective client should be worth one more free visit to them. Besides, with your many disguises and identities, you can go as someone else."

Eva shook her head. "I don't know why, but I have a bad feeling about that place. I don't want you anywhere near it, and it has nothing to do with jealousy."

CHAPTER 13: NATHALIE

"She's finally sleeping." Andrew walked into their bedroom and joined Nathalie on the couch they'd brought in there. Ever since Phoenix's birth, Andrew was back to sleeping in the master bedroom, but he didn't trust himself to join her in bed yet. The other reason was that she often fell asleep with the baby still at her breast, and he was afraid of accidentally rolling over the tiny bundle.

Andrew wrapped a gentle arm around her shoulders. "You should try and get some sleep. I'll take care of her through the night."

"You can't. You're back at work. Even you need a few hours of sleep."

"I'll put dark sunglasses on and catch a nap at my desk. No one will know."

Right. As if his loud snoring wouldn't give him away.

Only two weeks had passed since Phoenix came into their lives, bringing joy, love, sleepless nights, and achy nipples. Nathalie was exhausted, and her breasts felt as if someone had chewed on them. Well, someone had. The only thing that was helping were ice packs. Not to mention that her nipples were so oversensitive that she couldn't stand anything touching them and was spending most of her days in her bedroom.

Topless.

A sticky note on the other side of their front door asked visitors to wait for an invitation for after momma and baby felt better.

She sighed. "I feel like a bush woman." *And as sexy as a dishrag.*

Sleeping on the couch wasn't really necessary. Even without any of the guys babysitting Andrew at night, he had no problem staying away from her. It should've made her happy that they were sharing a bedroom again, but all it did was depress her further. At least before she'd felt desirable, so much so that her man needed guards to keep him from jumping on her.

Big belly and all.

Bridget had said it was normal for a new mother to feel overwhelmed and even depressed, but Nathalie doubted that her problem was postpartum depression. She loved Phoenix and was overjoyed about becoming a mom. But it was hard to be positive when she was having such a hard time with a simple thing like breastfeeding. It was supposed to be magical, a wonderful time for mother and baby. Instead, she was grinding her teeth to get through it.

"Switching to formula will make it so much easier on you," Andrew said for the umpteenth time.

Her resistance was starting to crack. She was a stubborn woman, determined to succeed at everything she did, but at some point she needed to admit defeat. "I know." The tears stinging the back of her eyes came rushing down. "Nothing worked the way I hoped it would. First the cesarean and now this."

"Oh, sweetheart." Andrew kissed the top of her head. "Life

is not neat, and things rarely work out the way we want. We adjust. I can't watch you torturing yourself like this every day and every night. I think having a happy mommy will benefit Phoenix more than breast milk. And let's not forget that as soon as you feel better you are going to take her to Annani's place and she'll turn immortal. Do you really think that feeding her formula instead of breast milk will have any long term negative impact?"

Nathalie reached for a tissue, wiped her eyes, and blew her nose. "The hormones must be still scrambling my brain. What you say makes perfect sense logically, but getting my emotions to agree is a different story."

"I'll tell you what. I'm going to get dressed and drive to the nearest twenty-four-hour pharmacy. I'm going to buy formula and bottles, and whatever else is needed so we can start tonight. You text Bridget and ask her what brand of formula she recommends, and also for something to dry out your milk. Tomorrow we start afresh."

Sweet, wonderful Andrew. Always putting her needs first. "Isn't it too late to call Bridget?"

"That's why I suggested texting her. If she's asleep, a text will have less chance of waking her." Andrew kissed her lightly on the lips and went to get dressed.

Turned out Bridget was awake. Not only that, she insisted on coming up and checking on Nathalie. Which meant that she would have to put something on. A silk night robe was the only tolerable garment, and Nathalie left it hanging loose, tying the belt only when Bridget knocked on the door.

"Hi, Nathalie," she whispered, so as not to wake the baby.

Nathalie motioned for her to come in. "Thank you for coming. I'm sorry for the late hour. I would've waited until tomorrow, but when Andrew makes a decision, he wants to implement it right away."

Bridget waved a hand. "Think nothing of it. I was parking my car when I got your text."

Given her bombshell getup, the doctor must've come back from a night on the town. A tight stretchy skirt hugged her beautifully shaped hips, and her four-inch heels made her legs look a mile long. The blouse was loose over her ample breasts, but for once Nathalie didn't envy Bridget her cleavage. Those things no longer symbolized sex appeal for her. Painful overstuffed balloons, that's what they were.

"Andrew went to get formula for Phoenix. Is there any brand that you recommend?"

"They are all good. But I'll save Andrew some time by telling him what to buy. Otherwise he'll be stuck in that aisle for hours, reading all the labels." Bridget pulled out her phone, her slim fingers flying over the screen as she texted Andrew a set of instructions that was obviously more than just a formula brand.

It hadn't escaped Nathalie's notice that Andrew's number was still on Bridget's favorites list.

Jealousy, hot and ugly, twisted Nathalie's gut. Was that the reason behind Andrew's supposedly subdued libido? Was he screwing his old girlfriend?

She shook her head. *Stop it.*

Andrew was with her every free minute he had. So unless he was cutting work, which she was sure he wasn't, he didn't have time for extramarital affairs.

Besides, it felt wrong to even think that way. It was time she banished the jealous monster living inside her. "When can I have sex with Andrew again?" The words just tumbled out of her mouth.

Bridget's expression didn't change. "My answer is the same as last time: no intercourse for six weeks. Could you open your robe? I want to examine your breasts."

Fernando was sleeping, so it was okay to bare herself in

the middle of the living room, but it felt awkward. And the fact that Bridget had seen everything already, inside and out, didn't make it any less embarrassing.

Damn Andrew. Out of all the possible immortal females, he'd had to hook up with the one that was the local clan's only medical doctor.

To her credit, Bridget was very careful with her examination, applying as little pressure as possible. It still hurt, but it could've been worse.

"The good news is that there is no infection. Your breasts are just too swollen which makes latching on properly difficult. Has Phoenix been fussy?"

With a wince, Nathalie closed the lapels of her robe. "Not more than usual. She still wakes up every two hours. Day and night."

Bridget nodded. "She's a big baby and needs a lot of food. You made a good decision switching her to formula. Easier on both of you."

"Can you give me something to dry out the milk?"

"Not yet. First we'll see how Phoenix tolerates the formula."

"Makes sense."

Bridget got up. "Not that I expect her to have problems, it's just a precaution. Your torment is almost over."

"I have another question."

The doctor sat back down. "Shoot."

Nathalie closed her eyes for a moment, gathering her nerve. "You said no intercourse, but what about other stuff? Is it okay if Andrew bites me?"

Bridget's professional composure was enviable. "Health-wise, I see no problem with that. In fact, the venom will speed up your healing. But the sex will be one-sided. You can pleasure Andrew orally, but he can't reciprocate."

Talk about awkward.

"That's fine. I miss the closeness, the connection. Besides, Andrew can't keep going like that."

Bridget frowned. "Is he still getting drunk every evening?"

"No. I know it's stupid, but it makes me feel even worse. I must be so unappealing to him that he's lost interest." Cue the sniffle.

Bridget reached for a tissue and handed it to Nathalie. "You're not the only one whose life has been turned upside down. You're taking the brunt of it, but Andrew is also tired and worried. I'm not surprised his libido has cooled down to at least a manageable level."

Nathalie wiped the few tears that had spilled out of her eyes despite her best efforts, and chuckled. "I'll finally get to experience a real bite. I wonder if it's really all that."

Bridget's professional façade finally cracked and her lips twisted into a grimace. "I wouldn't know."

Shit. She'd forgotten that most clan females had never gotten to experience a venom bite. "I'm sorry," she mumbled.

Bridget sighed. "Nothing to be sorry about. It is what it is. Hopefully, Amanda and Syssi will find more Dormants, and hopefully one of them will like me, and hopefully I'll like him back…"

Nathalie echoed Bridget's sigh. That didn't sound promising at all. Her heart ached for Bridget and the others. "Yeah, hopefully…"

Pushing up to her feet, Bridget collected her red purse and headed for the door. "One more thing," she said as she pulled the door open. "If Andrew bites you, you will transition. And if yours is as difficult as Andrew's, you'll be out for a few days. You need to make arrangements for someone to help Andrew take care of Phoenix."

Why hadn't she thought of that? Her brain was functioning at half capacity. Probably because she was so tired all the time. "Thanks for pointing it out."

The doctor cast Nathalie an indulgent smile. "It's difficult for a new mother to adjust to her new life. Until Phoenix is old enough to take care of herself, you need to consider the impact of every move you make on her. Eventually it will become second nature." Bridget stepped out into the hallway.

"I know. Even going to the bathroom or taking a shower requires planning."

"Welcome to motherhood." Bridget chuckled. "But it's all worth it."

True. The intense surge of love Nathalie felt every time she held Phoenix was incomparable.

"Thanks for coming."

"Any time."

As soon as Nathalie closed the door behind Bridget, she went back to her bedroom and took the robe off.

Damn, the exhaustion combined with the hormonal mess was making her stupid. How could she have forgotten about the main reason for the enforced abstinence?

Nathalie was more than ready for sex, in any form or shape, but she was definitely not ready for the transition. Not with a newborn depending on her. Who would take care of Phoenix when she was in a coma?

Oh, my God. What if I die? My daughter will become an orphan.

But if she didn't go for it, Nathalie was going to lose her husband. Andrew loved her, but there was a limit to what he could endure. Besides, she loved him too much to see him suffer like that. Letting him go would be the right thing to do.

He will probably go straight back to Bridget...

No! No way! Andrew was hers.

She had to take the risk and trust God or fate to see her through it.

No guts, no glory.

The thing was, Nathalie felt as if she was choosing her man over her daughter and it felt wrong.

I'm not going to win any mother of the year awards, that's for sure.

CHAPTER 14: KIAN

*K*ian's phone rang with the special ringtone he'd programmed for Syssi. "Hey, sweet girl. Miss me?"

"I do. When are you coming up? It's late."

Kian leaned back in his chair. "I'm waiting for Jackson. He wants to talk to me about something."

"Should I wait with dinner?"

"No. I don't know how long it will take." Kian chuckled. "I suspect he has some business proposition for me. The kid is all about making money."

"It's nice of you to humor him."

"I know. Normally I wouldn't have, but Nathalie and Bhathian speak so highly of him that I'm curious."

"I'm going to grab a bite of something and wait for you with dinner. So try and wrap it up quickly."

"I'll do my best."

Lately, Kian had been making an effort to leave the office at a decent hour so he and Syssi could share a meal after work. It wasn't that he had less to do, only that he was taking work to continue later in his home office.

Kian had finally caved and hired a young intern. The guy was a business major who was graduating in two months. Kian had high hopes for the kid. He had a sharp mind and was highly motivated. The question was whether he was a self-starter. Kian had no time to waste teaching a greenhorn what had taken him centuries to learn.

A soft knock on the glass announced his late evening visitor.

"Come in, Jackson."

"Hi, thanks for agreeing to see me," the kid said as he walked in and sat in a chair on the other side of Kian's desk.

"No problem. How can I help you?"

"I've met a girl." The normally cocky Jackson looked uncomfortable.

Kian snorted. "If you need help with courtship, I'm the last guy you should turn to for advice. Just ask my wife."

"What? No! I don't need any help with that."

Kian stifled a chuckle. No eighteen-year-old wanted to admit he had difficulties in that department. It took years of experience, centuries, to realize that when it came to understanding women, all men, regardless of age, were just as lost and confused.

"Of course not. My mistake."

"When she was younger, only fifteen, she ran away from her foster home and was picked up by slave traffickers. They hurt her badly, sexually and otherwise, then sold her to some guy that kept raping her until she managed to escape." The kid had admirable self-control. Jackson had delivered his speech in an even tone, but the glow in his eyes and the way his words started slurring toward the end had betrayed his rage.

"I'm glad she escaped. Does she need financial support? Is that why you came to me?"

Jackson shook his head. "No. The woman who helped her

escape took care of her and gave her a job. The girl is not hurting financially, but she is damaged. There is nothing I can do to fix that, but I thought you could help me avenge her. I don't even know where to start."

A noble sentiment, but naive.

"I wish I could help. I really do. But there is a lot that is broken in this world, and we are not all-powerful. We are doing all we can with what we have."

"You rescued the women from the Doomers."

"That was different. The Doomers had Carol, one of our own, and even then it was difficult to mobilize the old Guardians to help."

Jackson slumped in his chair. "I can't live with myself knowing that such evil exists, that kids are being snatched off the street and ruined, while I'm living my life and not doing anything about it."

Yeah, Kian knew that feeling well. A deep frustration, an impotence that left a sour taste in his mouth. But what could he do? Aside from the constant drip of information and ideas to help humanity help itself, he had no business trying to play savior and committing his clansmen to impossible tasks.

Taking care of his own was difficult enough.

"What if the girl I'm talking about is a potential Dormant? Does that change anything?

Kian shook his head. "Not really. As I said, I can mobilize warriors for a rescue mission, but not for revenge or even to help others. I would not risk my people. I'm sorry." The girl Jackson was talking about had to be one of Eva's two female employees. The only potential Dormants he was aware of. So unless more had been found and no one had bothered to tell him, it had to be one of them.

Jackson pushed to his feet. "Thank you for your time."

He couldn't let the kid go like that. Jackson was too young to carry such a burden on his shoulders.

"Sit down, Jackson."

"Yes, sir."

"I'll look into it. I'm not promising anything. But if there is something we can do, even on a small scale, like helping the human authorities with information about the whereabouts of those organizations, I'll consider it, but only as long as I don't have to put any of our clan members' lives on the line."

"That's all I can ask for. And if there is anything you need from me, please, I'm willing to do whatever it takes." Jackson got up, walked to Kian's side of the desk, and offered his hand. "Thank you."

Kian shook what he was offered. "You're welcome. I'll let you know."

Nasty business, human trafficking, Kian thought as he made his way up to the penthouse. Lately, it seemed as if the Fates were pushing it down his throat. First with Alex's operation, then with Carol's kidnapping, pulling him and his small force of Guardians into one rescue operation after the other. And then Jackson came to him about his girlfriend.

Was it all connected?

I wish you'd just tell me straight up what you want of me.

But of course the Fates didn't work that way. It was all about mystical mumbo jumbo and vague signs and premonitions. The problem was that anything could be perceived as a sign. It was very tempting to see patterns in random coincidence. The brain, human and immortal alike, was always trying to make sense of the chaos. But seeing imaginary patterns and acting upon them was dangerous.

Often catastrophic.

When he got home, Kian hugged Syssi tight. "I'm so glad I have you." What he meant to say was that he was happy she was safe.

She stretched up on her toes and kissed him. "Me too."

She touched a finger to the crease between his brows. "What brought that about?"

He sighed. "Jackson came to me with a story about a young girl that was abducted and sold into sexual slavery. Somehow she managed to escape, but the experience must've left deep scars because he described her as broken."

"Why did he come to you with that?"

Kian sighed. "He's under the impression that I'm some omnipotent force who can right all the wrongs in the world. I had to disillusion him."

"What did he want you to do?"

"Help him avenge her."

Syssi nodded. "I like Jackson. He is a good kid." She tilted her head. "Correction, he is a good man. I feel like calling him a kid makes light of his achievements."

"I agree, though I'm guilty of doing the same. It's not fair to give eighteen-year-old men automatic rifles, send them into battle, and still call them kids."

Syssi tugged on his hand. "Let's talk while we eat. Okidu is complaining that his creations are drying out in the warming drawer. I placated him by promising we will eat in the dining room and he could serve us."

Kian chuckled. "He is not human, Syssi. It's all an act."

She rolled her eyes. "A very convincing one. Come on."

Okidu must've been on standby. "Master, you are home. Please…" He ran ahead of them into the dining room and pulled out a chair, first for Syssi and then for Kian. "Soup will be out in a moment."

"How are Nathalie and the baby doing?" Kian asked as they waited for the soup to be served. Syssi's eyes always sparkled when she talked about Phoenix. But not this time.

She leaned back and crossed her arms over her chest. "She is having a hard time with the breastfeeding, and she's exhausted. I offered to come babysit so she could take a nap, but she refuses to accept any help. I don't know if it's because she feels like she has to prove that she is a superwoman, or because she doesn't trust me with her baby."

"Does Nathalie let anyone else take care of Phoenix?"

"Only Andrew and Eva as far as I know."

"Well, that makes sense. Andrew is the dad, and he's experienced. Eva is the grandmother and also knows a thing or two about taking care of babies."

Okidu came in with a tray loaded with two steaming soup bowls, and a baguette cut into thick chunks. It smelled as though it had just been taken out of the oven.

"Everything smells wonderful, Okidu," Syssi said.

"Thank you, madam."

Kian grabbed a chunk of the fresh bread and dug into the soup, happy to get a break from talking about the baby, which seemed to upset Syssi rather than make her happy.

Women were so difficult to figure out.

Was she mad at Nathalie for not sharing? Or were her feelings hurt because Nathalie didn't trust her with the baby? Or maybe it was something else?

Kian knew Syssi wanted a baby of her own. During Nathalie's last trimester, she used to joke about the pregnancy hormones making all the clan females baby crazy. But from what he had seen, she was the only one affected by it. Amanda and Bridget had seemed indifferent, as had Carol, who had been spending long hours with Nathalie and should've been the one affected the most. He wasn't an expert, but in his uneducated opinion, it just made sense.

Unfortunately, there was nothing he could do about it. It would happen when it happened. When the Fates decided it was time.

Fuck. I sound like my mother.

CHAPTER 15: AMANDA

*A*s Syssi walked into Amanda's office, there was a big smile on her face.

Amanda peered at her from behind her desktop. "You look happy."

"I'm always happy when I'm proven right. All three of Eva's employees tested positive as far as affinity. Anandur's report is on top. He gave Sharon a ten, Nick a nine and Tessa also a nine." She sat down and dropped a stack of papers on Amanda's desk. "Here. See for yourself."

Amanda examined each paper, reading the remarks several times over. "Looks impressive. But what if they are just cool, likable people?"

"That's why I wanted Brundar to come. He doesn't like anyone. But Kian needed him at the keep."

"Right. Who else do we have that doesn't like people?"

"A couple of months ago I would've said Bhathian, but he is all smiles now."

"Can you blame him? He has a mate and a baby grand-daughter."

Syssi snorted. "I doubt Nathalie lets him visit. She is

cooped up in her apartment with her baby, and the only one she allows in is Eva."

Amanda waved a hand. "Don't be so hard on her. It takes time getting used to being a mom. It's not as easy of a transition as everyone would like you to believe." Surprisingly, talking about motherhood hadn't brought on the choking sensation it used to. Being constantly exposed to Nathalie and her belly, and then to everyone obsessing about the baby was in a way therapeutic. After all, if one was afraid of snakes the best way to get over it was to get exposed to a lot of them.

"Anyway. What do we do with that?" Syssi pointed at the papers.

"We keep testing. I want to try it on more subjects."

"What about your flower girl? Do you want to lure her in here?"

"Nah. I'll send people to her shop. Anandur promised he'd stop by this afternoon. And William said he'd go tomorrow."

"Any progress with his facial recognition software?"

Until recently, the technology wasn't all that good, but in the past couple of years, huge advancements had been made. William was working on adapting it to their needs. If there were other undocumented immortals living in the West, he believed there was a good chance he would find them.

"I'm sure he'll tell us the moment it's ready. But the software is just one part of the equation. He needs access to the databases, and Andrew is in no shape to help."

"Poor Andrew. He looks like a train wreck."

Amanda waved a dismissive hand. "He'll be fine. As soon as that baby starts sleeping at night, and Mommy and Daddy start getting it on, everyone will be in a better mood."

Syssi rubbed the tip of her nose. "I've been thinking. What about Hannah?"

"What about her?"

"I like her. You like her. William likes her. Maybe she is a Dormant? If we factor in fate, it's a possibility."

Amanda tapped a finger on her chin. "If she were, she would've transitioned already. They've been together for a while."

"Not if they are not sleeping together."

"I'm not buying it."

"I am. William doesn't strike me as someone who would lie to your face. Besides, he is well aware of the damage repeated thralling could do to Hannah. That's why he keeps their relationship from turning into a romance. Imagine how relieved he will be if we tell him he can go for it."

Amanda seemed unconvinced. "I don't know. Hannah has zero paranormal talent. Even less than your run-of-the-mill human who has the occasional premonition about who's calling her before picking up the phone. Though I have to admit that William and Hannah's case lends itself perfectly to our experiment. With Eva's crew, we will have to play matchmaker in order to take it to the next step. William and Hannah are already a couple of sorts."

"Exactly."

Amanda smirked. "Who is going to tell him?"

"No offense, but I think a little diplomacy is needed here, and you have the same no-nonsense blunt attitude as Kian."

Amanda crossed her arms over her chest. "I don't know what you're talking about. I'm always diplomatic."

"Sure you are. For a cavewoman. Just bang it over the head and pound it into submission." Syssi demonstrated with an imaginary club.

"Fine. Be my guest. I can already imagine it. Your cheeks will get red like two ripe tomatoes." It had been a mean thing to say, given how much Syssi agonized over her inability to control her blushing, but so was comparing Amanda's style to Kian's.

Amanda was nothing like her brother.

Naturally, the taunt pinked Syssi's pale cheeks. "True. But I'm done letting that damn involuntary response dictate my actions or lack of them. If it wasn't cured by Kian's teasing and the transition, nothing is going to do it. I have no choice but to learn to live with it."

Amanda clapped her hands. "Bravo. I'm proud of you. And if you ever need it, I'll let you borrow my club." She winked.

"Thank you." Syssi sighed. "I wish I had half your chutzpah."

"As I said, my club is at your disposal."

Syssi snorted. "I need a driving course on it."

"No problem. It's simple. Don't give a shit about other people and what they think of you. Very few deserve your consideration. The only person you need to impress is you." Amanda pointed at Syssi's chest.

"Yeah, you're right. I'm too sensitive." Syssi pushed up to her feet and started pacing.

Amanda smiled. Husband and wife were rubbing off on each other, with Kian being the one benefiting most. He was calmer and happier and less explosive. Syssi had just picked up his habit of pacing while the wheels in her brain were turning.

"I was thinking," Syssi started. Sometimes it got annoying the way she always waited for an invitation to bring up a new topic.

"Yes?"

"About my visions."

Amanda rolled her eyes. "What about them?"

"I want to find a way to harness them."

"And how do you propose to do that?"

"I want to try hallucinogenics."

"Are you insane? Who knows what they can do to someone like you?"

"That's why I want you to help me. I want to start with something very mild, and I want you to be there with me."

"Did you share this crazy idea with Kian?"

Syssi snorted. "Of course not."

As a neuroscientist, Amanda knew a thing or two about hallucinogenic drugs, and some were indeed harmless. But there was always a chance of a bad trip. Taken by someone with Syssi's abilities, they could be very dangerous. She could end up with a severe psychotic episode.

"I've been reading up on mushrooms," Syssi said. "I can try a tiny amount and see how I react to it. Or, I can start with something as trivial as pot." She chuckled. "I think I'm the only one on campus who has never tried it. Everyone is doing it. Students and professors."

"I'm not."

Syssi arched a brow. "Really? You never tried anything?"

Amanda shook her head. "No. I don't even like alcohol. I can tolerate huge quantities of it until I get drunk, but I have no wish to. I value my brain too much to do anything to compromise it."

"I was so sure you did. You're such a rebel."

"Well, thank you. But I chose to rebel in different ways. What I want to know, though, is what brought it about? I was under the impression that you hated your visions, that they were always gloomy and dark and put you in a bad mood."

Syssi sat back down. "Not all of them. I predicted Andrew's daughter."

Aha, the puzzle pieces fell into place. Ever since Phoenix's birth, Syssi had been pining for a baby of her own. She'd been downplaying her craving, but Amanda had seen right through it. Her sister-in-law had it bad. Real bad if she was considering taking hallucinogens to induce a foretelling of her and Kian's future child.

"Is it about you wanting a baby?"

Syssi blushed. "Yes, but I started thinking about it even before that. What if I can predict when and where to find Dormants?"

That was an interesting idea. "Go on."

"Think about it. The Oracles of Delphi inhaled toxic fumes to induce their visions. What I think happens is not that the chemicals alter reality, but that they open the spigot to what the brain allows in. To process outside stimuli, the brain must filter most of it out; otherwise it would not be able to handle it all. The drugs change the filtering properties of the sieve. Things that are normally allowed in are blocked, and other things that are normally filtered out are allowed in."

It wasn't a new idea; Amanda had read the theories before. But unlike those long-winded and overcomplicated essays, Syssi's simple explanation made sense.

"When Kian finds out, he is going to lock us both in the dungeon."

"I can't help the feeling that the Fates can use me to guide us in our search. I feel compelled to try it."

"Are you going to keep it a secret from him?"

Syssi shook her head. "No. But I'm not going to say anything until I'm ready to try. Less time for him to build up steam."

"Good idea. I'm going to call my mother and ask her if any of the gods or immortals of her time messed around with hallucinogenics. It's not like they are a new invention."

Syssi got up, walked around the desk, and hugged Amanda. "Thank you. I knew I could count on your help."

Amanda hugged her back. "Always."

CHAPTER 16: BHATHIAN

How are my precious girls doing? Bhathian texted Nathalie, hoping she'd invite him over. He hadn't seen either of them for days. He even missed Andrew. It had been fun hanging out with his son-in-law, even when the dude had been medicating himself with booze. Andrew was a happy drunk.

But there was no more need for him to watch Andrew, and while Nathalie was recovering from surgery, she wasn't letting anyone other than Eva see her or the baby.

He missed her.

We are good. Phoenix is doing much better since we switched her to formula. She is not as fussy and sleeps longer between feeds.

When can I see her?

A moment passed with no reply, and then his phone rang. "I'm so sorry, Bhathian. I know I've been crappy about it, but I've been so exhausted all of the time. Give me another day. Okay?"

"No problem. Tomorrow then."

"Tomorrow."

With no classes scheduled for the evening, he had nothing

to do, and he'd already done his workout in the morning. Normally, he would head out to Eva's, but she was working late today. A local assignment by L.A.'s standards, somewhere out in Orange County.

Perhaps he could head over to her house and wait for her to come back.

Bhathian had gotten so used to sleeping over at Andrew's or Eva's that staying in his own place felt weird.

For several consecutive nights, he'd spent the night at Eva's, but he had a feeling she was growing uncomfortable with that. Getting used to sharing her bed was proving more difficult for her than it was for him. It seemed she still needed her solitude, while he was ready to toss it out the window and not miss it for a second.

Bhathian was ready for the next stage in his life.

Eva wasn't. Not yet.

Not that he was going to let her retreat into her shell. He was going to push and push some more until she got used to him being part of her life.

With that in mind, he stuffed a change of clothes into his duffel bag and headed toward her house.

Nick opened the door. "Hi, Bhathian, Eva is not back yet."

"I know. I'm going to wait for her." He walked in and joined Nick in front of the dumb box.

"What are you watching?"

"A surfing competition."

"Any hot surfer babes?"

"Unfortunately not today." Nick took a swig from his beer. "You want one?" he asked.

"I'll get it."

Bhathian got up and walked over to the kitchen. Regrettably, the only beer left was Corona. It was piss water, but he'd forgotten to restock the Snake's Venom.

Bottle in hand, he returned to the living room and sat on the couch. "Where are the girls?"

Nick's eyes remained glued to the screen. "Tessa is in the office, and Sharon is upstairs."

Unlike football or some other competitive team sport, watching guys surf was boring as hell. "I'll go say hi to Tessa."

Nick waved him off. "Okay."

The office was at the back of the house, in a room off the kitchen that was originally designed as maids' quarters. He found Tessa sorting through a pile of receipts and punching numbers at the adding machine.

"Accounting stuff?"

She lifted her head. "Yeah. Hi, Bhathian. Eva is not back yet."

"I know. How are things going for you?"

"Good." She narrowed her eyes at him. "Why are you asking?"

"No reason. Just making conversation. I'm bored."

"Oh. Surfing is not your thing, huh?"

He shook his head. "Not unless it's hot babes in bikinis."

She chuckled. "Don't let Eva hear you say that."

"Why? Is she the jealous type?"

"I don't know. You're the first guy I've seen her dating. But I wouldn't like it if my boyfriend made comments about other babes."

Eva had mentioned something about Tessa seeing a lot of Jackson lately. Were the two a couple?'

"Do you have one? Should I warn him?"

"No, I don't have a boyfriend. I have a friend who is a boy, but it's not the same."

"I guess not." He wondered what the deal was with that. Jackson wasn't the type of guy who had platonic relationships with girls.

He heard the garage door open, and a few moments later

Eva came in. "Hi, Bhathian, Tessa." She dropped her keys on Tessa's desk. "If you're going out to see Jackson tonight, can you take my car and fill it with gas on the way? I was too tired to stop for a refuel."

"Sure." Tessa pocketed the keys. "In fact, I'm heading out now."

"Say hi to him for me."

"I will."

As soon as Tessa was gone, Bhathian pulled Eva into his arms and kissed her. She seemed tense, her back muscles feeling tight under his palms. "A tough day?" he asked.

She pushed away from him. "Just tiring. And I'm hungry. Come with me to the kitchen?"

"Sure." He followed after her.

Eva pulled the fridge door open and cursed under her breath. "There is nothing left." She turned around. "Nick! Did you finish all the Chinese?"

"Sorry!"

She shook her head. "Damn selfish kid."

Bhathian reached for her hand. "Let me take you out to eat."

"I'm too tired. All I could think of while driving back home was digging into the leftovers from the Golden Palace and taking a long bubble bath."

"I'll tell you what. You go upstairs and take that bubble bath, and I'll order us takeout."

Her eyes softened. "Sounds wonderful."

"Chinese?"

"Yes please." She grabbed a banana from the fruit bowl. "This will tide me over until the food gets here."

As Eva headed upstairs, Bhathian placed the order, but instead of waiting for the delivery, he went to get it himself. Not only would it be faster, but he could stop by the liquor store and buy some decent beer to go with it.

When he returned, Nick and Sharon were gone, and Eva was still soaking in the bathtub.

Good. They had the house to themselves.

"Food is here, sweetheart."

"I'm getting out."

"I'll set up the table."

"Thanks."

It was a shame he couldn't have joined her in the large tub, but feeding his woman took precedence. Sex could wait.

Not for long, though. Eva came down wearing one of her fancy silk robes and looking good enough to eat. He pulled her into his arms. "Feeling better?"

"Much. But I'm starving."

"Let's dig in."

CHAPTER 17: EVA

"*W*ant to talk about it?" Bhathian put his chopsticks down.

As usual, he was attentive and caring, and it was difficult to get mad at him for just being there. But since the baby's arrival, he was staying over at her place every night, and Eva needed her space back. A few hours of alone time were crucial for her wellbeing. Especially after a tiring day of detective work.

"Nothing particularly interesting. A cheating husband." For some reason, those were the cases that got to her. She loved finding the suspected spouses innocent and hated to prove the suspicions right. Most of the time, the spouse hiring her hoped to be proven wrong. She loathed the devastating effect her proof to the contrary brought. It was like delivering news of a loved one's impending death. Though in that case, the soon-to-be deceased was the marriage.

"Did he give you the slip?" Bhathian got up and walked over to the fridge, pulling two cold beer bottles from the freezer.

"I chased him and his floozy all over town. First, they

went to eat lunch, then they went shopping, and then they stopped for coffee. But there was no handholding and no kissing, so I had nothing to show the wife. But from the way the girl was laughing at all of his stupid jokes and hanging on his every word, it was obvious he was banging her."

"Did you get them?" He put a tall glass in front of her and poured half the beer inside.

"Of course, I did. They ended up in her house, and I didn't need my super-hearing to hear them going at it. I snuck into the backyard and took a few pictures through the window."

Bathian didn't bother with a glass, drinking straight from the bottle, then put it down and wiped his mouth with the back of his hand. "It doesn't sound as if you're enjoying doing that."

"I'm not."

"So why did you take the case?"

She snorted. "The money, why else? I have bills to pay, and there isn't enough of the corporate stuff to cover all of my expenses. I need to make a reputation for myself in L.A."

Bathian frowned. "Maybe I can help. I know a guy, or rather Andrew knows him, who might send some work your way, or at least recommend you to his clients."

"Who is he?"

"Andrew's old boss from Special Ops who retired and now runs a civilian operation."

"Why would he want to send business my way?"

"The kinds of things he deals in are big and complicated. Maybe he gets requests for smaller stuff too and has to turn them down. It won't hurt to ask."

"Are Andrew and he good friends?"

Bathian chuckled. "Not at all. Turner is nobody's friend. But he is a businessman. If it's a good deal for him, he'll take it."

It could be nice to have a local contact, and even nicer to

dedicate all her time to corporate stuff instead of chasing after cheaters. "Do you have his phone number? Should I call and introduce myself?"

Bhathian shook his head. "No and no. The request needs to come from Andrew or Kian."

Eva grimaced. "I see. He is that kind of a guy."

"You got it. Full of himself doesn't begin to describe it. But apparently the guy is a genius. Even Kian was impressed with him. In fact, he paid a hefty sum for Turner's help in finding Carol."

"Speaking of Carol. What's the deal with her and Robert? Are they still together?"

Bhathian shrugged. "Who knows. At times they look as if they can't stand each other, and at other times they seem cozy. They still share an apartment, so I guess they are. Why?"

"I think Sharon would like Robert. Naturally, I don't want to suggest anything until it's clear he and Carol are no longer a couple."

"Matchmaking is not my thing." Bhathian got up and started clearing the table.

Eva yawned. "Mine neither. I'm so tired."

A month ago, the hint would've gone unnoticed, but Bhathian was getting better at reading her. "Do you want me to go?"

"I'm sorry. But I need some alone time to recoup my energy. I'm nasty when I'm tired. I'd rather be sweet for you." She batted her eyes.

Bhathian brought a dishrag and wiped the table. "You don't need to be sweet for me. Just be yourself. But if you need me to go, I will."

Damn. She hated hurting his feelings. "Make love to me first?" That should soften the impact of her dismissal.

He smiled. "I can do that." Walking over to where she was

sitting, he bent down and picked her up. Cradling her in his arms, he held her against his hard chest. "I'm a full-service kind of guy."

She appreciated that climbing up to the third floor with her in his arms was no problem for her big guy. "You're so strong," she murmured into his neck.

Tired as she was, mentally more than physically, Eva wasn't in the mood for games tonight. Simple and sweet was what she wanted.

As always, Bhathian picked up on her mood and delivered exactly what she needed. Laying her down on the bed, he helped her out of her robe then undressed quickly and got under the covers with her.

For a few moments, he just held her, caressing her back with his large warm palm. She lifted her head and kissed him, inviting him to kiss her back. His tongue swept gently into her mouth, entwining with hers in a slow dance of desire.

As he cupped her ass, she reached for the hard length trapped between their bodies. By now she was so familiar with the feel of it, warm and velvety, soft on the outside and hard on the inside, that she felt like she owned it. It might have been attached to his body, but belonged to her. Eva shimmied down Bhathian's body and took him in her mouth.

His powerful arms wrapped around her, and he lifted her on top of him, her entrance at his mouth. "That's more like it," he said before treating her to a long lick.

Bhathian was the most selfless lover she'd ever had. Most men would have been happy to let her please them while they did nothing, but not Bhathian.

It was an interesting angle, and the added sensation of getting her butt cheeks massaged while her sheath and her clit were getting expertly tongued hastened her climax. As she moaned around Bhathian's shaft, taking him deeper than she'd ever done before, he snapped, erupting inside her throat and sinking his fangs into her inner thigh.

So deliciously wicked.

They made love a couple more times, with Bhathian poised above her and thrusting gently. There was something to be said for the simplicity and closeness of that traditional position. Looking at the face of her magnificent male, feeling his smooth skin on hers, and knowing he would do anything for her, chased the shadows of her hard day away.

Sated, they lay in each other's arms, and Eva fell asleep feeling content. Bhathian could stay. She no longer needed time to unwind. He'd done it for her.

When she woke up, Bhathian was gone. He must've left sometime in the early hours of the morning because his side of the bed was still warm. For a moment, she entertained the hope that he was in the bathroom, or maybe making coffee downstairs, but he wasn't.

Disappointed, she went about getting ready for her day.

Confused? You bet.

CHAPTER 18: KIAN

"The Doomers are too quiet, which worries me. It can only mean that they are planning something big." Kian opened the Guardians' meeting. "Someone should've replaced Sharim a long time ago."

Andrew was the first to respond. "Nothing suspicious has been reported by airport security."

"How about Turner? Have his sources heard anything?" Bhathian asked.

Kian shook his head. "With Turner it's never a straight answer. He says there is too much going on locally for him to investigate everything. He doesn't know if any of the moving pieces are related to us."

Anandur snorted. "If you pay him, he'll make it his business to find out. The guy trades in information. He doesn't give it out for free."

"I offered to pay. He told me to keep my money because it wasn't worth it. As soon as he has something that he thinks relates to us he will let me know." Kian drummed his fingers on the conference table. "I wish the Malibu project was ready to move into. Our people are going to be safer there."

"It's almost complete," Onegus said. "But we have a few problems no one has foreseen."

That was news to Kian. As far as he knew everything was going fine and ahead of schedule. "What are you talking about?"

"Gardeners, window washers, trash collectors. Who is going to do all of these things? Not our clan members, that's for sure. And we can't bring in humans because it's supposed to be a secret location."

Fuck. He hadn't factored that in. It was always the small things that no one thought about but couldn't live without. "What are we going to do about it?"

Onegus lifted his hands. "You tell me. As I see it, we have two options. One is to offer the jobs to a bunch of humans who would be willing to stay for a long period of time. Once their contract expires and they wish to leave, we will erase their memories. But that's problematic on so many levels that it's undoable. The other option is to have William design smart robots and buy a robotics factory to make them."

Perhaps William could design something like that, but it would take him years. They needed a solution now.

"How is Sari handling that? Her castle is isolated, and there are no humans living with them," Arwel asked.

Kian grimaced. "The castle grounds proper are not big, and her people like gardening."

"What about the cleaning and the maintenance? And all those changes she made?"

"All in-house work. She trained her people well."

Onegus crossed his arms over his chest. "So that's what we need to do too. People will take turns taking care of the grounds."

Kian pinned him with a hard stare. "You think? We'll have a hard enough time convincing them to move in. Give them chores, and no one will agree to move."

"The Doomers solved that problem easy. Slaves," Anandur said. "They snatch girls off the streets and give them a choice between prostitution and household chores. And once those who chose prostitution get too old, they are switched to housekeeping. Dalhu says they work fourteen-hour shifts and get one day off a week."

Reminded of Jackson's sad story, Kian sighed. "Yeah, but we are not slavers."

"We won't be if we pay for the services provided," Anandur argued. "Like the girls we shipped to Hawaii."

"They are free to leave whenever they want."

"So will the people we hire be. A little memory scrub and they can go. They'll remember they worked for a secret facility but not where and for who. That will solve the problem of a time gap."

Why were Anandur's arguments starting to make sense? "Anyone else think it's a good idea?"

"I do," Arwel said. "Maybe we can also bring women. Professionals, of course. I like the idea of an easily available sex service. Saves time and effort."

Kian shook his head. How could he hate Doomers for doing exactly what his own Guardians were suggesting? They were supposed to be better than that.

Kian cut the air with his palm. "This idea officially killed the rest. No humans. We cross the line with one thing, and there will be no going back. Before you know it, we will be no better than the fucking Doomers."

The room went quiet. No one offered new suggestions or even looked him in the eye. Kian mellowed out his tone. "I concede that there is a big difference between hiring a full-time escort service for an in-house brothel and kidnapping girls off the street for a lifetime sentence of slavery in one way or another. But that doesn't make it right. A lesser evil is still an evil."

Anandur huffed. "Since when was paying for sex considered evil? Except for Kri and maybe Andrew, everyone in this room has done it at one time or another."

Kian shifted in his chair. He was guilty of the same. But those were different times... His own words came back to haunt him. It was no excuse.

"I feel so sorry for those girls," Kri said. "I'm daydreaming of the day we will storm that freaking island and free all of them."

Kian leaned toward her and patted her shoulder. "Me too. But there is no way to do it. We can't even send a spy to determine the island's defenses."

"What if we follow the girls' trail? Find the slavers who do the dirty work for the island, and cut off the supply side?" Andrew suggested. "I know it's a drop in the ocean, but it's better than nothing, and maybe we can get some information out of that."

As before, Kian had a nagging suspicion that he was being led by the Fates. He was supposed to do something about the slave trafficking.

But what?

Why push him in that direction?

As powerful and as influential as the clan was, it wasn't powerful enough for that. He couldn't even take out a small local operator without Turner's help. Fully mobilized, the Guardian force was too small. Besides, there was no way the guys would come for anything other than to help rescue a clan member.

"We can send a female spy," Kri said. "Hell, I'll go. There is no way to identify a female immortal. Not unless she is horny and the men know what to sniff for."

Kian had had his fill of stupid ideas for the day. "And what would you go as? A client?"

Kri snorted. "Why not? A rich lesbian looking for a

good time."

What was happening to his people? Had they all contracted the stupid bug? "As if they would allow gays or lesbians in there. You know what the Doomers' attitude is on the subject."

Kri deflated. "Right."

"Getting snatched and taken there is the only way." Brundar surprised everyone by saying something. "But no one will believe a woman like Kri was a runaway or a drug addict who got kidnapped off the street. Too big and athletic. We need someone who looks young and vulnerable."

Kri tapped her foot on the floor. "You've got a point. But I'm all there is."

"Carol fits the profile," Brundar said in his inflectionless tone.

The guy was the last one Kian expected to come up with idiotic suggestions, but apparently there was a first time for everything.

"The woman just escaped unimaginable torture, and you want to send her into the lion's den?"

Brundar shrugged. "I don't want to do anything. But if you asked my opinion of who could pull off something like that, I would say Carol."

"What if she wants to do it?" Andrew asked hesitantly.

Kian's temper was rising by the minute. "What if she wants to commit suicide? Should I aid her in that too?"

Andrew fiddled with his pen, twisting it between his fingers. "Eventually, we will need to go on the offensive and do something about that island. Sending an immortal female spy to gather information is the best idea we've had so far. Actually, it's the only one."

"And how do you propose to get her out of there?"

"We still need to figure out the details. All I'm saying is that the idea has merit."

CHAPTER 19: EVA

"Is that a new suit?" Eva raked her eyes over Bhathian's dashing good looks.

Striking a pose, with a hand inside his trouser pocket, he smirked. "Do you like it?"

"I do. It's a huge improvement from what you had on the last time you took me to that restaurant."

"I ordered a new one the next day. I was careful not to overdo it with the weightlifting, so my measurements didn't change."

She chuckled. "That's a lot of effort to go to just so you could take me to a fancy place."

Bhathian pointed a finger at her. "I paid a fortune for that membership, woman, and I intend to make the best of it. Now go get dressed."

"I'll be back in a few." Eva rushed upstairs, her bare feet making no sound as she climbed. It wasn't like her not to be ready, but Bhathian had arrived a few minutes early, catching her still in her bathrobe. Not a big deal. Her hair and makeup were done, and putting on the dress and her new designer shoes wouldn't take long.

"You look stunning," Bhathian said when she came back down. "Is this a new dress?"

So sweet. He probably wouldn't have noticed if she'd put on the same dress she'd had on the last time.

"No, but the shoes are." She lifted a foot and dangled it from side to side.

"Sexy as hell."

"I thought so too. They cost more than my car payment, but I couldn't help myself. Shoes and lingerie. Those are my weaknesses."

"I wish..." he started and promptly clamped his mouth shut.

Smart man. If he'd offered to help her out financially, she would've kicked him where it hurt. Eva managed just fine, and if business continued to be slow and finances became tight, she would cut expenses.

Eva was not going to be beholden to anyone. Especially not to Bhathian. They had a history with him offering her money and it wasn't good.

The drive passed with the two of them gushing about how adorable and cute their granddaughter was, and whether Nathalie would be okay with them buying Phoenix a teddy bear. Eva hadn't expected her practical and down to earth daughter to have all those New Age ideas about raising babies.

Things had been so much simpler in the Seventies, and babies grew up just fine.

When they arrived an attendant was waiting for them, and they followed him, holding hands, through the greenery leading to the restaurant. The guy introduced them to the hostess who led them to the same private enclave they had sat in before.

Bhathian removed his jacket and draped it over the

chair's back. "I don't like it that you're going out of town again."

"I don't like it either, but it's a well-paying corporate gig, and I like those." Eva took a sip of her wine. "This is good."

"Can I come with you?"

It was tempting. An impersonal hotel room would feel much more homey with Bhathian waiting for her. But how would he occupy himself while she was doing her thing?

It wasn't worth wasting his vacation days on.

"It's a lovely offer, but it doesn't make sense. I'll be gone all day and probably in the evenings too. So unless you're in the mood for touring Tampa on your own, you'll be bored out of your mind."

Bhathian smirked. "I have no intentions of staying in the hotel or touring. I want to follow you and see you in action."

That was unexpected. "You'll throw my concentration. I need to have my head in it and not worry about you giving me away."

Bhathian's lips narrowed into a tight line. "I'm not an untrained civilian. I know how to handle myself on an assignment."

She reached over the table and clasped his hand. "It's two nights. Three, tops. I want to do it fast and be done with it. I have another job already scheduled after that."

"Another one out of town?"

"No. Something local. By the way, did you talk with Andrew or Kian about asking that guy to meet me?"

"Oh damn, I forgot. We had a meeting yesterday, and his name came up, but I got distracted by what was on the agenda."

Curious, she leaned forward. "Anything you can tell me?"

"Yeah. But not here."

"Understood." Secrets should never be discussed in public places. Eva was proof of why it was such a bad idea. Most of her information gathering happened in cafés, restaurants, and bars. It was a rare occasion when she needed to go a step further and engage the target in conversation.

The waiter arrived with their meal, and for the next half an hour or so, they were too busy rolling their eyes in bliss to talk.

Bhathian wiped his mouth with a napkin. "I never knew Brussels sprouts could taste so good."

They must've been amazing because Bhathian was a meat man through and through. He rarely touched any greens.

"I should ask Gerard for the recipe. You need to eat more vegetables."

Bhathian laughed. "That's funny on so many levels. First of all, good luck getting that prick to share his recipes. And secondly, you don't cook."

"I know. But for a moment I entertained the idea. A girl can have her fantasies."

"I'm sure yours never include cooking."

Eva pouted. "Not true. When Nathalie was little, and Fernando and I were still good, I made an effort to make a home for us. But I couldn't compete with a husband who was a talented baker and cook. I was no good at it, and it was damn embarrassing to watch the faces he made while suffering through the meals I prepared. So I stopped trying."

He patted her hand. "If you ever get in the mood to play in the kitchen, you can experiment on me as much as you want. I'm not a finicky eater."

Eva crossed her legs, letting her dress ride up her thighs. "With how little leisure time we have together, I'd rather get busy playing other games. In the kitchen and elsewhere."

A wide grin split Bhathian's face. "I couldn't agree more."

CHAPTER 20: KIAN

For the past hour Kian had sat in his home office, mulling over and over again the idea of using Carol to infiltrate the island. Every instinct he had was shouting not to do it, and yet he couldn't stop thinking about it. If he didn't care so much about her, he would have considered it as a viable proposition. Not that he would've felt differently about any other clan member, but especially the females. The thing was that as a leader he couldn't afford the luxury of thinking with his heart. He had to use his head.

"What's eating you?" Syssi asked from the doorway.

He sighed. "A dilemma I can't reconcile."

"Do you want to talk about it?"

"Yeah. I need help."

Syssi chuckled. "That must be one hell of a conundrum if you're admitting that you're not omnipotent."

He pushed his chair back and got up. "It is. How about you make us coffee while we talk about it."

Her face brightened. "Cappuccino?"

His wife loved her cappuccino machine, pushing cups at

him and anyone else who ventured into their penthouse. "Sure."

"There are leftover pastries on the counter. Could you please take the plate outside? It's a warm night, perfect for sitting out on the terrace."

"No problem."

He did as instructed, and a few moments later Syssi joined him with the coffees. Putting her hand on his thigh, she lifted her head and looked at the sky. "Isn't it beautiful out here?"

"It is. Sometimes I forget how nice it is to sit out here, and I can't even remember the last time I took a swim in the pool."

"I know, right? We get so carried away with our jobs that we forget to slow down and take a breather, to enjoy life."

"Ain't that the truth." Kian raked his fingers through his hair.

"So what's the conundrum that is giving you so much trouble?"

He took a sip from his cappuccino. "Kri came up with the crazy idea of using a female immortal to infiltrate the island. Since there is nothing that would identify her as one, she could go in pretending to be a human."

Syssi's eyes narrowed. "What for? What can a female spy uncover that can be of any use? Even if we knew all there is to know about the island and all its strategic secrets, we still couldn't storm it with the force we have. Besides, even if we had an army of Guardians, what would you do? Kill tens of thousands of Doomers? That's genocide, Kian. I have no love lost for them. I feel sorry for the women they hold captive, I hate everything they stand for and the havoc they wreak time and again on humanity, but killing them all off is not the answer. We would be no better than them."

He loved Syssi's clarity of vision. In one minute, she'd

summed it all up beautifully and inadvertently pointed him in the right direction.

"You're absolutely right. We can't win using brute force. Only a change from the inside can put an end to the eons of their reign of terror. We need to start a revolution."

Syssi arched an eyebrow and crossed her arms over her chest. "With one woman?"

A smile tugged at his lips. "Sometimes all it takes is planting a seed, and there is no one who is better equipped to do it successfully than a skilled seductress."

"Kri?" Syssi's incredulous expression was almost comical.

He laughed. "No, not Kri. Carol."

Syssi's jaw dropped and she uncrossed her arms. "Are you crazy? Even if we put aside for a moment what she's been through at the hands of that sadist, the woman is a ditsy airhead, a drunkard, and a druggie. That's who you want to send on a mission like that?"

He nodded. "She's perfect. No one will ever suspect her of subterfuge. And let's not forget that she proved to be tougher than a hardened warrior. I know only a handful of men who could've withstood the torture she's been through and keep their mouths shut."

"But what about skills? She has no training, and frankly I doubt she is the kind who is willing to learn."

"She is skilled. Carol was a highly sought after courtesan. And as to the rest, we will put her through rigorous training. If she agrees, that is."

Syssi's rebuttals served to strengthen his conviction that Carol was the perfect candidate for the job. Kian could almost feel the Fates nodding in approval. Everything that had happened recently had been leading up to this. Including Carol's abduction. He would've never considered her for a mission of that caliber otherwise. She'd proven to him and everyone else that she was made of much stronger stuff than she seemed to be.

Syssi remained skeptical. "I still don't get it. What can she do to start a revolution?"

"Share fresh ideas. Describe a better future. We've been doing it with the humans since the beginning. On the one hand, we spread stories and myths that demonstrate a better way of life, that promote science, justice, and equality; on the other we trickle information that helps in other ways. Like better agriculture that grows more food to feed more people. Naturally, Carol will not peddle technology, but she can spin stories like no other, and she can manipulate males effortlessly. She'll have them doing things for her in no time."

"I'm starting to warm to the idea. But how will she communicate with us?"

"We still need to work out all the details. This is not a plan for tomorrow or even next month. First, Carol has to agree, and then she needs to go through rigorous training in a lot of fields. We need to prepare her for anything. As to communication, I trust William to come up with some gadget. And if not, she can send letters 'home' to her family with the guys she will trap. Obviously, they will have to be written in code."

Syssi shook her head. "You're putting a lot of faith in her abilities."

"I know."

CHAPTER 21: EVA

*I*t felt strange to be back in a city that had been her home for so long, and stay at a hotel.

Eva added the last few finishing touches to her handyman costume, tucked her long hair under a hard hat, and headed out. The meeting she was going to eavesdrop on was happening at the headquarters of her client's competitor.

Getting close enough was going to be tricky. Regrettably, the place was too well guarded at night, and she'd had to abort her initial plan of planting a bug in the room by sneaking in undetected. That kind of security required Nick's expertise, but she hadn't brought him along. Besides, it would've taken more time than she had to complete the mission.

Her best alternative was to go about it the old-fashioned way, acting like someone whose job was to take care of the place. Janitors and maintenance people were invisible. She'd go in, stick bugs in several places close to the conference room's door, and go back to her hotel to listen to the transmissions.

With a few phone calls to her informants, she'd found out

the name of the maintenance company servicing the high-rise office building. A couple of hundreds in the sticky hands of a petty thief got her the company's coveralls and protective headgear.

Armed with a ladder, a toolbox, and an armload of fluorescent bulbs, she sauntered into the receptionist's office. "I'm here to replace the bulbs."

"Which rooms?" the guy asked.

Eva gave her gum a few chews. "Wherever needed. Did you notice which ones are flickering?"

"Check out the one in the center of the corridor. It's making that annoying buzzing sound."

She hefted the folding ladder under her arm. "No problem. Can you get the door for me?"

The guy got up from behind his desk and opened the way for her. "You're the first female handyman the company ever sent over. Kudos to you for breaking the gender barrier."

You have no idea, buddy. "Thanks. But all I care for is the better pay."

A small smile crooked his lips. "Nevertheless, you and I are rebels."

"You've got it." She stepped into the hallway and headed for the buzzing sound.

"You need any help?" the guy asked when she unfolded her ladder.

"Thanks, but I got it. It's my job."

The receptionist nodded and went back to his station, closing the double doors behind him.

Perfect. Eva replaced the malfunctioning bulb and got down. Pretending to examine each ceiling fixture and replacing quite a few, she planted a bug inside one in each room that looked like an executive's office or had a conference table. Six bugs including the one in the corridor.

No one had paid her any attention.

Not to seem in a hurry, she stopped to chat with the receptionist before leaving. The competitor's offices took up the entire floor of the high-rise, so she didn't need to pretend to go into any others. It was into the elevator, and down to the parking garage to her borrowed pickup. The truck belonged to one of her snitches and didn't have the company's logo, but it was the best Eva could do on such short notice.

Her mistake was not sending Sharon and Nick to do the prep work. Under normal circumstances, Sharon would've gone to the building a few nights before and assessed the security for Eva. Then Nick would've done his magic. But budgetary concerns required cost cuts, and Eva figured she could do without, saving on two more plane tickets and several hotel nights. Her client didn't know that she'd moved to L.A., and Eva preferred to keep it that way. The airfare and hotel stay was on her.

No harm done.

The bugs were in place, and she had two hours until the meeting was scheduled to start. Enough time to get back to her hotel room and set up the equipment for the transmission. Theoretically, she could go shopping and then go over the recording later, but she preferred to listen to it in real time. If more investigating was needed, and not all of what her client wanted to know was discussed in the meeting, she'd immediately move to plan B.

Jerry, her snitch, was waiting for her in the parking lot of a mall.

Eva parked the truck and pulled out a pair of flip flops from a plastic bag. She removed her work boots, stepped out of her coveralls, and shoved them into the bag. Underneath, she wore leggings and a muscle shirt. The outfit did nothing to disguise her figure, but the blue contact lenses, blond wig, and makeup that made her skin look awful were enough to obscure her identity.

"Hi, Priscilla. How did it go?"

"Hunky dory." She used a Southern accent. "Thank you for the use of your truck."

"No problem." He took the hundred she handed him. The savings she'd been counting on were evaporating by the minute.

"Did you hear anything new through the grapevine?"

Jerry puffed out his chest. "I hear a lot of things. You need to be more specific."

"You know what I'm after. I still haven't found that missing girl." The imaginary one she was supposedly looking for. The cover story for why she was asking questions about slavers.

Jerry grimaced. "She's probably dead by now."

"Maybe. But I promised my client I will not stop looking."

He shrugged. "There are always kids gone missing. If you want a lead, I suggest snooping around Union Station. Lately, there are more creeps hanging around there than usual."

"I'm not interested in small-time crooks like pimps and drug dealers. How about the big guys who deal in flesh. Any new ones?"

"Not that I heard of."

"Okay, thanks for the info." Eva shook his hand.

If her surveillance provided what her client was looking for, perhaps she would check out Union Station after all and see what Jerry was talking about.

Should she?

It wasn't as if she was going after whatever creeps were hanging around there. Not her kind of targets. The bottom of the ladder was too easily replaced to bother with. She went only after the middlemen, and every mission took a lot of planning and careful preparation.

Eva wasn't stupid enough to be gung-ho about something that could land her in jail. No matter how satisfying taking out a few creeps could've been.

Damn. Her developing appetite for vengeance was worrisome. It was addictive. If she weren't careful to keep herself in check, it would consume her.

Back at the hotel, Eva took out the irritating contact lenses and removed the blond wig. She called room service and ordered dinner, then sat down and turned on her equipment. Each bug had been calibrated to a different receiver so she could listen to several conversations at the same time. Once she identified what she was looking for, she was going to turn off the rest.

"Are you still looking for her?" she heard someone ask.

"The little bitch killed my brother and then crawled into a hole in the ground and disappeared. I'm not going to rest until I find her. I have people all over the States looking. Unless she left the country, it's only a matter of time until someone recognizes her picture."

That didn't sound like two corporate executives discussing a merger. More like two thugs.

"She probably doesn't look the same. Five years make a lot of difference in a kid that young. How old is she supposed to be now? Twenty-one?" the other guy asked.

"Something like that. Women don't change that much when they get older. I'm going to find her, and when I do, she is going to pay."

Eva heard a door open and slam shut.

"Loraine, please have the Montesito file ready for me. I'm heading out." She heard the other guy. There was a pause, and then she heard him say. "The hotheaded idiot is becoming a liability. We need to get rid of him." Obviously, he wasn't talking to Loraine. There was another pause, and then he said, "Will do, boss."

Shivers ran up Eva's spine even though the chances the two had been talking about Tessa were slim... or were they?

No, not really.

The timeline fit. Besides, how many sixteen-year-old girls killed a man five years ago?

Not many. If at all.

Eva closed her eyes and thanked God for prompting her to move her operation out of Tampa. But the move didn't mean Tessa was safe. If the guy had provided her picture to a bunch of informants all over the country, eventually someone was bound to spot her.

Tessa needed a new face. Or at least a drastic change.

When she returned, Eva was going to take Tessa to a hair salon. A different hair color and a different hairdo would make a big difference. And of course the requisite contact lenses. Going from brown to blond and from hazel eyes to blue should do it. A change of style and attitude wouldn't hurt either. The biggest transformation, if Tessa could pull it off, would be shedding her mousy look and adopting a confident one.

For sure no one would recognize her then.

CHAPTER 22: TESSA

"*T*hat was such a fun movie." Tessa dropped her 3D glasses in the container outside the movie theater.

Jackson wrapped his arm around her shoulders. "Gal Gadot is hot. She made an awesome Wonder Woman. Did you see how she punched? There was nothing even remotely girly about it. The fight scenes were very well made. Kudos to the choreographers."

Tessa chuckled. "Our Israeli neighbor said that the movie should be called 'How to be an Israeli Woman 101.' Obsess over every baby you see, voice your unsolicited opinion loudly, and don't take shit from anyone."

"I like it."

"Yeah, me too. If there were a course like that, I would take it. I wish I could be more like that."

"Same as every guy wants to be Tony Stark. I think Iron Man is better than Superman. Generally, DC is not as good as Marvel, but Wonder Woman rocked."

Tessa was still having a hard time remembering Jackson's explanations about which superheroes belonged to the Marvel Comics universe and which belonged to DC. The one thing she remembered was that Wonder Woman was DC and Iron Man and The Avengers were Marvel.

"Have you ever watched the old TV series with Linda Carter?"

"No, I didn't. Have you?"

"When I was little, I dreamt I was her. Tall, beautiful, powerful, everything that I wasn't."

An odd look flitted through Jackson's eyes. "You got it all except for the tall part."

Tessa tossed the empty popcorn bag in the trash. "Yeah, I'm the all-powerful Tessa." She flexed her thin arm. "Fear me!" She deepened her voice as deep as it would go, which wasn't very deep at all.

Jackson opened the passenger door for her, waited for her to buckle up and only then closed it and walked around to the driver's side. "My place?" He turned the engine on.

"Are you going to make me a sandwich?"

"But of course, my lady." He bowed his head. "I'm on a mission to fatten you up."

She laughed. "When you accomplish your mission, are you going to eat me yourself or sell me to Hansel and Gretel's witch?"

Jackson cast her a lascivious glance. "No one is going to eat you but me."

As heat spread over Tessa's face, she was grateful for the car's dark interior. Careful not to trigger her fears, Jackson rarely made sexual innuendos, but some slipped out from time to time, especially when she supplied him with a perfect opening like that one. It was all talk; he hadn't made a move to even kiss her other than on the cheek. They were like a couple dating in the early days of last century.

Were they a couple, though?

Other than the sex, yes, they were. They were spending every evening together, and their emotional connection was getting stronger by the day. She didn't dare ask but was pretty sure Jackson hadn't been with another girl since they started seeing each other. The poor guy must have had blue balls the size of watermelons.

And yet, he never complained, never pressed for more, never even seemed moody or frustrated, but Tessa felt incredibly guilty nonetheless. Jackson deserved a woman who'd welcome his touch, who would pleasure him not as an obligation and not in spite of herself, but because she loved him and his body and wanted to be intimate with him, as much as he wanted to be intimate with her.

There must be something she could do for him without freaking out. Maybe she could handle a hand job?

After all, nothing about Jackson's body repelled her, which was a huge step for her. She should be able to put her hand on him. It was him putting his hands on her that she couldn't handle.

Tessa shook her head. Thinking about hand jobs before they had even kissed was ridiculous. But in some way a kiss was more terrifying. The thought of any part of a male's body entering her, even a tongue inside her mouth, was intolerable.

But what if he remained completely passive? What if it was her tongue that did the entering? Could she handle that?'

Would he?

Jackson was a dominant guy, but in a good way. The take charge way. She couldn't imagine him ever being abusive, physically or verbally, but she also couldn't imagine him passive.

Unless he did it for her.

He would, she had no doubt of that. But it wouldn't be easy for him and he probably wouldn't enjoy it.

Besides, she was too embarrassed to broach the subject.

It didn't make sense. After all that she'd been through,

nothing should have been embarrassing to her. Except, she'd spent the last five years pretending as if none of that had happened. More so, she'd spent them pretending she wasn't female at all. A sexless creature. That was what she wanted to be.

Before Eva had rescued her, Tessa had been starving herself to the point of being so underweight that she'd stopped getting her periods. It had been her only way to rebel. No periods meant she couldn't get pregnant, which had been her greatest fear. She would've rather died than brought a child into the nightmare of her existence.

The thing was, she kept limiting her food intake even in the safety of Eva's home. Having no periods was reassuring, as was looking like a scrawny, unattractive teenager.

All of that had changed when Jackson became part of her life. Tessa started gaining weight. Suddenly she had more appetite. Whether it was his friendship and the sense of normality he brought about, or the sandwiches he kept pushing at her, the result was that her pants were getting tight, and last week she'd gotten her first period in years.

The shocking part hadn't been the sudden appearance of spotting, but the relief at seeing it. Another milestone had been crossed on the road to recovery. And maybe one day, in the distant future, she could have a baby.

"Penny for your thoughts," Jackson said.

She waved a hand. "They are all over the place."

"I'm sorry about that remark. It just slipped out."

"I know. It's okay."

"So you're not freaking out because of it?"

"No. I'm good."

"*Pfft*. I was worried." Jackson pulled into a parking spot and killed the engine. Tessa waited for him to go around and open her door, not because it was something she expected, but because he insisted on doing so. In some ways, Jackson was very old fashioned for an eighteen-year-old.

"The usual?" he asked as they entered the kitchen.

"You know me. I'm a creature of habit. Same sandwich, same drink…"

"Same boyfriend?"

"Yeah. Same boyfriend."

Jackson paused with the fridge door open. "Did I hear you right? Have I just been promoted from a friend who is a boy to a boyfriend?"

"You heard me right."

Jackson lifted his eyes to the ceiling. "Thank you, merciful Fates."

Tessa frowned. She'd heard him say the same words before and thought them a joke, but maybe it was more than that. "Do you believe in fate, Jackson?"

"You don't?"

"No, I don't." If she did, she would hate the bitch with vehemence.

Jackson spread out the sandwich fixings on the work table she was sitting at. "I can't say that I'm a big believer. It's more of a saying. Like people who say thank God. I don't believe in any particular deity, so I invoke the Fates."

Made sense. Tessa often did the same even though she was an atheist. Some things were ingrained too deeply. Besides, since Eva was a big time believer, Tessa kept her own lack of belief private.

Getting into an argument about religion was just as bad as getting into an argument about politics. People clung to their version of the story regardless of any proof to the contrary. They just ignored it, or called it fake, or this or that phobic. It was a waste of time and energy to try changing someone's mind. Eva was entitled to her beliefs, as Tessa was entitled to hers, and Jackson to his.

They were lucky to live in a free country which was founded on the principles of freedom from oppression and the freedom of speech. Most of the world's population didn't enjoy those freedoms.

In some countries, girls as young as she'd been when her nightmare began were married off to men who were free to do with them as they pleased. She couldn't help thinking that some of them must've suffered as she had, but with nowhere to run, no legal recourse, and no chance of anyone coming to their rescue.

In that respect, she'd been lucky, and she owed it all to Eva.

"Here is your feast, my lady." Jackson put one plate in front of her and the other next to it, then pulled out two sets of cutlery wrapped in paper napkins. "What would you like to drink?"

"Coke, please."

CHAPTER 23: JACKSON

*T*essa finished the entire sandwich, a first for her, wiped her mouth with the napkin and leaned back in her chair. "I'm going to explode. My pants are, for sure. Nothing fits me anymore. I have to shop for new clothes."

"Can I come with you?" Maybe he could steer her toward the grownups' section of the department store. Jackson was pretty sure she was buying her clothes in the kids' section.

Tessa shook her head. "I order things online. Large department stores scare me, and small boutique salespeople are too pushy. And I hate malls."

"Can I help you choose?"

She narrowed her eyes at him. "Why that sudden interest in my wardrobe?"

"You're a beautiful woman, Tessa. I would love to see you celebrate it rather than hide it." Hopefully, he'd said the right thing. Usually, he was a smooth operator, the envy of his friends when it came to talking with girls, but Tessa was touchy.

She tilted her head and smiled. "Okay. Let's go up to your room and fire up your laptop."

Score! He still had it.

Sitting on his couch, Jackson had one arm around Tessa's shoulder, the laptop on his lap. "How about this dress?" A stretchy black number with a high neck and a short hem. Not too daring but still sexy.

"I like it."

"Let's add it to the cart."

"What's the price on it?"

"Sixty-five."

"That's good. I can afford that."

"What about this one?" The dress was a little old fash-ioned, with a flower print and a long loose skirt.

Tessa shook her head. "It looks too much like something Eva would wear. I don't want to imitate her style."

An hour later they had a cart with twenty-seven items, which they narrowed down to twelve.

"Ready to order?"

"Go ahead. If I don't like something, I can return it."

"Promise me you will model it for me before you decide."

"Okay." Tessa snuggled up closer to him and closed her eyes.

Feeling her small body pressed against his had the usual effect—instant hard-on that he was trying to hide from her.

Lately, she'd been doing it a lot. It was torture, but it was also a gift. It was a sign of trust he wouldn't have believed possible only a couple of weeks ago. Tessa was doing so well.

"Are you tired?"

"No. I just feel snugly." She lifted her face to him.

If she were any other girl, Jackson would've taken it as an invitation to a kiss. But Tessa wasn't ready for it.

"I want to ask you for something," she whispered.

"Anything."

"I want to kiss you, but you can't kiss me back. Can you do that?"

Jackson was dumbfounded. Tessa wanted to kiss him? "Hell, yeah. I'll take a kiss any way I can get it. I won't move a muscle."

"Lean back and put your hands under your thighs."

She was dead serious about it, and he was smiling like an idiot. Jackson schooled his features to give this the respect it was due and put his hands under his legs. Not to spook her, he needed to do everything exactly the way she wanted. It was monumentally important. If everything went well, Tessa would gain confidence and lose some of her fears.

When he was in position, she climbed up on the sofa and knelt next to him. Even seated, his upper body was so much taller than hers that she had to get up to her knees to reach his face comfortably.

Tessa's hands were trembling when she put them on his shoulders.

Waiting for her to make her move, Jackson barely breathed, his muscles locked so he wouldn't even twitch. She leaned forward and touched her lips to his, then retreated. Reassured that he was following her instructions to the letter, she leaned again, the press of her lips firmer this time.

When her small tongue darted out, and she licked at the seam of his lips, he parted them to grant her entry, but just a little. She did, hesitantly at first but then got a little bolder and started exploring.

It took Jackson all of his self-restraint not to wrap his arms around her and bring her flush against his body, then take over the kiss. Just imagining it he felt his balls contract and his shaft swell. At this rate, he was going to come in his pants just from that little kiss and scare the crap out of Tessa.

Closing his eyes, he tried to go over the day's profit and loss summary, adding the numbers in his head. Anything to stop that eruption. After weeks of abstinence, with only his right hand for company and a pillow to bite, he was in a sorry state.

Damn it. He felt his fangs elongate.

Reluctantly, he pulled his head back and turned it sideways. "I'm sorry, sweetheart, but I can't take much more of this. I don't want to embarrass myself."

A partial truth was better than a lie, right?

She leaned her head against his. "I'm sorry. I know how hard it is for you, and I'm grateful for your patience." Her whisper sounded desperate.

"Can I hug you? I think you need a hug."

She nodded, and in a split second he had his arms around her.

"It never fails to astonish me how fast you move. It's almost supernatural. Are you Superman?"

"Oh, gosh darn, you unmasked me. Yes, I am."

"And so modest."

"That too."

The joking seemed to break the spell, and Tessa heaved a heavy sigh. "We need to talk."

Damn it. Not that. Jackson felt his muscles stiffen.

"Don't get all tense. It's not something bad, it's good. At least I think it is."

Tessa shocked him completely when she sat in his lap and wrapped her arms around his neck. "I'm falling for you, Jackson. I never thought I would, but I am."

"Oh, Tessa." He held her to him gently. "I fell for you a long time ago."

She didn't try to refute his statement but didn't acknowledge it either. "It can't go on like this. I'm making you miserable. I need to break this barrier that is holding me back from getting intimate with you."

"There is no rush."

She lifted her head and smiled. "You must be the sweetest

guy who ever lived. But it's time. I've been thinking about it, a lot. And as long as it's me touching you, I should be okay. I know it's asking a lot and that it goes against your nature, but if you could do it for me, it might help me get over my fears. Small steps. That's all I can do."

This was like a dream come true, and if she needed to tie him down to the bed to feel safe, he would gladly let her do it. The problem was that when aroused, not only did his dick grow in size, which Tessa would expect, but his fangs as well. Not to mention that his eyes would start glowing like two fucking flashlights.

It wasn't a problem with other females when he was the one doing all the moves. They never saw the bite coming, and when it did, the euphoria that followed took care of their moment of panic. None of that would work with Tessa taking her sweet time exploring his body while he was immobilized.

He would have to tell her.

"Jackson? What's going on in that head of yours?" Tessa regarded him with worry in her eyes.

The lie came easily. "I'm trying to figure out a way for you to tie me down to the bed. It's a problem since my bed is a couch and has nothing you can secure a rope to."

Tessa laughed. A happy little giggle that made his heart soar. She didn't laugh often enough. "I see that you're one step ahead of me already. I was just waiting for a yes or no from you."

"Are you kidding me? Of course it's a yes. But I need to get a new bed."

"Are you serious?"

"Very. I want you to feel absolutely safe. Having me tied down should remove the last of your fears." He winked. "And mine."

He just needed to figure out how to keep his fangs

hidden. Maybe he could wear a mask? Right. As if Tessa wasn't scared enough already. A blindfold could take care of his eyes, but he doubted Tessa would be okay with a big Band-Aid over his mouth.

He had to tell her the truth about who and what he was. After all, there was a good chance she was a Dormant, and if they ever ended up going all the way, she needed to know about her chances of turning immortal.

Was it his decision, though, or did he need Kian's approval? Or was it Amanda's?

As far as he could remember from clan law classes, there was no mention of the proper way of going about turning a Dormant. Which created a loophole. If he didn't tell anyone and just did it, no one could accuse him of breaking a law that didn't exist.

On the other hand, taking responsibility for something as monumental as turning a Dormant was scary as hell.

CHAPTER 24: CAROL

*A*s Carol knocked on Kian's office door, her stomach felt as if she'd swallowed a nest of hornets. What could he want from her?

She hadn't gone out drinking in ages, and only smoked one joint a night out on her balcony after Robert fell asleep. Could Kian be mad about that?

"Come in." He waved her in.

She opened the glass door, closing it carefully behind her, then walked past the oblong conference table, stopping a few feet away from Kian's monstrosity of a desk. "You wanted to see me?"

"Yes. Please take a seat." He motioned to the armchair on the other side.

She sat on the very edge. "What is it about? Am I in trouble?"

Kian chuckled. "No, you're not in trouble. There is something I want to discuss with you."

Pfft, that's a relief. Carol got more comfortable in the armchair.

"I understand that the idea of interning with Gerard no longer appeals to you."

Aha, so that's what this was about. "No, not really. I'm thinking of taking a culinary course instead. After Nathalie comes back to work, that is."

"How about the Guardian training? Are you going to continue the program?"

"Sure. I love it. Not the endurance training Brundar wants me to do, but all the rest."

Kian seemed satisfied with her answer. "I'll cut to the chase. An idea came up to send a female immortal spy to the Doomers' island. Her job would be not only to collect information but to plant the seeds of rebellion. We can't attack the island, and we have no way of ever ending this conflict. The destruction of Navuh's organization and his propagation of Mortdh's destructive ideas must come from within."

It all sounded like a great idea, but why was he telling her that?

Kian chuckled. "From your bewildered expression I gather that you have no idea what any of that has to do with you."

She nodded, afraid to say something that would sound stupid.

"There is no one better for the job than you."

"Get out of here! Me?"

Shocked didn't begin to describe it. Kian must've been eating shrooms if he thought she was the right woman for the job. What in her past performance had led him to believe she was a capable person, let alone a superspy who could start a revolution? She was an irresponsible, pleasure-seeking airhead of average intelligence, who excelled at nothing other than seducing men. Not a great accomplishment by anyone's standards.

"Yes, you." Kian pointed at her.

"Thank you for the compliment, but you're mistaken. I'm not the right person for the job."

Kian regarded her with a contemplative expression. "I will understand if you don't want to do it. Most people would decline. It's an extremely dangerous mission, and it will probably span years if not decades. But as far as qualifications, you're perfect. After a lot of intensive training, that is."

Carol shook her head. "Explain to me like I'm a two-year-old why you think I'm perfect for the job." Too much was on the line to worry about looking stupid in front of Kian. Besides, he needed to see who he was dealing with.

"You look young and sweet, even naive, and you're a beautiful, fair-skinned blond—exactly the type slavers are looking for to deliver to the island. You're a skilled seductress, and good at manipulating men to do what you want. More importantly, you enjoy it. In addition, you have proven that you're extremely tough. What you lack are military and espionage skills, as well as the finesse of spreading the seeds of new ideas. A year or two of training with Brundar will take care of the first two, and our media expert, Brandon, can teach you all you need to know about the third."

Kian thought she was tough because she'd survived the sadist. But did it count? It hadn't been bravery, just stubbornness, endurance and to a large extent loyalty. There was no way she could've betrayed her family. Anything else she would've given up without much of a fight, but not her clan. To have their deaths on her conscience would have been worse than any torture the sadist could've put her through.

"You don't have to give me an answer now. This is a long-term plan, and you can take your time to mull over it. It's not a decision to be taken lightly. As to compensation, it's basically whatever you want."

An incredulous snort escaped Carol's throat before she

could stifle it. But what the hell? If Kian thought she was all that, she could at least talk to him as an equal. "Do you think I would do something like that for money? You're charging me with a task of gargantuan proportions. You're asking me to risk my life and leave everyone I care for behind for Fates know how long, maybe forever. And you think money can buy that?"

Kian lifted his palms in a sign of peace. "Of course not. It's just a bonus. I know that if you decide to do it, it will be because you love your clan. More than that." He paused for effect. "You, Carol, can singlehandedly change the world for the better. If you succeed, and the Doomers revolt against Navuh and forsake their agenda, every human and immortal on earth will benefit. There will be nothing to hinder progress and no one to instigate wars."

Carol looked at Kian with eyes peeled wide.

He leaned forward. "Imagine that, Carol. You can go down in history as the most influential female who'd ever walked the earth."

Wow! The buttering up was working. Kian was exaggerating, naturally, but if she succeeded...

Fates. Could she do it? Spend years pretending to be a human whore? True, she'd done it before, but there was a big difference between a courtesan and a common prostitute. Though given her experience and her skills, she could rise to the level of courtesan in no time. All it would take was to have one of the head honchos fall for her. Easy. She'd done it before. Many times. And once she had the guy wrapped around her little finger, she could start whispering the right things in his ear.

The idea seemed more exciting by the minute. So many hunky immortal warriors to play with. The only hitch she could foresee was that one of them would detect her unique immortal female scent and recognize it for what it was. A professional risk, since doing what she was charged with meant that she was going to be aroused a lot. Could a heavy perfume mask the scent? She needed to experiment.

"How soon do you need an answer?"

"Take your time. There is no rush."

She nodded. "I want to do some testing first. You know, with the scent of arousal. I need to check if a heavy perfume will take care of it. I know those guys have no point of reference, but after a while, one or more may grow suspicious of the only female in the brothel who smells differently."

"A valid point. If the answer is no, then I think we will have to scrap the idea. I will not send you there if there is the slightest chance of anyone figuring out you're an immortal. Your life and the success of the mission depend on no one ever discovering it."

There was another way she could get discovered. If a guy got rough with her, it would be hard to hide her rapid healing. Carol chewed on her lower lip. "What if I get hurt? How do I hide my quick healing from injuries?"

"According to Dalhu, Sharim was the only known sadist. Which doesn't surprise me. Doomers may be brainwashed to regard females as inferior, but that doesn't change their natural immortal instincts to protect them. Sharim was a rare deviant. But there are those who like it rough, especially among the humans. So it's a valid concern."

"I can pretend to hide bruises with lots of makeup. Or even better"—she smirked—"some stinky homemade poultice. That will keep the immortals away."

Carol was proud of herself. She was proving to Kian that she was much smarter than anyone gave her credit for, and quick on her feet.

Kian raked his fingers through his hair. "Both of us need to give it more thought. I'm starting to realize that I let myself run with the idea before thinking it through. I figured all the technical stuff could be solved out later. Like how to get you out of there or how to get information out. But the issues you raised are fundamental. Too many things can give you away. It's too dangerous for you."

Way to punch a hole in her excited bubble. He couldn't do this to her; dangle a chance of fame and glory in front of her nose then take it away. This was her chance to do something great. Carol the ditsy slut who smoked pot and drank too much would be no more.

Wait a minute. She'd have to give up pot?

"If we figure it out and I start training, will I need to stop smoking pot? Or drinking? I don't do it now as much as I used to before the kidnapping, but I don't want to give it up completely."

Kian's smile was sad. "If you don't overdo it, you don't need to give it up. On the contrary, a pot head fits the profile and will make your act more believable."

Carol let out a relieved breath. "Good. There is a limit to what I'm willing to sacrifice for my people." She winked. "I draw the line at pot. Risking my life is one thing, but giving up my recreational substances is another."

CHAPTER 25: ROBERT

*R*obert wrinkled his nose. "Why did you put on so much perfume?" Carol's perfumes were top quality, and when used in moderation they smelled terrific on her. But she'd overdone it this time.

"I'm conducting a little experiment. Come kiss me."

That would be tricky. He needed his mouth for breathing. But he wasn't going to turn down an offer of a kiss. "Come here." He reached for her, wrapping his arm around her narrow waist and holding her nape with his other hand. "I love your lips." He didn't start gentle. His tongue was in her mouth the moment their lips touched.

Carol moaned, her body going liquid in his arms as she pressed herself against his body.

He reached down, threading his arm around the backs of her knees to pick her up, but she stopped him with a hand to his chest. "Hold that thought. I'll be right back." She took off, running out of the apartment as if someone was chasing her.

What the hell?

A few moments later she came back with a big grin on

her doll-like face. "It worked. The perfume covered the scent of my arousal. Syssi confirmed it."

"You could've asked me. Who the hell can smell anything with that overwhelming scent you sprayed on? What happened? The bottle broke?"

She slapped his arm. "No, silly, it was a test to see if a heavy perfume could mask my special scent—the one that identifies me as an immortal female."

Suspicious, he narrowed his eyes. "Why are you suddenly worried about that? Are you planning on going clubbing again?"

She shifted her eyes away, a sign she was uncomfortable about something and was most likely going to lie. "Yeah. The girls invited me to join them to a club that has an erotic dance show, and I was worried we would get excited and that our scent could identify us to Doomers."

The story sounded plausible enough. But even though Carol was going with several other immortal females, it didn't mean that having witnesses was going to stop her from flirting with the human males, or worse.

"You don't need to worry about Doomers. None have ever met any immortal females. The males have no idea what scent to search for. But nevertheless, I don't like you going to a place like that. Who else is going? Because I can't see Kian letting Syssi go without him. Was it Amanda's idea?"

Dalhu and he weren't friends. The guy wanted nothing to do with him, but Robert had eyes. Amanda did whatever she pleased with no regard for her mate. Dalhu should've felt shamed by her outrageous behavior. Some of the things Robert had heard her say in public made his ears turn red.

But the guy seemed fine with that. As a warrior of some repute and a male who grew up on the teachings of Mortdh, Dalhu shouldn't have been so lenient with his female. Even Carol, who didn't consider Robert her mate, was more respectful of him and their status as a couple. She never told crude jokes, or remarked on the fine posterior of that actor or another and what she would've done to said posterior if she were to get her hands on it.

"No." Carol turned around and headed for the bathroom.

He followed. "So whose?"

She stepped into the shower and turned the water on. "No one's. I made it up."

"What?" Was she planning on going by herself? And seducing a fucking mortal? He'd been afraid the day would come when she told him it was over and kicked him out.

"I'll tell you after I'm done showering. I want to wash the perfume off." She started undressing.

"No. You'll tell me right now."

Nude from the waist up, Carol put her hands on her hips. "Fine. I'm training to become a special kind of Guardian. A spy. Part of my training is to pass for a human among immortals."

"Spy on whom?"

Carol arched a brow.

"Doomers?"

"Who else?"

Robert shook his head. "I don't get it. The Doomers' local base was destroyed, and as far as we know, no new one has been established."

"Eventually they will come and build a new base, and besides, I'm not ready yet. It will take time before I can go on an assignment. I'm just starting my training."

Something was missing from her story. Carol had been going to self-defense classes regularly, but she hadn't been taking them too seriously and hadn't said anything about plans to become a Guardian. He'd assumed she was treating it as a form of exercise. Besides, the woman was never going to make it through real training. She had the guts and resilience of a lioness but the lazy attitude of a spoiled house cat.

A spy, though, needed a different set of skills than a warrior. Maybe she had what it took for that. Was she cunning? Not so much. Could she lie convincingly? Hell, yeah.

Still, how was she going to spy on Doomers? How was she going to get close enough? The only contact they had with human females was—

"Over my dead body!" he yelled, fisting his hands as his anger rose to boiling. "You're going to fuck them? Is that the kind of spying you're gonna do?"

Carol took a step back and put her hand up to stop him from advancing on her. "Please calm down. You're scaring me. Go back to the living room and wait for me to finish showering. We'll talk then, like two rational adults."

The last thing he wanted was to leave before getting an answer, but she was right about his need to calm down. The fear in her eyes was real.

"Don't take too long," he managed to hiss through elongated fangs.

Robert poured himself a tall Lagavulin, emptied it and refilled the glass. The thirteen minutes it took for Carol to shower were the longest in his life.

Stepping into the living room, she pointed to the sofa. "Let's sit down."

"I'd rather not."

Carol sat and patted the spot next to her. "Come on, Robert, let's be adult about this."

Reluctantly, he did as she asked, sitting on the edge, and tapping his foot. "Start talking."

Carol sighed. "The training is going to be intense and long. I'm talking months or even years. So none of the stuff you're worried about is going to happen any time soon.

Eventually, though, it will. That's what I'm good at. More so than anyone I know. It may not be the most respected ability, but it is mine. I can seduce and manipulate males like no other."

"I can't believe Kian would whore you out like that." He was going to have a talk with the regent, and give the guy a piece of his mind. Not only was it despicable to use Carol like that, but it was also irresponsible. Kian was putting her in danger of the worst kind. Eternal hell. That was what awaited her.

Carol's eyes narrowed in anger. "Let's be clear about one thing. Kian is not making me do anything I don't want to do."

Robert pushed up to his feet and glared at her. "How can you even consider falling into Doomers' hands again? After all you've been through?"

"I'm doing it because of what I've been through, not despite it. I've proven to myself that I'm strong, and enduring the worst without breaking lessened my fears instead of intensifying them. I also experienced what the women endure whom the Doomers capture and keep. I got away. The ones who are delivered to the island are imprisoned for life. I'm their only hope."

Carol had given away more than she'd intended, and Robert felt his blood freeze in his arteries. "Did all of you go insane? This thing is about infiltrating the island? It's suicide! You'll be dead or wish you were before your feet ever touch the island's ground!"

Carol's eyes flashed in anger. "Don't twist my words around. Anything I discover will help liberate the women. I don't have to be physically there to do it."

Robert's arteries began to defrost, and he let out a relieved breath.

Anything was less dangerous for Carol than going to the fucking island. Even if she weren't discovered right away, she would be trapped there forever and eventually her secret would get out. It was a death sentence either way.

"You have no idea how glad I am this is not on the table. I don't want you to die."

A guilty look ghosted over Carol's features so quickly Robert wasn't sure it had been there at all. Had she been lying?

He sat back down and took her hands in his. "Tell me the truth, Carol."

With a sigh, she nodded. "The island is on the agenda. I don't know if anything will come out of it, there are no definite plans, but it's a possibility."

The prickling ice was back. "I can't watch you do it. I just can't. I was there when you screamed, Carol. I threw away my life to stop it. That time you were taken against your will, there was nothing you could've done to avoid that fate. But now you're going to hell willingly, intentionally." He shook his head. "I know you're not going to listen to me, and I can't watch you sign yourself up for an eternal nightmare."

Tears trickled down her cheeks, and she pulled out one hand from his to wipe them away. "I'm not crying because I feel sorry for myself, or because I'm suddenly afraid. I'm crying because I know I'm hurting you. I don't want to cause you pain, Robert, and yet no matter how hard I try I always do. You'll be better off without me. Find yourself an immortal female who will adore you, and forget about me." She chuckled through her tears. "I think the best thing I can do for you is to kick you out. If I don't, you'll just keep trying and keep hurting. One of us needs to be strong and cut the twisted string that binds us to each other."

CHAPTER 26: BHATHIAN

*W*ith Eva out of town and nothing to do, Bhathian fell back on old habits. He hadn't had an evening gym session in a while. Having no wish to outgrow his new custom-made suit, he'd been limiting himself to his two-hour-long morning workout.

The problem with going to the gym in the evening, though, was that it was overtaken by civilians who worked regular nine-to-five jobs. None of them was strong enough to act as his spotter, which wasn't all bad. It would force him to do cardio, which he needed but hated because it made him feel like a gerbil on a spinning wheel. Running outside would've been much more pleasant, but his unnatural speed would've attracted attention. Kian had ordered special treadmills for them, designed with Guardians in mind. Faster and stronger.

As he walked in, most people pretended not to see him, his perpetual frown warning them off. A few made eye contact, and he nodded at them. No reason to be rude. His mood improved when he saw Dalhu in the heavy weights area. The guy could spot him, and even better, no civilians loitered in that section of the gym.

"Dalhu, my man, am I glad to see you."

Dalhu arched a brow.

That probably wasn't a sentence the guy heard often. Except for the Guardians who had witnessed his bravery and dedication to Amanda and the clan, most of the others were still wary of him and kept their distance.

"I need a spotter."

Dalhu nodded. "You got it. But it will cost you."

"Name your price."

"You spot me in return."

"Good. I would hate to owe you a favor." Too late he realized how offensive that must've sounded to Dalhu. "I like to repay my debts on the spot. The last guy who did me a favor took my daughter as payment. I have to be careful. I have no more offspring to barter."

The joke softened Dalhu's hard expression, and he smiled. "You never know. Maybe Eva will give you another one."

"I should be so lucky." Bhathian sat on the bench. The barbell was loaded with weight plates totaling six hundred pounds, enough for a warm-up.

"Do you need me now or later?" Dalhu eyed the light weights.

"Later. After the warm-up."

"Good." The guy took the next bench over and started his routine.

"I'm surprised to see you here again. You've done quite a workout this morning." The Guardians, as well as Kian, Michael, and Dalhu preferred the early morning hours when there was no one else besides them in the gym. Bhathian thought that he was the only nutcase to go again at night.

"Amanda stayed late at work." Dalhu offered an explanation.

That explained it. "Eva is out of town."

"I'm used to spending the days alone," Dalhu said. "But in the evening, the place seems empty without her."

"Yeah, I know what you mean. We spend our entire lives alone and everything is fine, until a woman takes over our world and suddenly we can't be without her. A piece of us goes missing when she's away."

"Exactly."

Bhathian chuckled. "I'm glad no one is here to hear us. We sound like a couple of chicks."

Dalhu placed the barbell back on the rack. "I don't give a shit what anyone thinks. Except for Amanda, that is." He frowned. "Kian and Annani too. But that's it. Only three people whose opinions I value. Everyone else, I can take it or leave it."

"You're your own island."

"Precisely. Spending most of my life in the company of morons, I've gotten used to keeping to myself."

Bhathian put the barbell back and sat up. "The Doomers can't be all dumb. There must be at least a few who can think for themselves."

"Sure. Robert and I are examples of that. But flapping my gums to the wrong people could've led to deadly consequences. My strategy was to remain silent and listen. A man can learn a lot more if he keeps his mouth shut and his ears and eyes open."

Bhathian nodded. "Smart." Dalhu's comment got him thinking. Maybe he'd heard rumors about Doomers who'd deserted Navuh's camp. The immortal who'd turned Eva had most likely been one.

"I wonder if you've ever heard of other Doomers deserting? I'm sure you and Robert are not the only ones."

Dalhu pinned him with a hard stare. "Why do you want to know?"

143

For a guy who claimed not to care what anyone thought of him, Dalhu sure was touchy. Bhathian considered giving a vague reason, that he was just curious, but if he wanted the guy to answer honestly, so should he.

"I guess it's not a secret that Eva was turned by a mystery immortal. I questioned every male clan member, but none remembered her. I doubt very much that any immortals other than us and the Doomers survived. If any had, we would've found them. We've been searching for centuries. So the only logical explanation I can come up with is that it was a Doomer. But as far as we know, back then the Doomers had no presence in the States. A deserter, however, could've chosen to hide here precisely for that reason."

"I've never heard of anyone jumping ship, but that doesn't mean anything. All missing men were presumed dead."

That made sense. An organization like that would want to keep a lid on what would have been perceived as failure. "Did it happen often? Men not coming back from missions?"

"Not as far as I know. But I was just a lowly commander of a small unit. I wasn't told anything that wasn't necessary to my missions. You should talk to Robert. As Sharim's assistant, he would've been exposed to much more information. Sharim was pretty high up in the organization. The only ones above him were Navuh's sons."

"How many does he have?"

"There are the five older ones that run the organization, and several younger that are not as prominent. I'm not sure how many of them there are. They don't get any special treatment. Not unless they've proven they are better than everyone else and can be useful to their father. You should ask Robert about that too. He may know more about Navuh's progeny. Or not."

"I will."

Once Bhathian had finished his workout and spotted for

Dalhu, he headed straight for Robert's office. Most likely the guy was still there. Managing the supply side of the Malibu project was keeping him busy.

A shower would've been a good idea, but Bhathian preferred to avoid the one in the gym. A little sweat, or a lot in his case, should not bother a warrior, and especially not an ex-Doomer. Those guys were not known for their attention to hygiene.

Bhathian knocked on the door before pushing it open all the way. "Can I bother you for a moment?" he asked as he stepped in.

Robert looked surprised. "Any time. Please, take a seat." He motioned to the only spare chair in his office. Bhathian had been there only once before, and he didn't remember seeing the couch that was crammed into the small space. A neatly folded blanket covered a pillow.

Had Carol kicked Robert out?

That was probably what had happened, but Bhathian wasn't going to say anything about it.

It was none of his business.

"I want to ask you a few questions about your past in the Doomer camp."

Robert's face darkened. "What would you like to know?"

Damn it. Bhathian wished he had better communication skills. It seemed he offended people left, right and center. "It's not about you. I'm trying to figure out if the immortal who'd turned Eva was a Doomer deserter. I asked Dalhu about it, but he said he didn't know of any and suggested that I come to you since you were higher up in the organization and therefore better informed."

That seemed to mollify the guy, and he straightened in his chair. "No one ever dared to suggest that warriors deserted. But I always suspected that some of the soldiers who were presumed dead faked it and ran. Especially if an entire unit

145

was lost. When one or two died while the rest came home, it was for real because their comrades would not have covered for them. But not when a whole platoon went missing."

Bhathian whistled. "An entire platoon of immortals? How could that have happened?"

"World War II, Hiroshima." Robert leaned forward as if he was sharing a secret. "Not only that, the platoon was headed by one of Navuh's sons. Back then he was the youngest, and there was talk that he was going to rise in the organization. Not all of them do. If they are not exceptional, Navuh doesn't even acknowledge them. Out of shame, most try to hide their parentage, which isn't all that difficult since they are raised like the rest of the Dormant kids by the other dormant females and not their actual mothers."

"What the hell was he doing in Japan during WWII? Did Doomers mess with things there too?"

Robert snorted. "Of course. But for him and his men to perish in the nuclear explosion, they would have needed to be close to the epicenter. Seems to me like the perfect cover to make a run for it."

"Do you remember what he looked like?" It was illogical to assume that out of a group of forty to fifty deserters the one who'd turned Eva was the leader, but Bhathian was going with his gut instinct.

Robert leaned back in his chair. "I do, vaguely. But they all share the same build and dark coloring." He chuckled. "Either Navuh's genes are dominant, or all the females in his harem look the same."

"You never saw them?"

"None of the soldiers do. Total seclusion. Not even the sons themselves get to know their mothers. They are raised by the Dormants in the larger harem."

That was unreasonably cruel. Why would the despot treat his own children like that?

"Why does he do it?"

"Control. What else. A mother can have a big influence on her son. Navuh ensures the only influence is his."

Bhathian shook his head. "Only a sociopath could think that way."

"Read history, Bhathian. Harem politics were the downfall of more than one empire. Navuh is a very clever male."

That was true, as evidenced by his success. But history was full of smart despots who'd been brought down. Either from within or without.

Bhathian got up and offered his hand to Robert for a handshake. "Thank you. That was a very interesting talk."

Robert shook what he was offered. "Any time, man."

As he made his way to the elevators, Bhathian mulled over the new information Robert had provided him with. Maybe he could get Tim, Andrew's forensic artist, to draw the missing son's portrait from Robert's memory. The question was how to arrange for it. Perhaps Kian would agree to let Robert into one of the public areas of the high-rise, and Tim could meet him there. For the right amount of money, Bhathian was sure Tim would agree to come. That and a couple of pizzas and beers.

CHAPTER 27: NATHALIE

"Yes. Hallelujah!" Nathalie exclaimed. She'd never been so happy while sitting on the toilet in the morning, or any other time for that matter.

There was no blood on the pad.

It had taken nearly four weeks for the bleeding to finally stop, and Nathalie was more than ready for sex with her husband.

"Are you okay in there?" Andrew asked.

"No more bleeding. Tonight is the night," she called out.

There was silence on the other side of the door.

"Did you hear me? We can finally have sex."

"Yeah, I heard you. But are you sure? Bridget said six weeks."

Nathalie flushed the toilet, washed her hands, and opened the door. "She said the bleeding needed to stop first. And she also said that the venom would speed up my recovery. No more excuses, mister. Tonight you're going to pleasure me until I tell you to stop or faint from exhaustion." She stretched on her toes and kissed his lips.

Andrew wrapped his arms around her, lifting her and

148

twirling her around. "It's about time I paid you back for all those fabulous blowjobs you've bestowed on me."

"My thoughts exactly."

Their daughter's demanding wail pierced the sexy bubble.

"I'll get her," Andrew said.

"Thanks." Nathalie stepped back into the bathroom and turned on the shower.

Now that she was a mother, even a basic thing like when to shower had to be scheduled and planned. If she wanted to spend more than three minutes in there, Nathalie needed Andrew to watch the baby. It had to be done either early in the morning before he left for work, or in the evening when he got back.

She preferred the mornings. But if she was up all night, every additional minute of sleep counted. Flexibility was the name of this new game.

Which meant that if she wanted to make the first time in months she had sex with Andrew special, she needed to plan for it. Syssi could babysit Phoenix. Problem was that having her sister-in-law listening in was not conducive to wild lovemaking. She would have to ask her to take Phoenix to her place.

It was scary. Guarding her daughter's health, Nathalie had limited the number of visitors, letting only a few hold her, and she'd never taken her out of the apartment. If not for their large balcony, the baby would've not gotten any fresh air or direct sunlight. Nathalie's excuse was that there were no parks nearby, but the truth was that she was terrified of taking Phoenix out of the keep.

Should she consult with Bridget?

Nah, the doctor would probably laugh away her concerns.

Nathalie shampooed her long hair, put the conditioner on, and proceeded to shave everything that needed shaving. According to Syssi, the transition was going to take care of it.

Immortal females had no armpit or pubic hair, which were Nathalie's most problematic areas. Her leg hair was very sparse, but it was dark and therefore visible even on her olive skin. That too would be gone.

She couldn't wait.

For some reason, it seemed that the venom alone with no intercourse didn't do the trick. Either that or she was having difficulty transitioning. There was so much they didn't know about the process.

What if a Dormant couldn't transition after giving birth?

Bridget had said it was all nonsense and that Nathalie was seeing shadows where there were none.

The doctor's assumption was that pregnancy hormones might have prevented Nathalie's transition—which made sense from an evolutionary standpoint—to protect the fetus, and that their levels hadn't declined sufficiently yet.

Nathalie sighed. Her mood swings were so disturbing. One moment she didn't want to go through the transition at all, terrified that she would die and leave her precious baby an orphan. The next moment she couldn't wait to be done with it, and was afraid that it wouldn't work and she'd remain human.

When she stepped out of the bathroom, she found Andrew sitting on the sofa, baby-talking to Phoenix who was looking at her daddy with smiling eyes, cooing and gurgling back.

Precious.

Moments like that made it all worthwhile.

The couch was a reminder of darker days, but they decided to leave it in the master bedroom even after Andrew had gone back to sleeping in the same bed with Nathalie. It provided them with an intimate spot in the home they shared with her father.

"Who's the most beautiful baby girl? That's right, you are. Yes, you are. Who is Daddy's princess? Yes, you are—"

Nathalie sat next to Andrew. "How did she eat?"

"Sucked it all up in under three minutes. I think it's time to give her more. Maybe even start with baby cereal."

She'd been thinking along the same lines. It was a bit early, but Phoenix was a large baby and probably needed more food than the typical four-week-old. "I'll ask Bridget." She chuckled. "I'm driving the woman crazy. I'm calling her at least twice a day. She is a saint for putting up with me."

"That's her job, yes it is—" Andrew continued with the baby talk, getting more gurgles and coos out of Phoenix.

"I'm going to call Syssi and ask her to babysit tonight."

"That's a wonderful idea. Mommy and Daddy will be very busy tonight, yes they will—"

Nathalie rolled her eyes. It was cute but annoying. Especially given the topic.

"At her place. So we'll have privacy."

"What about Granddaddy? Is he going to a sleepover with baby Phoenix at Auntie Syssi's?"

Nathalie started laughing. "Is that how you're going to talk from now on?"

"Yes, I will, because it makes my baby girl happy. But not when Mommy and Daddy are alone. No, no, no. Mommy likes when Daddy says naughty things to her. Yes, she does."

"You're going to spoil her rotten, aren't you?"

"Oh, yes I will, yes I will."

"Daddy needs to give baby to Mommy because he needs to get ready for work." Nathalie imitated Andrew's silly tone.

Phoenix looked away from her daddy and gave Nathalie the sweetest smile.

Love, pure and all-consuming.

"Who is the cutest baby girl in the world?" Nathalie cooed as she took Phoenix from Andrew, kissing her soft cheek.

Bliss. The wave of endorphins made her light-headed. "You are. Yes, you are."

With a smirk, Andrew stood up. "It's addictive, isn't it? The sounds she makes are so adorable."

"Yes, they are." She stopped herself from repeating. If they didn't watch it, they would start talking to each other like that.

"I have an idea. How about we go out first? You haven't been out of this building in a month."

"Oh, God, that sounds wonderful."

Andrew bent and kissed her on the lips, teasing her with a quick lick. "I'll make reservations for By Invitation Only. Let's plan for six. I'll come home early so we can have more time."

"Let me check with Syssi first. I don't know if she'll be okay with babysitting for so long."

"She'll love it. But call me if there is a problem, early. Later in the day they might be booked."

"I will."

After she'd put down Phoenix for a nap, Nathalie called Syssi.

"Nathalie, what's going on?" Syssi immediately assumed something was wrong if Nathalie was calling her at work.

"Everything is fine. I'm calling because I need a favor. Could you babysit tonight?"

"Sure. Any time. You know how much I love that cutie pie niece of mine." The joy in Syssi's tone was heartwarming. Having a family rocked. The question was whether Syssi would be as enthusiastic about keeping Phoenix overnight.

"It's longer than usual, though. I'm finally ready to get out of here and then rekindle the romance with my husband. Could you keep her overnight at your place?" Nathalie chewed on her lower lip as she waited for the response. It was a lot to ask.

"Are you kidding me? I would love to."

"She still wakes up every four hours."

"Not a problem. You know that as an immortal I don't need much sleep."

"Thank you. You're the best."

"Any time."

"It will be good practice for you for when I transition." They'd talked about it, and Syssi had said she would take time off work and take care of Phoenix when Nathalie went through it.

"And for when I finally have a baby of my own," Syssi added.

Poor girl. The chances of her getting her wish were so pitifully slim. "You bet. Though after doing it full time for a few days, you might change your mind about wanting one. Motherhood is one hell of an adjustment. It takes over your life. Career? What career? Feeling sexy? Forget about it. Should I go on?"

Syssi snorted. "No. You made your point. I'll tell you what I think after the fact. All that matters to me now is that you come out okay on the other side."

Nathalie chewed on her lower lip again. "If I don't survive, I count on you to step in and help Andrew."

For some reason, Nathalie felt more comfortable entrusting Syssi with her baby than Eva. Her mother was too busy with her detective agency and with her crew, who she treated as if they were her children.

Syssi sniffled. "Don't you dare to even think it. You're going to be fine."

"I know. But it makes me feel better to know that she would be cared for if I don't."

CHAPTER 28: BHATHIAN

*B*hathian would've loved to pick Eva up from the airport, but she'd taken her own car to get there, leaving it at the airport parking for when she came back.

He'd missed her. It would've been so satisfying to be there at the gate when she got off the plane, pulling her into a crushing embrace and kissing her until she felt faint. Instead, he was waiting for her at her home, watching some stupid show with Nick. Those reality shows were so fake. As one who had been there and done that, he kept shaking his head at what the contestants were supposedly doing to survive.

"You know it's all fake, right?" he asked Nick.

"Yeah, so what? It's still fun to watch."

He pushed up to his feet. "I'm getting myself a beer. You want one?"

"That Snake's Venom brand? No thank you. It knocks me out. I need to drive in like half an hour."

"A date?"

"I wish. California girls are not as friendly as I thought they would be. I'm going to test a new security system. Supposedly it's foolproof. But we both know such a thing doesn't exist." Nick puffed out his chest. "As I have proven to your boss. You guys have one of the best I ever messed with, but I got through."

"And was immediately caught."

"That's irrelevant. I was doing it to prove a point, not to actually break in, and I did. Eva won the bet."

"That she did."

The kid was a wizard. William was still trying to figure out how his infallible system got hacked. It was also worrisome. If one hacker managed to infiltrate the keep, others could too.

In the kitchen, Bhathian pulled out a beer from the fridge and sat at the table. The Chinese takeout he'd brought was getting cold, but there was nothing to be done about it. Eva's flight was coming in an hour late.

Earlier in the day, he'd called Andrew and asked about Tim. Andrew had said he would talk to the guy and see if he was willing to do a side job for Bhathian. If Tim refused, Bhathian would have to find someone else. It would be a huge breakthrough if Eva recognized the guy Robert had described. It was a long shot. But he had a feeling about it.

Pulling out his phone, he began an internet search for a private service he could hire in case Tim wouldn't do it. They all looked amateurish. A gimmick for a party, a caricature artist. Maybe Andrew knew of someone else.

Sharon walked into the kitchen. "Bhathian, can I have some of that?" She pointed at the takeout boxes.

"Sure. I brought enough for everybody."

She clapped him on his back. "You're awesome. If at any point you get tired of Eva, give me a holler. I love guys who feed me."

"I'll keep it in mind." Not really, but that was what she'd expected him to say. Not that he thought for a moment that she was interested. He wasn't Sharon's type. Either that or the girl ignored his masculine charms because she was intensely loyal to Eva.

Probably the second one. Most women found him attractive. Mainly because of his muscles and other physical attributes. It sure as hell wasn't because of his charming personality or his pleasant disposition.

"It smells amazing." Opening a box at a time, she scooped a little of each item onto a paper plate and then shoved it into the microwave. "You sure you don't want any? I can warm up another plate for you."

"Thanks, but I'm waiting to eat with Eva."

Sharon leaned against the counter and crossed her arms over her chest. "You're a good guy, Bhathian. That frown of yours doesn't fool me."

He took a swig of his beer. "If you say so."

The microwave beeped, and she took out her plate. "I'll keep you company until Eva gets here." She put the plate on the table and sat down. "What's her ETA?"

"Depends on the traffic. She texted me twenty minutes ago that the plane had landed."

Sharon pretended to grimace. "Before she met you, Eva used to text one of us to tell us she'd arrived safely. But we are not important to her anymore. She has you."

Not deigning to answer, Bhathian just arched a brow. Eva loved her employees as if they were her own children, and they knew it.

"Where is Tessa?" he asked to change the subject.

Sharon finished chewing what was in her mouth and used a napkin to wipe off the sauce that had dripped on her chin. "You should know. She is hanging out with your cousin, Jackson. I think it's great that the two of them are getting close. Jackson is a good guy."

Bhathian chuckled. "Do you think everyone is a good guy?"

She shook her head. "Not at all. I think most men are jerks. But you and Jackson are different. I like you." She waved a hand. "Not like I have the hots for you or anything, though both of you are damn good-looking dudes, but as friends. You're good people."

Interesting. Maybe it was that affinity Syssi and Amanda were talking about. Apparently it went both ways.

"How would you know?"

As she thought of an answer, Sharon stuffed another bite of orange chicken in her mouth and chewed on it. "This is delicious. I can't tell you how I know. It's a gut feeling. I can always tell when a guy is a creep or a jerk, and when he is a mensch, like Jackson and you. Not many of those out there, unfortunately." She stuffed another bite in her mouth.

He bowed his head. "Thank you. From both of us." It had been a nice compliment. Bhathian didn't like it when people remarked on his looks, especially when women did it, it made him feel like a beefcake. But being called a mensch, a man of honor and integrity, he liked that.

"Do you have more hunky cousins in that big family of yours? Someone you can introduce me to?"

"I'm not into matchmaking. But once Nathalie is back to normal, she'll gladly snoop around for an eligible bachelor for you." If Syssi's hunch was true and Sharon was a Dormant, the girl would have so many suitors she wouldn't know what to do with them all.

"Speaking of Nathalie, when are we going to see that baby? Is she ever going to get out of her house?"

"She is a new mom, and everything must seem scary to her. Give her time.

Sharon shrugged and dug into her plate.

The window in the kitchen was open, and Bhathian kept his ears trained on the street, waiting to hear Eva's car engine. Every vehicle emitted a slightly different noise, and it wasn't difficult to differentiate one from another.

Pushing the chair back, he got up. "Eva is here. I'm going outside to help her with her bags."

Sharon narrowed her eyes at him. "Are you a dog or something? How do you know that?"

He shrugged and headed out.

At least one part of the welcome home scenario was going to play out. He opened Eva's door as she was cutting the engine, and offered her his hand to help her up. "I missed you," he said as an explanation for the crushing hug he pulled her into.

Eva didn't resist, molding her body to his as if she was his second skin. "I missed you too."

Burying his nose in her hair, he inhaled her scent. The one that meant home to him. Home wasn't about an address, it was about wherever Eva was. That was where he belonged.

Holding her close, he kissed her. She parted her lips for him, a small moan escaping her throat and sending a bolt of desire straight into his hard shaft. He couldn't wait to get her upstairs to her bedroom. But then her belly made a gurgling sound. "Are you hungry?"

"Starving. The sandwiches they had for sale on the plane were disgusting. All I ate was a bag of pretzels."

He kissed the top of her head. "I figured you'd be hungry and brought Chinese takeout. Pop the trunk, and I'll get your bags."

Eva stretched up and kissed him. "You're the best."

And wasn't that music to his ears.

Leaving her suitcase by the door, Bhathian clasped Eva's hand and pulled her toward the kitchen. Nick was there, eating at the table with Sharon.

Bhathian waited patiently as hugs and greetings were

exchanged, then pulled out a chair for Eva. "Take a seat, love. I'll warm a plate up for you."

A few minutes later Sharon and Nick exchanged knowing looks and excused themselves from the table.

Eva patted her belly and sighed. "That was so good. Thank you. It's nice to come home and have food ready for me."

"Can't your guys do that?"

"Tessa does. Sharon and Nick don't have the presence of mind."

"Well, you've got me now."

She smiled. "I do. By the way, where is Tessa?"

"Sharon said she is with Jackson."

"Good. He'll keep her safe."

Bhathian frowned. "From what?"

Eva folded a paper napkin over her plate. "While I was listening to the tab I put on my target, I overheard a conversation between two other guys in that office. I wasn't sure in which room the meeting was going to be held, so I put bugs in several places. Long story short, this one guy was talking about finding the bitch who'd killed his brother five years ago. He also said, or was it the other guy, I'm not sure, that she was so young then and probably looks much different now. The timing fit Tessa's story. I'm not aware of any other murder committed by a teenage girl five years ago. It might be a coincidence, but I'm worried."

"Did the murder Tessa was involved in make it to the news?"

"Only that a businessman was found dead in his apartment, and the police were investigating. They ruled out burglary because nothing had been taken. They said it was probably revenge on a deal gone wrong."

"You have your answer. No teenager was mentioned in this case, because no one knew she existed. He was holding her captive, and her clothes were the only clue that he had a woman living with him. The same can hold true for other cases you've never heard about. Besides, not everything gets the news attention. The guy could've been talking about a hit-and-run accident that had killed his brother, the driver of which had been a girl Tessa's age."

"Maybe. But I can't help feeling anxious. The guy said he has people looking for her. I'm going to take Tessa to the hairdresser's to change her hair color and buy her contact lenses. I hope that will be enough to change her appearance."

Bhathian got up and pulled two beers from the fridge. "Taking a precaution is always a good idea. But I really don't think you should lose any sleep over it. For five years you guys lived in the same city the guy had died in, and no one came looking for Tessa."

He handed Eva a bottle and a glass.

"Thank you. I need that." She emptied the bottle into the tall glass. "Your turn. What new and exciting things can you tell me about?"

"I have a good lead on your mystery guy."

"Oh, really?" Eva leaned forward.

"I talked with Dalhu and then with Robert. Apparently a whole platoon of Doomers disappeared during the Second World War. They were in Hiroshima at the time of the nuclear bombing. When they failed to come back, they were presumed dead. The clincher is that they were led by Navuh's youngest son." Bhathian crossed his arms over his chest. "I think the guy took the opportunity to slip his father's clutches, and he and his warriors traveled to the States after the war. Back then, there were no Doomers here. A perfect place for them to hide."

Eva leaned back with her glass in hand. "An interesting assumption but there is no way to verify it."

"There is. Robert can describe the guy, and I can have the"

same forensic artist that drew your portrait from my memory, draw that guy from Robert's. You said you'd recognize him if you saw him."

She nodded. "It's a long shot, you know that, right?"

"I do. But I have a gut feeling about this."

"Then let's do it. What's the worst that can happen? We just find out that it wasn't him."

CHAPTER 29: ROBERT

*I*n his office, Robert leaned back in his chair and stared at the ceiling. There was nowhere for him to go. He was sleeping in the blasted office, taking his meals in there, and showering in the gym. Basically, he was spending most of his days in almost complete isolation.

It was starting to get to him.

Combined with the seething rage Carol's decision had brought about, Robert was a walking time bomb waiting to explode. If he could spar with the Guardians, he could've taken some of his aggression out on the wrestling mat, but he was loath to ask. If even Dalhu shunned him, a fellow ex-Doomer, what were the chances that one of them would agree to train with him? And the civilians were just that—civilians. None of them posed a challenge.

He needed to talk to Kian. The guy had said to come to him if he needed anything. And besides, he had no one else to talk to.

His only companion wanted him out of her life.

She was right, though. It was time to move on. Banging

his head against the wall and hoping for a miracle was a loser attitude.

There was a reason he'd risen in the Doomer organization despite his limitations. Hard work and determination compensated for average intelligence and less than average social skills. Robert made himself useful and readily bowed to authority—two qualities highly valued by his commanding officers.

Kian's office was on the same level of the underground as Robert's, and given the guy's work habits, he wasn't surprised to find the clan's regent still there despite the late hour.

Robert knocked on the glass panel of his door.

Kian lifted his head, then waved him in. "What's up?"

"I need to talk to you. Do you have a minute?"

"Of course. Please, take a seat." The regent motioned to one of the chairs on the other side of his desk.

There was no point in talking in circles, not that Robert knew how to do it if he wanted to, so he got straight to it. "Carol and I broke up. I've been sleeping in my office for the past four days, but it's not a good solution. Is there an apartment you can assign to me? Or a room? I don't mind flatmates or even roommates." On the contrary, that was how he'd lived most of his life. The Doomer compound was sprawling, but that didn't mean that warriors had their own quarters. As an officer, Robert had shared lodgings with fewer men than the rank and file, but it was still two men in a room. That was what he'd been used to. He preferred cohabiting with others. Even a silent roommate was better than none.

"Why haven't you come to me sooner? You must've been going crazy cooped up in that small room twenty-four-seven."

"I didn't want to impose."

Kian shook his head. "Let me check with Ingrid." He pulled out his phone and typed a quick text. A few moments later it pinged with a response.

"She has a room available in an apartment with two other guys. It's one of the larger three-bedroom ones."

"That would be great. Thank you." Two roommates were better than one.

"Her office is on the third floor. Suite 304. She'll meet you there in ten minutes to give you a key."

"Thank you." Robert debated whether he should ask Kian again about what was in store for him. The guy had gotten pissed the last time Robert had voiced his concerns. But he had to make sure that he knew where he stood. "I'm still okay? Right? Nothing changes because I'm no longer with Carol?"

"Nope. Nothing changes. You still got your job and a place to stay. In time, after you have proven trustworthy beyond a shadow of a doubt, you'll become a full-fledged clan member."

"How can I help hasten the process?"

Kian drummed his fingers on the glossy surface of his desk. "I don't really know what to tell you. It's not easy for us to trust an ex-Doomer. Dalhu has a true-love mate, and that in itself guarantees his loyalty. He will always choose Amanda above anyone and anything else, and that extends to her family. He also went through a trial few could've survived, let alone done so with such honor and dignity. Not only that, but he'd also proven himself in battle. And still, even after all that, not everyone is happy about him being here, and some still eye him suspiciously."

Robert sighed. "I appreciate the frank response, but it's far from encouraging."

"That is true. But on the other hand, time will do its thing even if you do nothing to hasten the results. People will get used to your presence, and after years of your loyal service their suspicions will shrink and eventually evaporate. Lucky for you, time is not an issue."

Robert nodded. He would've liked to find a quicker route, but then nothing he'd ever achieved came fast or easy. Slow and steady was his way. He pushed to his feet and offered his hand for a handshake. "Thank you. For everything."

Kian shook it. "You're welcome."

When he got to Ingrid's office on the third floor, she was already waiting for him with a key, a note, and a big smile. "Here you go, Robert. I wrote down the apartment number and the names of your roommates. Charles is a civilian plane pilot, and Edgar flies a helicopter. Both are young immortals I'm sure you'll get along splendidly with. They know you're coming and are waiting for you."

"Thank you." He stuffed the note and the key in his back pocket.

Ingrid leaned over her desk, giving him a view of her rounded backside, and scribbled another note. "Here is my number. In case you need anything for your room." She handed it to him. "If you don't like the pictures or the bedding, anything at all, I can order you something else."

Robert glanced around her office. "You're the interior decorator, right?"

"Yes, I am."

"Then I'm sure I'm going to love everything in that room. You have great taste."

Her smile was wide, and she put a hand on her hip, striking a pose. "Flattery is always appreciated. Thank you."

"It's not flattery when it's the truth."

"Even better."

"Well, I'd better go and say hello to my new roommates. I already took too much of your time."

She waved a dismissive hand. "My pleasure. And please, call me. I'm at your service." She winked.

Robert felt the tips of his ears heating up. "I will. Good night." He rushed to the door.

Dear Mortdh, he was indeed dense. It'd taken him a while to realize that Ingrid was coming on to him. Kian had been right. The moment his relationship with Carol had officially ended, the females, or at least this one, got much bolder in their pursuit of him.

Maybe that was the answer to his loneliness?

The men didn't trust him, maybe the women didn't either, but they wanted him. Even if they were only interested in sex, he should take whatever he was offered.

It beat being alone.

CHAPTER 30: SYSSI

*K*ian hung up the house phone. "The security guy says there is a package for you downstairs."

Syssi put down the book she'd been reading and pushed to her feet. "I'll go get it."

Kian pulled her into his arms. "I hope it's sexy lingerie."

"Why would I order sexy things? You like me best in the nude."

"True. So what is it?"

"A surprise." And not one Kian was going to be happy about. She still hadn't told him about her plans to try shrooms.

Ugh, he was going to hit the roof. But keeping it a secret from him wasn't an option. As much as Syssi hated confrontations, there was no avoiding it this time.

After all was said and done, it was her decision, and Kian could do nothing to prevent her from carrying it out... Except locking her down in the dungeon, or taking the shrooms and flushing them down the toilet.

She was fully prepared for their first colossal fight.

Was it worth it?

Time would tell. If the hallucinogenic achieved what she hoped it would and kick-started her foresight, then the answer was yes.

When she came back up, Kian eyed the small brown envelope she was holding. "Now I'm really curious. It's not clothes or shoes. Is it makeup?"

Most of her shopping was done online, and Kian was used to her getting packages in the mail and showing him what she'd gotten.

"No, it's not. Come sit with me on the couch and I'll show you."

His eyes smiling, he sat next to her and cocked a brow.

Damn it. Kian was expecting something fun.

With a sigh, Syssi tore the top of the envelope. "Promise you'll let me explain before you start yelling."

Kian frowned. "Yelling? Since when do I yell at you?"

"You don't. But I have a feeling this time you will." She pulled out a small plastic bag with a few dried mushrooms at the bottom. "These are shrooms." She lifted the bag and gave it a little shake.

"Mushrooms?" He wrinkled his nose. "Why would I be angry about some stinky mushrooms? Unless you want to feed them to me, in which case I'll politely decline. No yelling."

There was no way Kian didn't know what shrooms were. People had been using them to enhance visions since time immemorial.

"The shrooms are for me."

"What are you going to do with them?"

"You really don't know what these are, do you?"

For a moment he looked puzzled, but then realization dawned. "Don't tell me those are the kind that cause hallucinations?"

She nodded. "I want to try them. Maybe they will help my foretelling. I'm sick and tired of being at the mercy of my visions. I want to control them."

"You mean you want to force them to come?"

"Yes."

"Is it dangerous?"

He was taking it surprisingly well, and he wasn't faking the calm either. His scent betrayed worry but not anger. "No. Most people report very mild effects, and they are not harmful or addictive in any way."

"But you are not most people, Syssi. You are a seer, and a hallucinogenic can bring about visions too powerful for you to handle. The foretelling hits you hard enough when it comes without any prompting."

"I know. And I won't lie to you and tell you that I'm not scared. But I have to try. I feel like I'm sitting on a goldmine of information that I have no access to."

Kian wrapped his arm around her and pulled her closer. "I don't like it."

She leaned against him, thankful for his warmth and strength and his unwavering support of her. "I know. I'm going to start with a tiny amount, and have you and Amanda watch over me."

"Before you do, I want to read about it."

"I already did. Don't you trust me?"

"Of course I do. But reading about it myself will help assuage my concerns."

Syssi grabbed a throw pillow and twisted the fringe between her fingers. There was one more tiny secret she'd kept from him from the beginning. "I dreamt about you. Before we met, that is. Night after night for weeks. It didn't feel like a premonition, but in retrospect, I realized it was."

He smirked. "Oh, yeah? What were the dreams about?"

That was one of the reasons she'd never told him. Kian's ego was overinflated as it was. "It was a nightmare."

His smile wilted. "That's why you never told me?"

She chuckled. "No. Your part in it wasn't nightmarish at all; you were the hero who came to my rescue. In the dream, I was alone, running in the dark from a pack of wolves. I saw you, or rather your shadow, in the distance and ran toward you, but I always woke up before reaching you."

"So how do you know it was me?"

"Because shortly before I met you, I did. And it was one hell of an erotic dream."

The smirk was back. "Tell me."

"Later. I know you. If I tell you now, you'll want to recreate it right away."

"And that's a problem because?"

She punched his bicep. "Because I want to try the shrooms first."

"Why haven't you told me about the dreams?"

She shrugged. "It seemed silly. At first, I was embarrassed to admit it, and later it felt weird to mention something I've kept from you for so long. But lately I've been thinking a lot about them. It's another manifestation of my paranormal ability, and it isn't as traumatic as the visions. I wish I could do something to encourage the dreams.

"And you hope to do it with the shrooms?"

Syssi lifted her hands. "I welcome anything. Visions or dreams. I just hate to feel useless."

He mussed her hair. "Don't be ridiculous. You're the furthest from useless a person can get."

"Thank you. I meant my talent. It's wasted. There must be a way to harness it."

Kian smoothed the hair he'd mussed. "I get it. Being at the mercy of those visions must be frustrating. I'll look into it

while I'm reading up on the shrooms. Maybe I can find legit-
imate psychics who can give you guidance."

"Most are charlatans."

"I agree. But we know that some are not. You're the proof
of it."

"Okay. You go and conduct your search, and I'll tell
Amanda to come over in half an hour. Is it enough time
for you?"

"It will do."

As Kian ducked into his office, Syssi texted her
sister-in-law.

A moment later her phone rang. "How did Kian take it?"

"Surprisingly well. He is in his office researching the
topic. I told him he has until you come."

"Girl, I'm so proud of you. You've changed that man. I
was sure he was going to go ballistic on us."

"You mean on me."

"To start with. But then he would've come after your
accomplice, me."

Syssi chuckled. "True. Now that you know it's safe you
can come over."

"I thought you wanted me there in half an hour."

"Changed my mind. We can have a cappuccino while
Kian is surfing the net."

"Fabulous. I'm on my way."

She and Amanda were on their second cappuccino when
Kian came back, his laptop tucked under his arm. "I found a
documentary about a western anthropologist who tried
Ayahuasca. I thought we should watch it."

Amanda waved a dismissive hand. "Comparing shrooms
to Ayahuasca is like comparing a regular bell pepper to the
Red Sabina Habanero."

"What's that?"

"One of the world's hottest peppers. There are hotter

ones, but the others were bred to be like that. This one is nature's child."

Syssi shook her head. "The things you store in that head of yours."

Amanda lifted her chin. "What can I say? Curious minds want to know. Now dig into that plastic bag and take out a small shroom. We can watch the documentary while we wait for it to kick in."

Syssi took a deep breath. "Okay. Let's do it." She pulled out the smallest piece and put it in her mouth. The taste wasn't as horrible as she expected. In fact, the dried mushroom was pretty tasteless. And chewy.

Syssi swallowed the last of it. "That wasn't so bad. How soon should it start working?"

"Half an hour tops," Amanda said.

His expression disapproving, Kian voiced no further remarks. He put the laptop on the coffee table and started the documentary.

As she watched, Syssi became convinced of two things. The first was that she was never going to try Ayahuasca because no visions were worth the terrible side effects of intense vomiting and diarrhea. The second was that the shrooms had no effect on her.

"How do you feel?' Kian asked for the fifth time.

"Nothing. They didn't work."

Amanda frowned. "Maybe the shrooms are fake."

"It's a reputable site. Carol recommended it. She said she orders from them all the time."

Kian looked relieved. "You tried, it didn't work, case closed."

Syssi shook her head. "I ate too little. I should eat more." She reached for the bag.

Kian stayed her hand. "Not tonight. If you insist, we can try again in a few days after this dose is out of your system.

This needs to be done scientifically." He pinned Amanda with a hard stare. "Does it say the net weight on the packaging?"

Syssi pulled out a piece of paper from the brown envelope and read through it. "Yeah. Fifty-seven grams."

"I'm going to weigh what's left and make a note of the difference."

"We kind of went willy-nilly about it. Shame on us," Amanda admitted.

Syssi hadn't thought about the experiment in scientific terms. Carol claimed that each person was different and there was no way to tell how much would be needed or how strong the effects would be. She'd advised caution—starting with a small amount and not doing it alone. Syssi had followed the advice to the letter. But if it helped Kian to worry less, then so be it. Let him do the weighing and the notating.

Next time she was going to double the dose.

CHAPTER 31: ROBERT

"We have a schedule," said Charles, who preferred to be called Charlie. "When it was just me and Ed we took turns. One day I cooked dinner and one day he did. Now that you're here, we each get to cook twice a week. Sunday is off. We eat out."

"Works for me."

"Can you start tomorrow?"

"Sure. But you guys need to do the grocery shopping. I can pay my share, but I can't go out to the supermarket. I'm not allowed out of the keep."

"That sucks, man." Ed patted him on the back.

The guys were nice, treating him as if he was just another clan member and not an enemy they were wary of. Maybe it was because they were so young. The two hadn't had a reason to develop the deep resentment toward Doomers the older ones had. Growing up in the United States of America, they hadn't been exposed to the devastation Navuh's influence had caused.

Robert wondered if they'd gotten to witness any war at all.

"Can I ask you something personal?"

Ed lifted his hands defensively. "I'm not into guys, dude."

Robert smiled. "That was a leap. All I wanted to know is how old you guys are."

"Oh. I'm thirty-eight, and Charlie is forty-five."

They were babies.

"How old are you?"

"Much older. Let's say I count my age in centuries, not decades."

"Hey, Charlie," Ed called out. "Our new flat-mate is an old geezer."

"I'm not that old."

"Just kidding, man. Do you want a beer?"

"I'd love one."

"Charlie, get us some beers."

"Fuck you, Ed. I'm not your maid."

"You're already in the kitchen."

"I'm eating."

Ed grimaced. "Sometimes he is such a dick. I'll get them."

Glancing around the apartment, Robert felt at home. Ingrid must've ordered the same furniture for all of the apartments in the keep. The fabric covering the couch he was sitting on was a different color than the one in the apartment he'd shared with Carol, but it was obviously the same brand. Even the pictures on the walls looked to be from the same line.

"A cold Snake's Venom." Ed handed him a bottle. "There is nothing better than that. But it's pricey. We take turns buying these too."

"I'll pay my share." Robert flicked the cap off and took a sip. "It's really good."

"You've never had one of these before?"

"No."

"You'll never want another beer. That's the only one that can get an immortal in a good mood."

"Good. I need it."

Ed put down his bottle on the table. "You being here, I'm assuming that you and Carol are no longer together."

Damn it. The keep was worse than a beehive. Everyone was in everyone else's business. Even those two had heard about him and Carol. "You assume right."

Ed clapped him on the shoulder. "That's a bummer. Charlie and I would've taken you clubbing, but you can't leave the keep. There is so much free pussy out there that you would've forgotten about Carol in no time."

"Don't feel sorry for him, Ed." Charlie walked in with a beer bottle of his own. "He can have his pick of clan females. They will be fighting over you, dude. You don't know how lucky you are that Carol dumped you."

"She didn't dump me. It was by mutual agreement."

Charlie took a swig from his beer. "Whatever makes you feel better. But as I was saying. It's a good thing. Who wants to be stuck with one woman? Right?"

Obviously, these guys knew nothing about relationships and had the level of maturity of a teenage human male.

Damn, he missed his crew from Vegas. Those were men, even though they were much younger than Edgar and Charlie, except maybe for the supervisor. That guy was in his mid-fifties.

When his phone started vibrating in his pocket, Robert's breath caught in his throat. He pulled it out, hoping it was Carol asking him to come back. But it was Bhathian.

"What can I do for you, Bhathian?"

"Are you busy later this evening?'

"No. Why?" Actually he was. Robert had brought over the one bag he'd kept in the office, and he was planning on picking up the rest of his stuff from Carol's later. But it could wait for tomorrow. He wasn't ready to be alone with her yet. It had been difficult enough to see her at the café—the only place he could get food in the keep.

"After we'd talked, I thought about what you'd said, and I figured we can have a forensic artist draw Navuh's son's picture from your memory. Andrew knows a guy who can do it this evening."

"Where?"

"I'll come get you. Kian is letting me use one of the offices on the third floor."

"I'm not at Carol's. My new place is on the fifteenth floor. Apartment 1507."

"You're rooming with Charlie and Edgar?"

"You know them?"

"Of course I do. They are the pilots who fly us places. Nice guys. You're going to like them."

"I already do."

"Good to hear. I'll be there in a few minutes."

"Okay."

Charlie lifted his beer in salute. "Any friend of Bhathian is a friend of mine."

Even though the guy was mistaken, Robert returned the salute and then gulped down the remainder of his beer. Bhathian was no more than an acquaintance, and he was talking to Robert only because he needed a favor.

Exactly ten minutes later, there was a knock on the door and Robert got up to open it.

"Ready?" Bhathian asked, nodding hello to the two pilots.

"Let's go."

As they entered the elevator, Bhathian pressed number three and leaned against the mirrored wall. "I'm sorry about the breakup. Must be a bitch."

Finally, a man who understood what Robert was going through. "It's difficult."

"I bet."

The doors opened and they stepped out. "She wasn't your true-love mate, though. You can get over her."

"I don't know if she was. Is there a way to tell?"

"Give it time. That's all I can tell you. If the feelings you have for her fade, then she wasn't the one."

Robert had been thinking the same thing. How did one know what was love and what was attraction? Maybe being with others would make it clear—help him forget her.

The office they stopped next to was three doors down from Ingrid's, and as Bhathian pulled out a key card and inserted it into the lock, Robert wondered if the interior designer was still there. Maybe after he was done with the forensic artist, he could knock on her door.

They stepped into a room that was appointed much in the same way as Ingrid's, but without all the personal touches she'd added to her workspace. It looked as if no one was using it.

"Take a seat. I need to go down to reception and get Tim." Bhathian turned on his heel, leaving Robert alone.

A few minutes later, he returned with a short, balding man.

"Tim, Robert. Robert, Tim." Bhathian made the introductions.

They shook hands briefly, with Tim pulling his away as quickly as possible. It seemed the human didn't like touching other people.

The guy pulled out a large drawing pad from his portfolio carrying case, flipped it to a new page and put it down on the desk. Next, he pulled out a thin metal case, put it next to the pad, lifted the lid, and chose one of the drawing pencils.

Tucking the pencil behind his ear, he lifted the pad and leaned back in his chair. "Shall we begin?"

Robert nodded.

Tim cast Bhathian a quick glance. "Get the pizza and beers. Extra pepperoni and onions on mine."

Bhathian seemed oblivious to Tim's rudeness. "What would you like on yours, Robert?"

"Thank you. But I don't like pizza."

"Beer?"

"Always."

"I'll go get it."

"Hurry up. I'm hungry," Tim said.

Bhathian flipped him the bird behind his back. "You had better be almost done when I come back."

Tim shook his head. "You can't rush art. It will take as long as it needs to."

Bhathian rolled his eyes and stepped out.

A smile spread over Tim's face. "He's paying me by the hour, and he thinks I'm going to be quick about it? Moron."

Robert took offense on Bhathian's behalf but said nothing. The human seemed like the type who would get up and leave if he didn't like something.

"I was asked to provide two drawings. A close up of the face and a full body. I'm going to start with the face."

CHAPTER 32: BHATHIAN

Staring at the portrait Tim had drawn of Navuh's son, Bhathian was torn between the urge to punch the smiling face or take it up to his apartment and hang it on the wall.

Apparently, the guy's smile was what people remembered about him best. Both Eva and Robert had remarked on that.

With the food service closed for the day, the café was mostly empty. Smart girl that she was, Carol had gotten two vending machines for after-hours snacking. One was a Nespresso and the other offered pastries from Jackson's café. For a buck and a half, an immortal could have a decent cup of cappuccino and a pastry. Which was exactly what he had on his table.

"Bhathian, what are you doing here so late?" William clapped him on the shoulder.

"Drinking coffee."

"That's what I came here for. And one of those delicious pastries. They are my Kryptonite. I can't stay away."

"Yeah, they're good," Bhathian muttered without lifting

his eyes off the portrait. He liked William, but he was in no mood for chitchat.

"Is Eva out of town again?"

"No." But she was working on a case at home, busy analyzing two weeks' worth of surveillance recordings.

When he said nothing more, the guy got it that he didn't want to be bothered. "I'm going to check out what's left in the machine. See you later."

Bhathian nodded, flipping to the other portrait Tim had drawn, the full body one.

That son of a bitch who'd taken Eva's virginity and turned her was annoyingly good-looking. No wonder the young Eva had succumbed to his charms so easily. He was well-built, had a charming smile and intelligent eyes, and exuded confidence. The perfect combination to get into any college girl's panties.

The question was whether he'd done it with her consent or without. Not that there was any way to find out. Eva didn't remember it, and Bhathian couldn't fault the guy for thralling her to forget what had happened. It was the standard order of operations for immortals after sex with humans. Especially for the males. Even Doomers weren't stupid enough to leave women with a memory of their fangs and their bite.

To keep his rage in check, Bhathian had to assume that Eva had participated willingly. And besides, by turning her, the guy had put in motion the sequence of events that had brought her into Bhathian's life. If not for her enhanced senses, Eva would've never thought of becoming an agent, would've never worked undercover as a flight attendant, and would've never met Bhathian.

In addition, the guy deserved an honorary space on Bhathian's wall for escaping his father's grip and taking with him an entire platoon of Doomers.

His motives, though, were anyone's guess.

There could've been a number of reasons for the son to desert, ideology being just one of them.

He might've wanted out from under his father's control, or craved a power position he could not have achieved in the Doomer organization. It remained to be seen what the guy had done with his freedom. He might've become a force for good or for evil, or just neutral, living his life and enjoying the privileges his abilities no doubt provided him with.

The name Robert remembered was Kalugal, which in the old language meant strong king. A very presumptuous name that didn't match the more mundane names Navuh had given his other sons. Had he been expecting that particular one to rise to greatness?

Why him and not the others?

The barely there sound of light footsteps could've only belonged to a Guardian. Bhathian turned, expecting one of his comrades. But it was Dalhu. The big guy was a warrior through and through, and his recent metamorphosis into an artist had done nothing to diminish his skills. Bhathian had witnessed those when Dalhu had defeated Sharim, a master swordsman.

"Is this the guy?" Dalhu asked.

"Recognize him?"

Dalhu pulled out a chair and stared at it. "No, but I recognize Navuh in him. The sons look a lot like their father, even though I'm sure each one was by a different mother. I can show you if you want. I drew portraits of all the main players in Navuh's camp for Kian. The five older sons run the operation."

"Robert says his name is Kalugal. Does it ring a bell?"

Dalhu shook his head. "He must've been a junior commander before he went missing. There are many of them."

"He commanded a platoon."

"There are many of those too. I only paid attention to the leaders."

Dalhu pointed at the portrait. "Can I take a look? Professional curiosity."

"Sure." Bhathian handed him both.

"The guy is good—especially since he is drawing from someone else's descriptions. I'm not sure I could've done it. I have to see the face, or at least a picture."

That was a shame. Bhathian had been toying with the idea of commissioning another portrait. This time from Dalhu. Eva's story about the guy at the club who'd looked a lot like Kalugal kept nagging at him. What if that man was another one of Navuh's sons?

Dealing with Tim was a pain in the ass, and he would've preferred for Dalhu to do it. But apparently it required skills the guy didn't have.

Except, maybe one of the portraits Dalhu had already done was of that guy.

"Do you still have those portraits, or does Kian have them?"

"I gave them to Kian. Why?"

"I want Eva to take a look at them. She saw a guy that reminded her a lot of that Kalugal individual."

Dalhu shook his head. "That was probably a coincidence. Navuh's older sons never leave the island unless it's for a major mission, as in a large-scale war."

"It won't hurt for her to take a look."

"Sure. Come over tomorrow, and I'll ask Kian to part with them for a couple of hours."

"That would be great. What time?"

"Preferably in the evening. Amanda will be mad if she misses a visit from you guys. She comes home around six."

"How does eight sound?"

"Perfect."

CHAPTER 33: BHATHIAN

*T*he café was teeming with clan members, as people rushed to get their sandwiches before Carol called it a day.

Sitting at a table, Bhathian stared at the large plastic bag he'd put on the other chair to make sure no one got any ideas and tried to join him. He was saving it for Eva. Maybe she would want to grab a bite or have some coffee before they headed up to Nathalie's.

The idea was to spend time with their granddaughter, not to burden Nathalie with serving them food. After that, they were going to Amanda's, and that wasn't a social visit either. The prudent thing was to eat something first.

They could chat a little, and he could somehow ease into telling her about the portraits.

Damn it. He should've told her over the phone.

The thing was, Bhathian wanted to observe her reaction. To see her expression as she glanced at the immortal who'd changed her life. Her first lover. His jealousy was irrational but calling himself an idiot didn't help to stop it from consuming him.

Bhathian rubbed the back of his neck, trying to school his face into an amiable expression for when Eva arrived. She didn't deserve the deep frown that had etched itself into his face since Tim had completed the portraits last night.

He felt her eyes on him as soon as she entered.

Turning his head, he watched her walking past the green barrier separating the café from the rest of the lobby. With her head held high, her dark hair perfectly done and cascading in thick waves around her shoulders, she looked beautiful and regal. In comparison, the other immortal females sitting in the café seemed plain. Dressed in one of her long flowing skirts and a puffy white blouse that revealed her shapely shoulders, she stood out from the crowd of jeans and T-shirt wearers.

His Eva was a lady.

Pushing up to his feet, he walked up to her and pulled her into his arms. "You look lovely."

She returned the embrace and kissed him lightly in greeting. "Thanks. Are you ready to go up and see our girls?"

"Don't you want to grab a bite first?"

"I had a huge lunch. I can't even think of putting anything else in my mouth right now. Maybe later."

The best-laid plans of mice and men...

"Let's go." He took her hand and walked back to his table to retrieve the bag.

"What do you have in there?"

"A surprise. The question is whether you want to stop by my place to see it before we go to Nathalie's or after."

She eyed the bag suspiciously. "Am I going to like it?"

"I don't know."

"Ooh, now I'm really curious. Let's go to your place first."

Bhathian couldn't help but smirk. He was getting to know Eva pretty well, and the woman couldn't stand a mystery unsolved.

"Show me," she commanded the moment he closed the door to his apartment.

"Please, sit down. Make yourself comfortable." He motioned to the couch. When she did, he asked, "Can I offer you something to drink?"

He was teasing her on purpose. The longer she waited, the more telling her response would be. Though he wasn't sure what he expected to see. Her pupils dilating in desire from seeing her first lover?

He hoped not.

"Stop dragging it out, Bhathian, and show me what you're hiding in there."

With a sigh and a shake of his head, he pulled out the two drawings and put them upside down on the coffee table.

"God, you're a tease." Eva grabbed the first one and flipped it over, then frowned and leaned to get a better look.

"Where did you get it?"

"Do you recognize him?"

She lifted the portrait and tilted it toward the natural light coming from the balcony's glass doors. "He looks a lot like the guy who turned me. But not exactly. The lips are thinner, and the hair is not the right color."

That was a relief. Eva wasn't excited at all about looking at the guy's face. "Could it be him, though?"

"I guess so. Who is he?"

Bhathian sat next to her. "That's Navuh's youngest son. The one who went missing. Robert remembered him well enough to describe him to Tim, who drew the picture. The other one is a full body portrait so you can see his build."

Eva flipped the other drawing around. "It looks about right."

Crossing her legs, she swung one foot up and down. "So now we know who he was. It still doesn't help us find him."

"Yes, it does. William is working on tweaking the facial

recognition software, and if the guy is still in the States, he must have a driver's license. We might be able to find him if Andrew gets William access to government records."

Turning to look at him, Eva narrowed her eyes. "I hope you are not harboring any nefarious intentions toward him."

"Am I allowed at least one punch?"

She laughed. "What if he punches back?"

Bhathian lifted a brow. "You think I'll refuse an invitation to dance?"

"Seriously now. Why do you want to find him?"

"Finding other immortals who are not affiliated with either of the camps is of utmost importance. If the guy deserted his father's organization on ideological grounds then we might negotiate some form of cooperation. And maybe if he and his men are decent people, like Dalhu and Robert, they could become potential matches for our females. The more new blood we can infuse into our clan, the better our chances of survival."

"Then I hope you find him. Now can we go to see the girls?" She started to get up.

Bhathian pulled her back. "Not yet, love. There is one more thing I wanted to tell you about. One more surprise."

She crossed her arms over her chest. "You're full of them today, aren't you?"

"That's what happens when you leave me alone, and I have to find something to keep me busy."

Her eyes softened, and she leaned to kiss his cheek. "Poor baby, have you been lonely?"

"Yes, I was."

"Sorry about that. But I'm finally done with that job. I wrote up the report and sent it before coming here."

"Hallelujah."

"Now tell me all about your other surprise."

"After Tim had finished the portraits, I ran into Dalhu,

and he confirmed that the guy looked a lot like Navuh's older sons—the ones who run the Doomer organization. By the way, your guy's real name is Kalugal, pronounced Kal-lugal, which means a strong king in the old language."

"Cool name."

"It is, and uncommon. Anyway, I remembered what you said about that guy in the club reminding you of him, and I wanted to ask Dalhu if he could draw a picture from your memory. But then he said that he had drawn portraits of all the main players in Navuh's organization for Kian. I asked him if you could take a look at them. Long story short, he invited us and we are going to visit Amanda and him after we are done at Nathalie's."

CHAPTER 34: EVA

"What's that secretive smile about?" Bhathian regarded her as he called for the elevator.

Eva pushed an errant lock of hair behind her ear. "Andrew and Nathalie look so good together. I've never seen them so affectionate with each other."

"The baby is sleeping better, and they are finally having sex. Things are getting back to normal. That's how they were with each other before Andrew's venom glands became active and they had to abstain because of the pregnancy. It would've put a strain on any couple."

"It sure would."

The elevator arrived, and Bhathian held the doors open for her even though it was unnecessary. Still, she liked being treated like a lady. Women's Lib was fantastic, and Eva loved that the barriers that had kept women at a disadvantage for eons were crumbling more and more each day, but she was sorry to see chivalry disappear along the way. There was no reason for one to negate the other, and yet it was happening. Young men didn't hold doors open for women or their elders, and could watch a woman struggle under a heavy load, or trying to push a stroller while holding the door open, and not offer help.

The elevator stopped at the penthouse level and the doors opened on an opulent vestibule. There were only two sets of doors, which meant that each of the penthouse apartments occupied half of the building's footprint.

"Who lives here?"

"Kian and Syssi are on one side, and Amanda and Dalhu on the other."

"Royalty, eh?"

Bhathian chuckled. "You could say so. Annani's only son and her youngest daughter."

Eva wished there was a book she could read about the clan. There was still so much she didn't know. Like how many children the goddess had. Bhathian had said Kian was the only son and Amanda the youngest daughter, which meant they had at least one more sister.

"Where are the goddess's other daughters?"

Bhathian knocked on one of the doors. "Elena is with her mother, and Sari is running the Scottish arm of the clan."

"I wish I could meet them. And Annani too. I get butterflies in my tummy just thinking about being in the presence of a living breathing goddess. The only one on earth."

Bhathian leaned and whispered in her ear, "They are guaranteed to come for a wedding ceremony." He winked at her.

The door had opened before Eva had a chance to ask him whose wedding he had been referring to. But then the wink and the smirk were clues the size of Hummers.

Amanda threw the door wide open. "Come in, guys." She took Eva's hand and pulled her behind her. "I'm so glad you came. I was thinking about inviting you over for so long, but something always came up, and I didn't get to it. I'm so happy that Dalhu took the initiative."

Amanda sat on the couch and Eva had no choice but to join her since the woman was still holding on to her hand. The goddess's daughter was a stunning beauty, but that was the only clue to her divine origins. She was dressed in jeans and a loose button-down shirt, with a pair of black ballerina flats on her feet.

"Thank you for having us."

"My pleasure. And I mean it." She squeezed Eva's hand. "Dalhu! Our guests are here. Drop your paint brush and come out!"

Bhathian took a seat in one of the overstuffed armchairs.

Amanda's outfit might have looked simple, but it was clearly top designer stuff. The penthouse was lavishly appointed and designed to perfection. Eva had seen enough high-end homes and luxury apartments to know that everything in that living room was the best money could buy. Annani's children lived like the royalty they were.

Someone knocked on the door, and Amanda jumped up off the couch and rushed to open it. "Hello, darlings, come in and join the party."

Syssi walked in with Kian right behind her. He was holding a large portfolio case, which must contain the portraits Dalhu had made for him.

"Hi. Eva, Bhathian." Syssi sat next to Eva and gave her a quick hug. "How is my little niece doing?"

At the mention of her granddaughter, a wave of tenderness and unconditional love washed through Eva. "She's adorable. I could spend days just watching her smile and hear her gurgle those cute bubble sounds."

Bhathian chuckled. "All true. The problem is that she is not always smiling and making cute noises. Her wails could bring down the walls, and her stinky diapers require hazmat protective gear to change."

Kian nodded in agreement. "Phoenix is cute until she

starts crying. As soon as she does, I'm ready to give her back to Nathalie. I don't know how Syssi tolerates those ear-piercing shrieks."

Eva cast the men an indulgent smile. "You are spoiled babies. Toughen up, guys."

"Sorry I kept you waiting." Dalhu walked into the living room. "I had this one little detail to finish before I let the paint dry."

"I heard you're taking a course at the university," Eva said.

He nodded. "Landscapes. That's my new pastime. Portraits have become a job."

"That's right." Kian lifted the portfolio off the floor and placed it on his knees. "We came here to look at these." He pulled out a stack of laminated black and white drawings and put them on the coffee table in front of Eva.

"Thank you." She looked at the first one.

A shiver ran through her, but not because the face staring back at her was familiar. It was the expression, and she wondered whether the man really looked like that or it was Dalhu's impression of him. Never before had the saying that the eyes were the windows to the soul made so much sense to her. So much could be gleaned from the look in a person's eyes. And with a dense, stylishly trimmed beard and mustache covering most of the face, the eyes became even more prominent.

Power. Arrogance. Disdain. Indifference. A dangerous man. "Who is he?"

Dalhu shifted in his chair. "Navuh."

She'd guessed as much. Even the guy from the club hadn't had such an effect on her. The charisma was almost palpable. Dalhu was a talented artist to capture the essence of the man so well.

The next one was almost a clone, but his face was a bit

softer. The chin was less pointy, and the beard was shorter and a shade lighter.

The third one also sported a beard. And so did the fourth and the fifth. The man at the club had been clean-shaven, and Eva doubted she would recognize him with a beard. But she did. The seventh portrait was of a man who looked like a watered-down version of Navuh. Not regal or charismatic at all, he looked soft and amiable except for one thing—the sharp intelligence that shone from his eyes. She wasn't sure who was the more dangerous of the two, the charismatic leader or the one with the eyes.

The Brain.

"That's him." She pointed at the portrait. "That's the man I saw at the club. He didn't have a beard when I saw him, but I would recognize those eyes anywhere."

Dalhu leaned to take a look. "It must have been a case of a doppelgänger. Losham never leaves the island. The other sons occasionally do, but not Losham. The other sons are military commanders. He is not. His main job is to keep Navuh company. I heard rumors that he is Navuh's top advisor, but it's not his official title. Navuh is too arrogant to admit he listens to anyone. As far as everyone is concerned, Navuh is the chosen successor of the God Mortdh, and the only one who makes important decisions."

Eva lifted the portrait again and looked at it up close. "I don't know what to say, Dalhu. It's either him or a doppelgänger as you said. But I doubt there are two identical men who are both brilliant. Just look into these eyes. That was what gave me the creeps when I saw him. A brain like that on someone with no morals is an extremely dangerous thing."

"Losham was Sharim's adoptive father, right?" Kian asked.
Dalhu nodded.

"He could've come to check what happened to his son and stayed longer. I would be surprised if the guy wasn't plotting revenge. If he is as smart as Eva thinks he is, Losham might be busy putting things in motion that will have a long-term effect. I think his appearance in a local club is worth investigating."

Amanda patted Eva's knee. "Is that the club you were asking about while we were in the waiting room? Allure?"

Eva nodded.

"We should check it out. Maybe go on a girls' night out?" She looked at Syssi and then at Eva.

A snort escaped Eva's nostrils. Embarrassed, she put a hand over the bottom part of her face, then lowered it with a sheepish smile. "It's not that kind of a club. Allure is a high-class, members-only sex club."

Amanda's eyes widened. "We have something like that in L.A.?" She turned to Dalhu. "I want to go."

The guy's ears turned red. "Over my dead body."

Amanda was taken aback. "Darling, I would never dream of going there by myself. I meant the two of us."

He shook his head. "Not going to happen."

Amanda crossed her arms over her chest and pushed her chin up. "We will discuss it later."

"No, we won't, and that's the end of it."

Eva cast a glance at Kian to see what he thought about Dalhu talking to his sister like that. The guy was holding a hand over his mouth to stifle a laugh. Apparently, he found the confrontation humorous.

She decided to come to Dalhu's rescue. "I don't think it's what you think it is. People go there to find partners for their sexual fantasies, or to indulge a kink. So unless you're both into voyeurism or exhibitionism, it's probably not a place for you."

Uncomfortable with the whole exchange, Bhathian pretended to observe the portrait Tim had drawn. Which gave Eva an idea for a quick change of subject. "Bhathian, can you put Kalugal's portrait next to Losham's? It will be interesting to compare the two."

Bhathian arranged the portraits next to each other, waited for a moment and then flipped them upside down for Dalhu and Kian to look at.

"It's obvious they are related," Kian said.

Dalhu shrugged. "Or just look alike."

As the guys continued to discuss the portraits, Amanda turned to Eva. "I want to talk to you about another round with your crew."

"What do you have in mind?"

"The affinity thing is hard to prove or quantify. I want to conduct a larger scale test before we decide what to do next."

Eva narrowed her eyes. "Do what next?"

"Offer Sharon and Nick the opportunity to transition. I know Tessa is off limits, at least for now, but I want her at the event."

For some reason, Eva hadn't thought about where the testing was leading. If her crew were Dormants, then it made sense to offer them immortality.

"I think you can approach Sharon and Nick without further testing. Both are very open-minded."

"I don't want to offer anyone false hope. And it's not an easy process for either one. Nick will have to fight a male, and Sharon will have to have sex with one. A decision like that shouldn't be taken lightly."

"What do you suggest?"

"I want to arrange a bigger gathering. Something under the pretense of a lecture about paranormal abilities and a reception after that. I'll invite both humans and immortals who haven't met your people yet and have them mingle. If the immortals still gravitate toward your guys, then I think it's a good enough indication. If the results are mixed, then I'll need to come up with a different way to test it."

"Sounds good to me. My crew would like attending a lecture like that. I think most people find the subject fascinating."

"I need you to make sure they will. I'm going to too much trouble and expense for them not to show up.'

"I'll make sure they do."

"That's what I wanted to hear."

CHAPTER 35: AMANDA

"You can't stay, Jackson." Amanda gave him a light shove to hurry him out the door. They were in the classroom adjacent to the one she was going to deliver her lecture in. After the class was over, everyone would come to this one for snacks and games.

"Why? I'm already here. Why can't I stay and listen to your lecture? I heard you're an amazing teacher and your classes are so interesting."

Smooth. The boy was a pro. But this time flattery wasn't going to help him.

"Thanks for bringing the pastries and for not charging for them. But if you stay, Tessa will hang out with you instead of mingling with the others. The whole point of this experiment is to introduce the suspected Dormants to new immortals who have no idea who they are. That's why there are so many other humans here."

Jackson nodded. "I get it. I'll go."

"Smart boy." She patted his arm.

He didn't like her calling him a boy, but he was too polite

to say anything. "Don't forget to mention Fernando's Café. I need to make my money back."

"I won't. And I had the name and address printed on the back of the pamphlet." She decided a little flattery would compensate for the 'boy' remark. Jackson wasn't the only smooth one in the room. "It was a genius idea. After they get a taste, they will not only come for more but bring their friends."

The compliment did the trick. Jackson smirked and pointed at his head. "I always think ahead."

"Yes, you do. Now out." She walked him out of the room, watching him stride down the hallway before she entered the other classroom.

Amanda surveyed the faces of her audience.

Thirty-two immortals, none of whom had met Eva's crew before, twenty-three students, Eva's crew, and the flower girl had been invited to the lecture. Hannah couldn't come, which was a relief. The girl was too smart and too involved in Amanda's work. The lecture and the games Amanda had planned for after would've made her suspicious. If it were a fundraiser, it would've been a different story. The unscientific flavor of the event would've made sense.

Everyone had shown up, including a few uninvited students who'd heard about it from their friends.

A nametag had been given to all participants to stick on their shirts.

"Good evening, everyone. My name is Professor Amanda Dokani, and I'm a neuroscientist. Today's lecture is about paranormal phenomena in general and individual paranormal abilities in particular. We will also discuss the various methods we use to test these abilities. After the lecture, we will move to the next room and play games that are designed to test your own talents. You'll discover that most people can feel when someone is staring at their back, some can tell when others are talking about them, and a few can guess what the other person is thinking. Refreshments will be served, and it will be a lot of fun. So don't skip this part."

As was the case with all her lectures, her audience, including the immortals, hung on Amanda's every word. And as always she wondered if it was the fascinating topic or her delivery style that kept them captivated. At least with the immortals, she knew for sure that they weren't obsessing about her looks.

When she was done, no one snuck out and everyone followed her to the next room. The promise of snacks was irresistible to students.

"The amazing pastries are courtesy of Fernando's Café. They are also inviting you to try the café and offering a free cappuccino to all who attended this lecture. All you have to do is show them this." She lifted the pamphlet each participant had received.

More than a few eyes rolled in pleasure after tasting the pastries. Jackson would gain a lot of new business from this event. Hopefully enough to compensate for not being allowed to join his girlfriend.

Amanda glanced around the room, searching for Tessa. She spotted her hiding behind her boss. That wouldn't do. Sauntering over, Amanda offered her hand to Eva. "Darling, I'm so glad you could make it and bring along your lovely entourage."

Eva shook it. "Fascinating lecture. Right, Tessa?" She turned to her assistant.

"Yes, and thank you for inviting me. My head is still spinning from it all."

"Come, let me introduce you to some people." Amanda clasped her hand. Eva hadn't said what Tessa's problem was, but she'd hinted it had something to do with men. Pulling the girl behind her, Amanda scanned the room for a female immortal who wasn't busy talking with a human. She spotted Ingrid just as she was about to move to her next.

"Ingrid, sweetheart, I want you to meet Tessa. I think the two of you will make a great pair for our first game."

"Nice to meet you." Ingrid offered a hand to Tessa, who looked relieved to be paired with a woman and shook it enthusiastically.

"Same here. Have you played games like this before?"

Ingrid smirked. "Plenty of times. I'm an old pro."

"That's good. Because I'm clueless."

"That's why I paired you two." Amanda patted both on the shoulder and moved on to introduce the next pair. A random student this time. It was important not to tip off the immortals as to who the suspected Dormants were.

"Okay, people." She waved a hand in the air. "Does everyone have a partner?"

"Good. Time for the first game of tonight. Are you ready?"

A few murmured a yes, others nodded.

"I can't hear you! Are you ready!"

"Ready!"

"Turn your back to your partner and lift a random number of fingers. From one to all ten. Look at them and say the number in your head several times."

She waited a full minute. "Partners. Guess the number and write it down in the pamphlet."

A few moments later it seemed everyone was done. "Okay, turn to your partner and look at the number she or he wrote."

A few murmurs and giggles sounded.

"Partners, raise your hand if you guessed right."

Five pairs did.

"Excellent. Everyone write down the name of your

partner in the space provided for game one, and those of you who guessed right mark it with an X. Both partners."

She waited a few seconds. "The reason I asked both partners to mark it with an X is that either one could've been responsible for the result. As I explained in the lecture, telepathy can be of the receiving kind or the projecting kind. Now everyone switch partners."

They played for over an hour, and when Amanda ran out of games, the room filled with murmurs of disappointment.

"I'm glad you all enjoyed yourself. Before you leave, please tear out the answer sheet from the pamphlet and leave it in this basket." She pointed.

It took another half an hour for everyone to say their goodbyes and leave. Tomorrow, she would get the results from the immortals.

Syssi took the basket and tucked it under her arm. "Great evening. I hope we'll get the results we are hoping for. And I'm not talking about what's in here." She shook the basket.

"I'm crossing my fingers." Amanda crossed them on both hands.

They walked out together and headed for Amanda's car.

"These results are not worth much because of the large number of immortals participating." Syssi put the basket in the back seat. "I'm sure most of the positive results are from the pairs they were in. But we can arrange for a similar evening with humans only. It should be interesting what results we will get then."

"Not a bad idea. And with Jackson supplying the food, the costs are minimal. The university gave us the use of the rooms free of charge, and all I have to pay for is the cleanup."

CHAPTER 36: JACKSON

A box of pastries in hand, Jackson walked into Amanda's lab. His previous plan to speak with her after the lecture had crashed and burned. He'd hoped to soften her up by providing the refreshments free of charge, but she'd kicked him out.

Therefore plan B.

"Can I help you?" The woman whose desk was facing the entry eyed him and his box suspiciously.

"I'm looking for Professor Dokani. I brought pastries." He pointed at the pink cardboard box. As he was discovering lately, that was his entry ticket to most places. If he ever wanted to be a spy, he would use a box of pastries to get into high-security areas. No one had turned him away yet.

"Her office is over there." The woman pointed.

"Thank you." He walked over and knocked on the door even though it was partially open.

"Come in."

He pushed the door open, then closed it behind him.

Amanda lifted her head. "Jackson, what are you doing here?"

He put the box on her desk. "I brought more pastries. Advertisement."

"Right. Why are you really here?"

"I wanted to find out the results from last night. Did you have time to analyze them yet?"

Tapping her pen on her desk, Amanda stared at him for a moment. "You want to know about Tessa."

There was no reason to lie about something that was becoming obvious to anyone who knew him. "Yes."

"How serious is this thing between you two?"

"Very serious. I think she is my one."

Amanda dropped her pen on the desk and leaned back. "Oh, boy."

His heart sank to his gut. "Why? She is not a Dormant? Please tell me."

"She might be a Dormant. Our testing provides no definite proof."

Damn it. She was talking in circles. He already knew all that. "What were her results?"

"All four of the suspected Dormants scored high on the affinity test. But so did a few of the humans."

"Maybe they are Dormants too?"

"Or maybe they are just charming people who others gravitate toward. That's why this is not a foolproof method of identifying Dormants."

"Tessa is shy. She barely talks to strangers. If any of the immortals felt an affinity toward her, it wasn't because of her outgoing, friendly personality."

"I agree. Which is a good thing because she doesn't have other indicators like Nick and Sharon do."

Jackson ran his fingers through his hair, pushing the long bangs back and smoothing them. "I want to tell her about me. I have to."

Amanda nodded. "She is resistant to thralling."

"No. I never tried to thrall her. She is very skittish. I've worked hard on gaining her trust, and I'm not going to do anything to undermine it."

"That's very admirable, Jackson. I'm proud of you."

"So can I tell her? I can't even kiss her. How am I going to explain the fangs?"

Amanda frowned. "I'm sure you figured it out already. From what I hear she is not your first girlfriend. You have quite the reputation for someone so young."

Damn. This was so frustrating. "It's not the same. It's easy to hide the fangs when I'm the one with my tongue inside a female's mouth; it's impossible the other way around. I can't be the aggressive one with Tessa. I need to let her explore. Do you understand? I really don't want to say more."

Given her pained expression, Amanda knew exactly what he was talking about and was saddened by it. "I understand. What if she never gets past it? You won't be able to turn her."

"She will. It will take time and patience but eventually she will. I'm sure of it."

Amanda sighed. "You're too young to take upon yourself such a task. But then again only the young have that much hope in their hearts. You still believe that you can change the world and fix whatever is wrong with it."

"I'm not naive, and I'm not hoping to fix everything. Just this one thing. Tessa deserves a life. I won't let the monsters win." Crap, he shouldn't have said it. It was one thing to hint and another to practically spell it out.

"I wish you luck from the bottom of my heart. But before I give you the green light, I need to ask Kian's permission."

"Is there a chance he will refuse?"

"He might. But I can be very persuasive." She winked.

"Can you do it now?"

Amanda chuckled. "Sure. Wait outside, please. And I mean way outside. There might be some yelling, and language unbecoming to a lady that I don't want you to overhear."

"How long?"

"Give me half an hour."

Setting the alarm on his phone to go off in thirty minutes, Jackson went out of the building and spent the time pacing back and forth on the walkway in front of it. Any other time he would've been busy flirting with the babes passing him by, but he didn't pay them any attention, not even when they came up to him.

He must've aged a decade until the damn thing finally buzzed that it was time.

"Well?" He burst into Amanda's office.

"Take a seat, Jackson."

She was killing him. "For crying out loud just tell me yes or no!"

"It's a yes."

Feeling light-headed, he closed his eyes and slumped in the chair. "Thank you, merciful Fates."

"With conditions."

His eyes popped open. "What conditions?"

"Kian wants Tessa to come to the keep, accompanied by Eva and Bhathian and you. He wants to talk to her while you're there and swear her to secrecy. Tessa owes Eva her life. She needs to understand that by exposing her she will jeopardize her safety and that of every member of the clan."

It wasn't an unreasonable request, and yet Jackson knew how difficult it would be for Tessa. Mainly because of Kian. The guy was intimidating as hell.

"Will Sharon and Nick have to be brought in front of Kian too?"

"That's a long way off. First, they will have to be matched with immortal partners. When that happens, they will be told. If they decide to go for it, they would have to stay at the keep for the duration of the experiment. If they refuse or fail to transition, their memories would be thralled away. Tessa is different. Because you guys are not intimate, and it's not clear when you will be, the period of time during which she will know about us and remain human is going to be prolonged. Too long for successfully thralling her without causing damage, or for keeping her locked in the keep."

Amanda's detailed explanation made one thing very clear. Kian was doing Tessa and him a big favor by agreeing to this at all. Sharon and Nick's induction process ensured the clan's safety. Tessa was a wild card. And yet Kian was allowing it.

Jackson owed the guy a big debt of gratitude.

CHAPTER 37: NATHALIE

*N*athalie put Phoenix in her bassinet. After spending time with Auntie Syssi, then pooping a big stinky and having her diaper changed, Phoenix had gulped down every last drop of formula in her bottle and fallen asleep.

Things were getting much easier, and life was returning to normal. More or less. Nathalie no longer felt exhausted and bedraggled, their sex life was back on at full swing, and the biting part she'd been so concerned about was just as incredible as Syssi had told her it would be. Everything was perfect except for the nagging worry about her transition.

Or non-transition as it was.

In her nonscientific opinion, at eight weeks post-delivery her hormone levels should have gone down sufficiently. And to think of the torment she and Andrew had gone through to prevent it from happening, when her body knew it had to block it all along. Not that she would've done anything differently. Who knew what the venom could do to the baby, even if it did nothing to the mother?

Syssi collected the baby toys scattered on the living room couch and put them into their basket. "Why the frown?"

"I'm worried. It's been a month since Andrew and I started having sex again and yet nothing."

Syssi blushed. "Did you talk to Bridget?"

"Yeah, she keeps giving me the same lame answer."

"Which is?"

Nathalie rolled her eyes and plopped down on the couch. "To be patient, that my hormone levels are still high. Yadda, yadda, yadda. I'm sick of hearing it."

Syssi took a peek at Phoenix in her bassinet. "She's so adorable. Just look at those pudgy cheeks. I can't stop kissing this baby."

Nathalie chuckled. "She will grow so sick of everybody kissing her that as soon as she is old enough, she will punch anyone who tries to kiss her. Those cheeks of hers are just irresistible."

Sitting next to Nathalie, Syssi grabbed a throw pillow and hugged it to her. "Maybe you should go talk to Bridget again. Have her run some blood tests to see where your hormones are at."

Nathalie let her head drop back. "I'm scared. What if I can't transition at all? What if motherhood negates a Dormant's ability to change permanently?"

To Syssi's credit, she didn't immediately dismiss Nathalie's concerns as nonsense. "Did anyone think of asking Annani? Maybe she remembers a similar case from the times where mixed pairings were common."

Nathalie regarded her sister-in-law with new appreciation. The woman had one hell of a head on her shoulders, and thought outside the box. Like her idea for a new method to identify Dormants.

"Should I ask Kian to do it for me? It's not like I have the goddess's phone number on speed dial."

"I think Bridget should do it. A formal request to Annani as a doctor."

"I'll talk to her when Andrew comes home."

Syssi glanced at her watch. "How come he is not back yet?"

"He said something about meeting with the hacker. William wants access to the driving license records so he can run his facial recognition software when it's ready. He is looking for cases of two different names with the same face decades apart."

"That could really help us to find any immortals hiding in the States. If there are any."

"And it can put Andrew in jail. I hate that he's taking such risks."

Syssi smirked. "If he gets caught, we'd take care of it. Send several immortals to eliminate evidence and thrall everyone involved to forget."

"You can do it? I thought it was against clan law."

"Not if security is at stake. Then anything goes."

That was news to her. "Good to know. Did anyone tell Andrew?"

Syssi crossed her legs. "I'm sure he knows."

"I'm not sure at all. My poor guy might be stressing for nothing."

Syssi sighed. "I wish we could employ that hacker of his instead of Andrew having to ask favors of him all of the time."

"We can't. Apparently Roni had been a naughty boy and hacked into government stuff when he was a kid. They made a deal with him. He works for them and is kept under semi-house arrest. He can't go anywhere without a handler accompanying him."

"So how does he manage to do the things he does for Andrew?"

Nathalie shrugged. "At work, under his supervisors' noses."

Syssi frowned. "If he gets caught, and it's only a matter of time until he does, I'm not sure Kian can authorize a swipe to save his ass, only the minimum required to protect Andrew. Without that kid, we will have no one to hack for us."

"I don't think they will put Roni in jail. He is too valuable to them."

"But they will keep a better eye on him."

The door opened, and Andrew walked in. "Keep an eye on who?"

Nathalie felt her cheeks get warm. She wasn't supposed to talk about the work-related things Andrew had told her.

Too late. He'd caught her red-handed, or was it red-mouthed?

"Roni. I was telling Syssi about how he does his hacking under his supervisors' noses. Syssi says it's only a matter of time before he gets caught."

Andrew walked over to the kitchen and pulled out a cold Coke can from the fridge. "I agree. But there is not much I can do about it. I wish we had someone else who was as good. I'm tired of playing matchmaker for that kid."

Syssi arched a brow. "Matchmaker? What do you mean?"

The tips of Andrew's ears got red. He popped the lid on the Coke and gulped it down as if he hadn't heard Syssi's question.

She crossed her arms over her chest. "I'm waiting, Andrew."

"I don't need to tell you anything."

She huffed. "Fine. Be like that."

Andrew's shoulders slumped, and he plopped down on one of the armchairs.

"I guess I can tell you since it's not a government secret. But I'm not proud of it. For his first gig for us, Roni asked me to arrange a hookup for him. He'd just turned eighteen and was confined to the apartment they gave him in the office building. There was no way for him to meet girls. Besides, he was a scrawny nerd with an overinflated ego and an unpleasant attitude. I doubt he could've scored with anyone even if he were free."

"And you did it? How?"

"Sylvia agreed to meet him. It was up to her to choose; either to thrall him and make him believe that he was a virgin no more, or actually do it. Long story short, the two are still seeing each other. I don't know why, but she likes him."

Syssi tapped a finger on her chin. "You say he's a scrawny nerd with an attitude and she still likes him?"

Andrew took another long gulp from his Coke can. "He's no longer that scrawny, he started working out, and his attitude has improved a lot, but his ego is still overinflated. Sylvia has a positive effect on him."

Syssi smiled and uncrossed her arms. "Your Roni might be a Dormant."

Andrew almost choked on the Coke. "Say again?"

"Think about it. He has a special ability. Hacking undetected from a government office where everything is under surveillance and recorded requires one hell of a talent. And then you have Sylvia liking him enough to keep seeing him even though he is far from charming or good-looking."

Andrew slapped his thigh. "You may be right. Wow, the implications are tremendous. Imagine him working for us full time. Between Roni and William these two could rule the world."

Syssi chuckled. "We wouldn't want that. Maybe it's not such a hot idea after all."

Andrew's loud slap must've startled Phoenix, and she whimpered in her sleep. Nathalie put her hand on the bassinet and started rocking it gently. "Even if he is a Dormant, how do you propose to test it? We can't bring him here for a sparring match together with his handler, and have Roni bitten right in front of him."

Andrew got up and sat next to Nathalie. "No, we can't. But if we put our heads together, we can figure something out. He could become a huge asset to the clan."

CHAPTER 38: TESSA

*P*retending to dust the bookcase closest to the sliding doors, Tessa tried to listen to what Eva and Jackson were talking about out on the patio. But it was no use. The slider was closed, and they spoke in hushed voices.

What had Jackson to talk about with her boss? And why hadn't she been invited to join the conversation? Were they talking about her?

Most likely.

Crap. She hoped it wasn't about Eva's misguided attempts to protect her and scare Jackson off. Not that he was easily scared. Even the formidable Eva couldn't do that. But it would be a shame if the two people Tessa cared most for in the world were fighting because of her.

Damn it. She needed to adopt some of Wonder Woman's attitude.

Tessa pushed the slider open and stepped out onto the small backyard. It was eerie the way both Eva and Jackson stopped talking and turned to look at her. She kept going until she was standing between the two of them.

They were both so much bigger than her.

Whatever. Size didn't matter. Attitude did.

Tessa put her hands on her hips and glared first at Jackson and then at her boss. "Whatever the two of you are talking about you can do it in front of me."

Jackson reached for her hand. "You're right. I was just asking Eva's advice about something I wasn't sure about."

"Are you sure now?"

"I think so. Your boss likes the blunt, take-no-prisoners approach. So here it goes. I need you to come with me to meet my cousin Kian, but I can't tell you what it's about until we are in his office. Eva and Bhathian are going to be there as well."

Oh, God. Did it have anything to do with going after the monsters who'd hurt her? Did Jackson want her to tell Kian about it with all of them present?"

She'd told him she would talk to his cousin, but he'd told her it wouldn't be necessary. And now he wanted her to do it with an audience?

She pulled her hand away. "No. I'm not going to do it."

Jackson looked puzzled. "What the hell are you talking about?"

"You know what I'm talking about."

"No, I don't."

Tessa rolled her eyes. If he wanted to play dumb so be it. "The things I told you in confidence, and you asked my permission to tell some of it to your cousin—the big shot who could do something about it."

Jackson slapped his forehead. "I'm such a moron. It has nothing to do with that, but I totally see why you'd think it does. It's about something completely different."

She narrowed her eyes at him. "Like what?"

"I can't tell you yet. But I can promise that you'll be doing very little talking and a lot of listening. Does that help?"

Of course, it did. Jackson knew her well. "Am I going to like it?"

"I'm pretty sure you will."

"Fine. When are we going?"

"He's expecting us at nine-thirty."

"Tonight?"

"Yeah. It's urgent and that's the only time he had available today. Kian is a very busy man."

Tessa glanced at her watch. "It doesn't leave me much time to get ready."

"You're fine the way you are."

"I'll feel more comfortable wearing something nicer."

"Then go for it."

Eva took her elbow. "I'll help you choose."

Jackson opened the slider and let them go in first. "I'll wait for you in the kitchen. Is there anything to eat?"

"Leftover sushi."

"It will do."

Fifteen minutes later Tessa walked into the kitchen in a pair of cream-colored pants, a black short-sleeved blouse, and black, two-inch pumps.

"You look very elegant."

"Thank you. That was the intention. I want to make a good impression on your big shot cousin."

"Where is Eva?"

"She'll be down in a minute." After having helped Tessa choose an outfit and do her makeup first, Eva needed a few minutes to touch up her own appearance. Not that it was needed, the woman was always perfectly put together.

On the drive to downtown, Eva turned on the radio, and they listened to a comedy station, but no one laughed.

Tessa was too busy stressing over what the hell Kian wanted with her, while Jackson and Eva seemed deep in thought.

Turning into an underground parking of a high-rise, Eva kept going down until she reached a huge garage door. The thing started rolling sideways as soon as her car got nearer. Did she have a sensor? And if yes, why would Eva have one?

Did she know Jackson's cousin?

Tessa got the strong feeling that the people she cared most about were conspiring against her. It seemed they were all in cahoots. Including Kian, Jackson's big-shot cousin.

When the big door finished its trek, Eva drove in and parked next to a black Porsche. There weren't many cars on that level, but the few there were looked pricey. Whoever this private parking belonged to was affluent.

Eva cut the engine and stepped out. Jackson got out from the back seat and opened the door for Tessa.

He looked nervous as he offered her his hand. "Let's go. We are cutting it fine. It's almost nine-thirty and Kian appreciates punctuality."

They entered one of the elevators and Jackson pressed a button that looked like it marked another parking level, one that was a few floors below that one. But when the elevator doors opened, she saw a wide corridor with a wall made of white painted concrete blocks. Not what she imagined Jackson's cousin's offices would look like.

After passing several plain looking doors, they reached one that was double in size and had glass panes. Behind it, was a very lavish office.

Jackson knocked on the glass panel and then opened the door for Eva and Tessa to go in first.

Bhathian, who was already there, got up to welcome them, his large frame blocking from view whoever was sitting behind the desk in the back, which was probably Kian. He kissed Eva's cheek, shook Tessa's hand, and then Jackson's. "Let's sit over there." He turned sideways and motioned to the large conference table taking up most of the space in the room.

Tessa glanced at the other man, who at that moment got up from behind the desk and started walking toward them.

Her breath caught.

The imagery that came to her mind defied her atheistic views. Where Jackson's beauty was that of a naughty angel, and Bhathian's that of an enforcer leading sinners to hell, Kian's was that of a god.

So blindingly beautiful that he seemed not of this earth. He smiled and offered her his hand. "Hello, Tessa. I'm Kian."

Even his voice was perfect.

She just stared, too awestruck to move a muscle. It took Bhathian's chuckle and Eva's hand on her shoulder to break the spell. Her hand shook as she lifted it.

Kian's touch was very gentle. "I promise I'm not as scary as I look. You're perfectly safe here." The tone of his voice, more than his words, had an oddly reassuring effect. Tessa felt herself relax.

It was on the tip of her tongue to tell him that he wasn't scary, only too beautiful, but despite his friendly tone, she had a feeling Kian would've not appreciated her being so forward.

She needed to act respectfully.

The man exuded an aura of importance. Despite wearing jeans, not even a designer brand, he had the bearing of royalty.

"Hi, Kian. Can I call you Kian? Jackson didn't tell me your last name."

"Kian is fine. Please, make yourself comfortable." He walked her over to the table and pulled out a chair for her. Right next to his at the head of the table. Jackson sat on her other side. Bhathian and Eva sat across from them.

A short man dressed like a butler entered the room with a

large tray. "Good evening, master. Would you like me to put the tray of hors d'oeuvres on the table or on the buffet?"

"On the table is fine. Thank you, Okidu."

The man bowed his head. "Yes, master."

Tessa's mouth gaped and then snapped shut. Master? What century were these people living in?

On the other hand, it fit with her impression of Kian being a royal. Was he some kind of prince? Did it make Jackson royal too?

While holding the large tray in one hand, the butler proceeded to place in front of each of them a small plate, a tiny fork, a crystal goblet, and a folded cloth napkin. When he was done with that, he put an oval platter of snacks right in the middle. Next, he walked over to a cleverly concealed fridge and brought several bottles of sparkling water.

He bowed again. "Should I serve the coffee now, master, or later?"

"Later. Thank you." Kian dismissed the butler who retreated walking backward and closed the door behind him.

Kian waved a hand at the platter. "Please, help yourselves."

"Don't mind if I do." Bhathian picked up his plate and loaded it with several little treats.

Jackson reached for one of the sparkling water bottles, opened it, and filled everyone's goblets.

Tessa wished they would all be done with the niceties and get to the point of this meeting. Her throat felt tight, and she wasn't sure she could handle a single sip of water.

Kian surprised her by reaching for her hand and covering it with his. "You're probably wondering why we are all here."

Duh, you think?

Instead, she said, "Yes, I do."

"You're a very special woman, Tessa. We believe that

you're a carrier of very unique genetic traits. We are not certain, but the indicators are strong."

"What are you talking about?"

"Immortality." He chuckled when her mouth fell open. "It's difficult to accept, but I ask that you listen to what I have to say with an open mind and reserve your questions for after I'm done. Can you do it?"

She nodded.

"Good." He took a sip from his goblet. "Except you, all of us here are immortal. Eva, Bhathian, Jackson and myself. Nathalie who you've met is one too. In fact, she is Eva's and Bhathian's daughter."

As bizarre and as unbelievable as what Kian was saying sounded, it had a ring of truth to it. A lot of little things that seemed weird to her before suddenly made sense. Like Eva's motherly attitude toward her crew, like her aversion to reading things off the screen, even her style of clothing. Everything except her looks fit someone from a different generation. Besides, Eva was right there to vouch for Kian's veracity. She might have kept things from Tessa, but she had never lied to her.

Kian smiled. "I see the wheels turning in your head. You felt that something was off about us before."

"Eva always behaved like a woman in her late fifties and not her late twenties."

Eva chuckled. "Late seventies. But thank you for the compliment."

Tessa's eyes widened, and she turned to Jackson. "How old are you? Are you really eighteen? Or are you ancient too?"

"I take it back," Eva murmured.

Jackson took hold of her other hand. "I'm really eighteen." That was a relief. "And Bhathian?"

"I'm older."

That wasn't saying much, but maybe he was sensitive about his age.

"The reason we are telling you this is that there is a way for a dormant carrier of our genes to be turned immortal. It's a complicated process, and you're not ready for it yet. But because you and Jackson are getting closer, it's becoming exceedingly difficult for him to keep hiding from you what he is, and he asked my permission to tell you the truth."

She cast Jackson a puzzled look.

He smiled and gave her hand a little reassuring squeeze. "Patience. We'll get to the details soon."

"I agreed, but under certain conditions," Kian continued. "As far as the human world is concerned, we don't exist, and it's crucial for our survival that it remains that way. We entrust you with a secret that if revealed will destroy us. I know that Eva is dear to you, and so is Jackson. Their lives and the lives of all of us are now in your hands. Do you understand how serious it is?"

"I do. Your secret is safe with me. You can ask Jackson. I'm very good at keeping secrets."

"I need a binding oath from you."

"What's a binding oath? Do I need to swear on a Bible? I will if you want me to, but as an atheist, it will not mean much to me."

"Not the Bible. Swearing on Eva's life will do."

Tessa cast a quick glance at Eva who nodded her approval. Pulling her hand out of Kian's, Tessa put it over her heart. "I swear on Eva's and my own life that I will never tell anyone about you or any other immortals. No one will ever hear me say that immortals exist."

Kian nodded. "That will do." He looked at the others. "We are done. If you have questions, which I'm sure you have, Jackson can answer them for you. If you need a more scientific explanation about the genetics and the process of transitioning, I suggest talking to my sister. Amanda is the real expert on that."

As everyone prepared to leave. Tessa offered her hand to Kian. "Thank you for granting Jackson's request. It must've been a difficult decision to make."

Kian shook what she'd offered. "You're welcome. Don't make me regret it."

"I won't."

They said their goodbyes and Bhathian escorted them out to the car. It was still strange to think that he and Eva were Nathalie's parents. They all looked more or less the same age. The bigger question, however, was where had Nathalie and Bhathian been for all the years Tessa had known Eva?

CHAPTER 39: EVA

*E*va glanced at Tessa through the rear view mirror. The girl must've been mad at her to sit in the back with Jackson instead of the passenger seat the way she'd done on the way to the keep.

She had said hardly anything on the drive home.

Or maybe she just preferred his company. With her head resting on his bicep, and his arm wrapped around her shoulders, they looked like a young couple should.

It warmed Eva's heart.

Thanks to that boy, Tessa was healing. Not that Eva thought Jackson had such a profound therapeutic effect. But he gave Tessa a strong reason to fight her way back from her self-imposed stasis, and blossom into the woman she should've become if not for the trauma she'd suffered.

And to think Eva had tried to scare him off.

Good thing the boy was stubborn and not easily intimidated. Heck, she doubted there was anything he shied away from. To get what he wanted, Jackson had approached two of the most intimidating people Eva had ever met—Amanda and Kian.

He fought for Tessa, and in turn she fought for him.

These kids were meant to be.

Fate, or God's will.

Eva shook her head. Poor Tessa was so angry at God that she proclaimed herself an atheist. Maybe when her life got better, her beliefs would change. Eva wasn't going to say anything, though it always astonished her how others didn't see God's hand in everything around them—from the smallest blade of grass to the universe at large and all of its wonders.

To each her or his own. Belief wasn't a rational thing, even she was ready to admit it. Where Eva saw God, others saw evolution and natural selection. In her mind, there was no contradiction, but others disagreed, sometimes vehemently.

When did people become so intolerant of others' opinions?

Closed-mindedness was the new epidemic.

Nowadays it was more acceptable to talk about one's sex life than to discuss religion or politics.

Though soon, with all the gender and non-gender brouhaha, that too would become a controversial topic.

And anyway, doing it was better than talking about it.

Eva smiled as she saw Bhathian leaning against his car, waiting for her outside to see her home safely. Now that was a proud example of the male gender. There was nothing ambiguous about him. Just the way she liked it.

"We are here, kids." It felt so good to finally talk freely with Tessa and stop pretending that she wasn't old enough to be the girl's grandmother.

Bhathian pushed away from his car and walked over to open her door. "What took you so long?"

She took the hand he offered. "Unlike you, I'm a safe driver."

He pulled her into his arms and kissed her hard. "I was in a hurry."

"Were you now?"

Behind them, Tessa and Jackson exchanged a few hushed whispers, promises of talking the next day and some sweet endearments.

"He is good for her," Bhathian said.

Eva agreed.

Jackson walked Tessa to the door and kissed her cheek goodnight like a boy from Eva's girlhood. Adorable.

He walked up to them. "Thank you for being there for Tessa and me."

Bhathian clapped his back. "Any time. You make me proud, Jackson."

The boy looked uncomfortable. "Thank you. Though I'm not sure what I've done to deserve it."

Bhathian smiled. "You're a mensch."

"What is that?"

"Look it up."

"I will. Goodnight."

Jackson and Bhathian did the manly hug and clap thing, and Eva put her hands on the boy's cheeks, kissing each one. "Goodnight, Jackson."

They watched him walk to his car before getting inside. Maternal instincts were a weird thing. Jackson could handle himself just fine without any help, and yet she felt responsible for him.

"I can't wait to get you in bed," Bhathian whispered in her ear as he opened the front door for her.

She answered with a coy smile.

There was no one in the living room, but the familiar sounds coming from the kitchen meant that Tessa was there, making tea.

"Wait for me upstairs? I think Tessa needs to talk."

Bhathian's shoulders sagged. "How long will it take?"

"It might take some time. Just get comfortable on the bed." She stretched to nuzzle his ear. "Naked."

The smile was back on his face. "Yes, ma'am."

In the kitchen, Tessa sat with her elbow propped on the table, her ear against her palm, dunking her teabag in and out of the mug in slow motion.

Eva sat at the other end. "Do you want to talk?"

"What's the deal with Nathalie and Bhathian? Where have they been through all the years I've known you? Have you been seeing them on your trips? And why the sudden decision to move to be next to them?"

Eva sighed. "It's a long story. But I can give you the gist of it. Bhathian was a one-night-stand, or a hookup as you kids call it today. He knocked me up with one try. I was forty-five, looked the same as I do today, but didn't know I was immortal. A Dormant who transitioned without knowing it. Bhathian didn't realize I was an immortal either. When I found him a month later to tell him that I was pregnant, he offered to pay for an abortion."

Tessa gasped. "He didn't."

"He did because he thought I was a human. As you learned today, immortals have to guard the secret of their existence, which means they can't have real relationships. Sooner or later a partner will start noticing things and get suspicious. Not to mention the different lifespans. Anyway, I told him no thanks and left. I found a nice man who I believed would be a good father to my child and married him. For a while, everything was fine, until I could no longer attribute my unchanging looks to luck. I didn't know why I wasn't aging, and I invented all kinds of crazy scenarios like the government experimenting on me without my knowledge and stuff like that."

"You must've been scared."

"I was terrified. People would pay a fortune to get their hands on a fountain of youth. I would've been dissected like a lab rat. Worse, they would've gone after my child and dissected her too. Things between me and the man I married went sour, and we got divorced. I hung around as long as I could, using makeup and baggy clothing to look older. But as soon as Nathalie left for college, I ran. I missed her every day since, but I was convinced that I had to stay away to keep her safe. I let her believe I was dead."

"Ouch."

"Yeah. It hurt. I was walking around with a big hole in my heart. But God hadn't forsaken me. Apparently, Bhathian never stopped looking for me, but since he met me while I was working undercover and using an alias, he couldn't find me. When he met Andrew, who had a high-security clearance, he asked him to try and find me. Andrew had access to government data and found who I was. From there it was easy to locate my ex-husband and my daughter. But not me. Bhathian and Nathalie got closer, she and Andrew fell in love, and they kept looking for me. There was only one thread they had to follow—my government pension. But I was very clever at hiding. I donated the pension to an orphanage in Brazil. Bhathian traveled all the way there only to discover that my trail ended at that orphanage. He left me a letter in the hopes that I would come back. I did, got the letter, and the rest is history. I discovered that I'm not the only immortal, and more importantly that no one is looking for me and my mutant genes."

"That's when you decided to move here?"

"Yes. I wanted to be near my daughter."

"What about Bhathian?"

Eva ran her fingers through her hair. "He was a stranger to me, and I was angry at him for the way he reacted all those years ago."

"But it seems like you guys are really into each other."

"Bhathian is convinced I'm his destined mate. I'm sure Jackson will explain that nonsense to you. The immortals believe that there is only one person who is their true love match. Finding her or him is considered the greatest blessing one can hope for. Most never do."

"That's sweet. Very romantic."

"Yes. And it's also bullshit. But Bhathian believes it and tries to convince me that we are fated mates. I'm enjoying his company, but that is all. I'm too old to believe in mystical love."

Tessa lifted a brow. "How about just plain love?"

"I'm not sure I know what it is. I know mother's love, but not romantic love."

"Do you miss Bhathian when you're away?"

"I do. But that doesn't mean anything."

"You're wrong. If you miss him, and if being without him makes you feel hollow inside, then you love him."

It was on the tip of her tongue to tell Tessa that she knew nothing about love and shouldn't dispense advice on something she'd never experienced. But it would've been unnecessarily hurtful. Besides, the girl obviously had feelings for Jackson, maybe even loved him.

"I'm used to being alone, and I need my space. True, sometimes when I'm away, I miss Bhathian, but other times I want him to go home so I can have room to breathe. I'm not ready to share my life with another. I may never be ready. Having Bhathian as a boyfriend is good enough for me."

"But it's not for him."

"I know."

"What if he despairs and decides to move on?"

She hadn't thought of that. But it was a viable concern. Would she be sorry to see Bhathian go?

Yes, she would.

But then, contrary to what Bhathian believed, committing to him didn't guarantee that he would never leave. Fernando had been a perfect example of that. By cheating on her, he'd left her even though she'd been the one to file for the divorce.

"He can leave even if we are married. My husband, Nathalie's adoptive father, was unfaithful despite claiming he loved me. There are no guarantees in life."

Tessa snorted. "You're telling me? But I know that fear of being hurt can rob you of the best things in life. Letting it rule you means that whoever hurt you is still doing it because you're stuck behind the protective shield you've built for yourself. My fear and my pain will never go away because I can't forgive those who wronged me. And still, I try to push through it. You, on the other hand, can forgive those who wronged you and move on. You can forgive your ex-husband for being weak, and you can forgive Bhathian for making a mistake he's regretted from the moment he made it. When you do, you can open your heart for love."

Words of wisdom, no doubt. There was one problem with what Tessa had said. Fernando and Bhathian weren't the only ones Eva had to forgive. She needed to forgive herself first, and that was going to be much more difficult.

CHAPTER 40: BHATHIAN

*B*hathian got in bed and flicked the television on, flipping channels until settling on a rerun of *Cosmos*. It was one he'd seen before, but that show never got old, especially with Carl Sagan's unique style of narration. Bhathian turned the volume up.

With his hearing, it was hard to avoid eavesdropping on Eva and Tessa's conversation. Sagan helped.

The episode was nearly over when Eva came up.

Bhathian flicked the television off and dropped the remote on the nightstand. "Tessa must have had a lot of questions."

"She did, but not the ones I expected." Eva pulled her blouse over her head and draped it on the back of a chair.

"What did she want to know?"

"About you, me and Nathalie."

"That's surprising. I was sure she had a thousand questions about immortals and Dormants and what it all meant to her. What did you tell her?"

Eva sat down on the bed and unstrapped a sandal, dropping it to the floor, then the other one. "Our story. More or less." She popped the button on her silk trousers, pulled them down, and got up to drape them over the blouse.

As usual, what was under her clothes was fancier and sexier than the outer layer. This time the matching set of bra and panties was light blue. The back of the bra was a lattice of strings, and so was the back of her panties.

He whistled. "Is that new?"

Eva lifted her arms and slowly turned in a circle. "You like?"

"You know I do. But I like you even better naked."

"Give me a minute." She ducked into the bathroom.

He waited with bated breath.

A few minutes later she emerged, striking a pose with one hand on the door frame and the other on her hip. A vision of female perfection, she took away what little breath remained in his lungs.

He patted the bed. "Come here, beautiful."

She sauntered over and climbed. Kneeling, she looked down at him. "How do you want me, lover boy?" She cupped her breasts, thumbing her perky nipples in slow circles.

He patted the bed again. "On your belly."

"Oh yeah? And what are you going to do to me?"

"You'll find out."

"Ooh, what could it possibly be?"

She did as he asked, lying on her belly and stretching her arms over her head.

As Bhathian got up to his knees and regarded the beauty sprawled before him, he wished he had Dalhu's talent so he could paint a picture of her in that pose. Her hair, dark with a reddish undertone, spilled in thick waves over her shoulders and down to the white pillowcase. Her back, smooth and creamy, was muscular but not overly so. Her legs were shapely and long. And that ass, flaring gently from her narrow waist, heart-shaped and plump, was so perfect that he wanted to worship it with his mouth.

But first, he was going to give his lady the treat he'd been planning on. The lotion he'd put under the blanket was all warmed up from being pressed against his body. He pulled it out and squirted a generous dollop into his palms, then straddled Eva's thighs and went to work.

"Ahh." She moaned. "That feels wonderful."

He kneaded the tight muscles below her shoulder blades. Eva carried so much tension in her body. He was going to massage all of that away until everything was loose and Eva was relaxed.

"I've died and gone to heaven," she murmured into the pillow.

Bhathian chuckled. "I don't hear such loud moaning from you when we are making love. Should I be offended?"

"Just keep doing what you're doing, and I promise to moan even louder later."

"You've got yourself a deal." He moved to her shoulders.

"Ohh, yes, just like that, don't stop."

Bhathian couldn't help the laugh that bubbled up. "What will the neighbors think?"

"Fuck the neighbors."

If his Eva was saying fuck with such ease, then he was doing a good job. She was loosening up.

"I don't want you to fuck the neighbors. Just me."

"Ha, ha."

He moved down and started kneading her butt cheeks. "That's my favorite part. Your ass is a work of art."

"But I have no sore muscles there."

"And I should care because?"

"No reason. Just saying."

He played with her ass a little longer, sneaking a few feathery swipes down her moist labia folds, then moved down to her thighs, then her calves, and finally her feet. Each little toe at a time.

"You're spoiling me."

"You deserve to be spoiled, love."

He felt her tense. "Did I say something wrong?"

"No, but I think I'm ready for the front."

Tight-lipped as usual. Getting Eva to talk was harder than getting information out of prisoners of war.

"Okay. You can turn over."

She did, her arms flopping lazily down her sides. "I feel boneless."

"Good. Now spread those lovely legs of yours a little."

He lifted one leg and pulled, stretching it, then repeated with the other. With Eva's puffy petals beckoning him, it was getting harder to focus on the massage. All he wanted to do was to dive in there and lick her all over.

Eva lifted a hand and put it on her belly, then let it slide down to her center, her fingers parting her folds. "I think I need a little massage here. I feel achy and needy."

Bhathian couldn't refuse an invitation like that. The rest of the massage could wait for later.

His fingers replaced hers on the seat of her pleasure, and he rubbed gently, gathering some of the dew seeping from her core and spreading it over the sensitive bundle of nerves.

As promised, Eva moaned loudly and lifted to meet his fingers. When he didn't react fast enough, she grabbed his hand and guided one finger inside of her.

He pushed in, then retreated and came back with two, eliciting another throaty moan.

"I see you like the massage, love."

"I like your hands on me."

Ahh, music to his ears.

Bhathian dipped his head, adding his tongue to the play,

and Eva went wild, bucking under the double assault and clutching at his head.

His fingers and tongue unrelenting, he went faster and faster, building up her pleasure until it crested in a powerful tidal wave.

Eva's body sagged, and he cupped her gently, coating his palm in her copious juices.

His woman was easy to please. Sexually, but not otherwise.

CHAPTER 41: EVA

*T*he climax combined with the massage Bhathian had given her banished the last traces of stress she'd held in her body, and Eva felt as if she was floating even though the bed was firm under her. It was more than a post-orgasmic float. It was nirvana.

Propped on his arms, Bhathian hovered above her, his fleshy lips delivering gentle kisses to her flushed face.

With a smile, she opened her eyes to look at his handsome face and wrapped her arms around his massive torso, barely reaching past his sides. "Make love to me, big guy."

He didn't say a thing, but his eyes spoke volumes. Love and admiration pouring out of them in a light show of warm colors.

In the back of her mind warning bells chimed. A woman could get used to feeling like that but shouldn't. There was nowhere to go from there but down.

Before that thought had a chance to destroy her blissful contentment, Bhathian slid into her in one gentle thrust and began moving inside her. Slow and steady, he was like a wave, retreating and surging, and retreating and surging again, his tempo increasing in barely there increments, stoking the fire inside her one tinder at a time.

Eva had had sex aplenty in her long life, but very little lovemaking. With Bhathian, even when they were playing games and it got intense, the sense of connection underlying everything made it feel like love.

Though gradual, the buildup soon reached critical velocity, and the loving turned into no-holds-barred, immortal style fucking. As the orgasm hit her, Eva's mouth opened on a scream, but Bhathian smashed his lips over hers and swallowed what came out of her throat.

His name.

When he let go, she turned her head sideways, offering him her neck.

Bliss. Then oblivion.

The next time Eva opened her eyes, her bedroom was bathed in the gentle gray light of early morning's sunlight filtered by the thick marine overcast.

Carefully, she lifted Bhathian's heavy arm, slipped out of bed, and ducked into the bathroom.

Done with her morning routine, Eva opened the bedroom door and looked at her man's amazing body sprawled over her bed. It was so tempting to crawl back under the covers and cuddle with him. But she had a busy day ahead of her and staying in bed meant finishing her work late.

She'd better get dressed.

But Bhathian…

Undecided, she rubbed at her bare arms. The sound must've woken him, and he turned around, regarding her as if she was a marvel of beauty.

Eva smiled. "Every time you see me naked, you have the same awe-struck look in your eyes as if it's the first time. I love it." She wondered how long it would last.

"I'll never get tired of the vision you make. You are female perfection." He lifted the blanket and beckoned her with a crooked finger. "Come back to bed, and I'll warm you up. I kept it nice and toasty for you."

For some reason, that small gesture brought a sting of tears behind her eyes.

It was nothing, really, but the fact that he was mindful of her little quirks meant a lot to her. Eva tended to get cold easily and hated getting into a chilly bed.

Why did it make her so emotional, though?

Maybe because love wasn't about the big things. It wasn't about extravagant gifts or elegantly phrased declarations, and it wasn't even about grand heroic deeds or flowery sentiments. Love was about the small things, like remembering that your loved one hated cold beds, or that she liked her coffee with a spoonful of sugar, or that spiders creeped her out. It was knowing what her favorite show was, and bringing home her favorite takeout, and a thousand and one other things that meant you paid attention and that her comfort and enjoyment were important to you.

Maybe it wasn't everyone's definition of love, but it was hers.

Bhathian loved her.

The certainty of it hit her like a bolt of lightning, and she swayed on her feet.

Between one blink of an eye and the next, Bhathian was out of bed and at her side, holding her up. "What's the matter? Are you dizzy? Do you need a glass of water?"

She put a hand on his chest. "I'm fine. Thank you for caring."

He lifted her up and put her in bed, covering her with the blanket that was still warm from his body. "That's an odd thing to say. Thanking me for caring for you? It's as much a part of me as breathing. I don't expect to be thanked for it."

She cupped his cheek. "I know you don't." Those tears were still there, waiting to spill out of the corners of her eyes. She held them back. It would be too difficult to explain why she was getting emotional. "I think you're right and I'm a little dehydrated. Could you bring me a glass of water?"

"Of course."

Bhathian grabbed his pants off the nightstand and pulled them on, then headed downstairs to the kitchen, giving Eva a few moments to collect herself.

He'd said he loved her before, but she hadn't believed him. Not in the sense that she thought he was lying, but that he was misguided, and that he couldn't possibly love her.

But he did, showing his love in all the little things he did for her, the ones she took for granted and didn't even notice.

Tessa was right. Eva had doubted Bhathian's love because she thought of herself as undeserving. And she wasn't.

Did she do nice little things for him? Did she know what his favorite show was? Well, she knew that one. He loved watching *Cosmos* and football games.

What else?

When he drank coffee, he liked it black, but he wasn't a fan of it. Bhathian drank mainly water and a beer or two in the evenings.

He loved Nathalie and Phoenix. He was good friends with Andrew, but other than that she didn't think he had a lot of friends. Bhathian was a loner. But he loved being with her.

She needed to find out more about him. To show him that she cared for him.

God, I want to love that man.

As it dawned on Eva that she was incapable of letting herself love Bhathian, the tears she'd been holding began dripping down her cheeks. Tessa was right about that too. Until Eva let go of the past and forgave the men in her life as well as herself, she couldn't open her heart to love.

CHAPTER 42: JACKSON

"*V*lad, don't you and Gordon have something planned for tonight?"

Tessa was on her way, and Jackson wanted his buddies gone so he could answer her questions without them over-hearing. Intentionally or unintentionally.

"Why? Is your girlfriend coming over?" The sarcastic undertone in Vlad's voice was new.

Jackson frowned. "I thought you liked Tessa."

"I do. But it's started to feel as if this is your place and not ours. Every evening you can't wait to get rid of Gordon and me so you can be alone with her. I get it. But we can't hang out in bars or go to the movies every night, and I'm forced to spend more and more time at my mom's. You know how much I like that. I love her, but she's bat-shit crazy."

Jackson cringed. Vlad's mom's craziness was fun in small doses, but being exposed to it daily? Not so much.

Maybe he should get a place of his own. But with all his talk about the big money he was making, it wasn't that much, and the cost of rent was insane. Especially since he could have no roommates and would have to pay it all himself. Last he heard, a crappy studio apartment went for fifteen hundred. He could make the payments, but then his monthly savings would dwindle to basically nothing.

Being a coffee shop manager wasn't his life goal. It was a stepping-stone to something better. Jackson needed to save up as much as he could.

Damn. The rule about having to either finish college or be twenty-five to get a share of the clan's profits was so stupid. Kian should change it.

Maybe he could talk to the guy, or maybe not. Kian had already done him a big favor. He couldn't bother the regent with more requests. Not that asking would help. Kian wouldn't change the profit sharing rule just because of Jackson. He needed to come up with a solution on his own.

"I'm sorry, dude. You're right. I can't expect you guys to be gone every evening. Give me this one time, and I'll try to figure out something for the future."

Vlad lifted one of his thin brows. "The solution is simple. Soundproof your room, and keep your girlfriend there."

"Do you know how? Because I don't have a clue. It's not like soundproofing a recording studio."

"Maybe it is. I don't know. I'm going to ask around."

"Thanks, man."

Vlad saluted with two fingers. "All for one and one for all, bro."

By the time Tessa knocked on the door, Vlad and Gordon were long gone.

Why the hell did she still knock instead of just walking in? As he opened the door for her, Jackson was about to say something to that effect when the words died on his lips.

The girl standing outside was Tessa, but different.

A lot different.

"What have you done?"

She shifted her weight from foot to foot. "You hate it."

Damn it. "I don't hate it, I'm just shocked." He shook himself, and pulled the door open all the way to let Tessa inside.

Her hair, which used to be brown, wavy, and reaching past her shoulder blades, was now light blond with darker shades weaved through it, stick straight, short in the back and chin length in the front. Long bangs covered her eyebrows and made her small face look even smaller. Other than that, she was also wearing a lot of makeup, including a bright red lipstick.

Tessa looked like she was on the verge of tears. "Eva said I needed to change my looks drastically so no one from my past could recognize me."

Jackson took her by the hand and led her to the front booth where they usually sat when there was no one in the café. "If that was the objective, then it was achieved. But why? Is someone after you?"

"She said it was a precaution. Because I didn't change much over the years, I'm easily recognizable. This was just the first stage." She pointed to her face. "Tomorrow she is taking me clothes shopping. She says I need to drop the mousy look and adopt a confident one." Tessa grimaced. "She wants me to start wearing heels and elegant skirts and look like a sophisticated professional woman."

Jackson couldn't imagine Tessa looking like some snooty socialite. But he had to admit that with such a drastic change no one would even think to compare her to her old self.

"Eva is right. And if anyone knows how to change looks completely it's her. She is the master of disguise."

Tessa sighed. "I can deal with everything except the heels. How am I going to walk? I'll twist my ankles for sure."

"Start with low ones and keep upgrading."

"I guess."

She looked so despondent that he felt like an ass for

reacting the way he had. The new haircut was cool, and Tessa looked pretty, she just didn't look like herself.

Wrapping an arm around her shoulders, he pulled her against him. "You look hot. And I can't wait to see you in a tight skirt and high heels. My only problem with this new look is that I'll have to beat up any guy who looks at you funny."

Tessa's body tensed. "I don't want men to look at me."

Dammit. Eva should've thought of that. There was a reason Tessa dressed like a kid. She didn't want to look like a woman. Out of the outfits they had chosen together, she'd only worn the pants and shirts. He hadn't seen her in that tight black dress even once.

A different angle was needed.

"It's not going to be so bad. You don't go out much. Right?"

She nodded. "Now I'm not going to go out at all. Grocery shopping in heels is ridiculous and uncomfortable. I don't know what's going through Eva's head."

Jackson had a feeling he knew. Now that Tessa was making a real effort to overcome her fears, Eva was expecting her to go out more.

"I'll tell you what. We'll go out together. I'll take you to the mall on Sunday."

"I'm not sure about it."

"You know that I can protect you, right?"

Tessa shrugged. "I guess you can handle one unarmed guy. But what if there are more?"

He chuckled. "Did you already forget what you were told last night? I'm an immortal."

She shrugged again. "That's good because they can't kill you. But they can still take me."

He'd forgotten that Tessa still didn't have a clue what being an immortal meant. "I'm stronger and faster than a human male. All my senses are more acute: hearing, eyesight, smell. Immortal males are the most dangerous predators on the planet. That doesn't mean that a group of humans armed with knives and guns can't take me down, but I doubt gangs are hanging around shopping malls looking for trouble."

She turned to him with a wide-eyed look. "If I become immortal like Kian said, will I also get stronger and faster?"

"Yes, you will."

"How much stronger?"

"Strong enough to take down an average human male."

For the first time since she'd arrived a smile bloomed on her face. "How soon can I do it? And what is it going to take?"

CHAPTER 43: TESSA

*J*ackson tilted his head, a questioning expression on his face. "Don't you want to find out more first? I would think you'd have a thousand questions."

Tessa waved a hand. "Of course I do. But this is the most important part." If she could become a superwoman, she wanted to do it yesterday. It was a dream come true, and the immortality was just the cherry on top of finally feeling safe.

She could kick ass. A miniature-sized Wonder Woman. She could go to a martial arts class and learn how to do it properly. Or maybe she should join her neighbor's Krav Maga class. The woman had offered Tessa, Sharon, and Eva a discount if all three enrolled together. The class was just for women, which was perfect for her.

But then if Tessa became as strong as Jackson had said she would, her strength would look suspicious. She should join the class before becoming immortal.

"Immortal males have fangs," Jackson said.

Tessa had been so immersed in her daydreaming that she

wasn't sure she'd heard him right. "I'm sorry. What did you say?"

Jackson raked his fingers through his hair, pushing his long bangs back. "I said that immortal males have fangs."

That was weird, but whatever. "So what?"

"And we also have venom glands. To induce the transition, I'll have to bite you."

"Where?"

He chuckled. "The neck is the most common place, but not the only one."

"Then it's a good thing I cut my hair. Here, bite me." She tilted her head, presenting him with the expanse of her thin neck.

Jackson cringed. "It has to be done during sex."

That complicated things. For some reason, she wasn't scared of him biting her, maybe because she'd never been bitten before, but she was scared of everything else. "I see."

Jackson clasped her hand. "There is no rush. I don't want you to try to force things before you're ready just because you want to hasten your transition. It's not a guaranteed thing. You're a potential Dormant, but it may turn out that you're not."

"Is there a test for that?"

Jackson shook his head. "There are a couple of indicators. One is paranormal abilities, and the other is affinity. But I'm not an expert. Amanda is."

"What do you mean by affinity?"

"It's a certain feeling you get—like recognizing like. You feel more comfortable around your own people. That was the whole reason behind Eva's housewarming party and Amanda's lecture. She invited immortals to meet you and Sharon and Nick, then asked them if they felt something."

"You mean Sharon and Nick are also potential Dormants?"

"Yes. They have some special abilities, and Eva picked them up because she felt the special something for them. But they don't know yet, and you can't tell them."

"So why was I told?"

"Because of me. Us. Remember when you kissed me?"

Tessa nodded.

"My fangs got longer, and I had to pull away. I went to see Amanda and begged her to let me tell you."

That was sweet...

"Wait a minute. So how did you kiss other girls?" Jackson hadn't kept his past hookups secret. She knew he'd been a player.

The guy looked more uncomfortable than she'd ever seen him before. "When I'm the one doing the kissing, I'm controlling what's going on. I wouldn't have let you enter my mouth."

He'd let her lead because there was no other way she could get close to him.

"And then you started talking about taking it further, and I was totally on board with that. But in a situation like that, when I'm aroused, my fangs elongate, and my eyes glow, and you would've freaked out."

Tessa tried to imagine Jackson with fangs and glowing eyes, testing the image to see if it was scary, but it wasn't. His fangs and his glowing eyes weren't half as scary as his hands and what was between his legs.

"If your fangs get longer when you're aroused, does it mean that you always bite during sex? Not only to activate a Dormant?"

"Yes."

"How the hell did you keep that a secret from your partners? I would assume it hurts pretty bad. Not something they might've not noticed."

"First of all it only hurts for a second or two. When the

venom hits, the euphoria it brings wipes away any pain. It's the most intense pleasure possible. Later, I thrall the memory of the bite away. Make them forget."

"Thrall?"

"Yeah, like in the vampire movies. That's our survival mechanism. We can get into humans' heads and make them forget things, remember things that never happened, and so on."

She narrowed her eyes, pinning Jackson with a hard stare. "Have you ever done it to me?"

"No. And I never will."

That was a relief. "Thank you."

He smoothed his hand over her new hairdo. "I never felt right about thralling girls after I've been with them. But we have no choice."

Even though it wasn't a newsflash, Tessa cringed every time Jackson mentioned his past lovers. She couldn't help it. The jealousy would rise, and no amount of self-talk helped make it hurt less.

Especially since he hadn't done it with her.

Jackson was going to be a phenomenal lover, she just knew it, but couldn't imagine how. Nothing in her past experiences had been about pleasure. It had been about pain and intimidation and control.

Tessa shook her head, banishing the dark thoughts from her head. This was the past. The future would be the exact opposite. "Did you get a new bed?"

Jackson smiled sheepishly. "It was an excuse. A way to buy myself time. You don't need to tie me up to anything. I can keep my hands to myself. Besides, I can probably get free no matter what you tie me to. I can break the bed frame."

Jackson was that much stronger than a human?

"How do you manage to be so gentle when you're so strong?"

247

He shrugged. "The same way you hold an egg or a baby. You just know."

Could she do it without him being tied up and at her mercy? Only one way to find out.

"Let's go up to your room."

Jackson swallowed. "Are you sure you're ready?"

"For what we talked about. Nothing more."

When Jackson got up and offered her his hand, it wasn't as steady as it usually was. Could he be nervous?

No way.

She followed him upstairs, her anxiety mixed with a tinge of arousal. It was hard to believe that she was actually going to do it. To touch a man of her own volition and perhaps even enjoy it.

As they entered his room, seeing Jackson's sofa messy as usual made her relax. He hadn't been expecting her to follow up right away. Otherwise he would've tidied up.

"Excuse me a moment." He started collecting the various items of clothing strewn about the floor. When he was done, he bundled them all together and tossed them out into the hallway.

"You should at least put them in the laundry basket."

"I don't have one." Jackson closed the door. "Out of sight will do."

True. A messed up room was not conducive to a romantic atmosphere. Tessa walked over to the sofa, picked up the blanket, folded it, and draped it over its back.

Now what?

For a moment, they each remained rooted in their spots, unsure what to do next. She'd told Jackson that she wanted to be in charge, so she should act accordingly. Her timidity was one of the things she wanted to get rid of.

Tessa sat on the couch and waited for Jackson to join her. He sat close to her, but not so close that they were touching.

Now what to do? Should she kiss him first? Have him lie down and put his head on the pillow she'd fluffed?

Yeah, that would work.

"Could you lie down on the pillow and put your hands behind your neck?"

Jackson seemed relieved to be told what to do. "I'm yours to command, my lady."

Tessa got up to give him room to sprawl, then when he pressed himself against the couch's back, sat down and looked at the magnificent man at her mercy.

How the hell did she get so lucky? Jackson was gorgeous, smart, and kind. He could've had any girl he wanted, and yet he'd chosen her. A broken soul with issues from there to Timbuktu.

Perhaps there was something to the mate thing that Eva had talked about, and Tessa was Jackson's. Or maybe he liked a challenge. Or maybe he wanted to be the hero who saves the girl. Though in her case it wouldn't be any dragon he'd be saving her from, just the demons in her head.

CHAPTER 44: JACKSON

*T*essa ogled him, making Jackson hard faster than the best porn flick he'd ever watched—including the kinky Japanese ones.

Perhaps the prolonged deprivation had done it, allowing one needy look to make him go from zero to sixty in a split second. Whatever it was, he couldn't wait for her to put her hands on him.

She was taking too long, just watching him while nibbling her red tinted bottom lip. That new look of hers was growing on him. There was no mistaking her for a kid now.

Tessa was a woman.

But she was hesitant like a middle-schooler. He wasn't allowed to touch her, but she'd said nothing about talking.

He could encourage her.

"Do you want to kiss me? Put those lipstick-covered lips of yours on mine?"

His words seemed to wake her from her trance. "Oh shit, I forgot all about it. I probably have lipstick all over my teeth." She rubbed her finger over them, and sure enough, it came away red. "Ugh, gross. I need to wash it off." She made a move to get up.

He almost broke protocol and grabbed her, remembering at the last moment to keep his hands under his head. "No, don't. The lipstick is sexy. I want you to smear it all over my face."

"Why?"

"Because when you look at me, you'll know you did it—that you put your mark on me and made me yours." Jackson had no idea whether what he was saying even made sense. He was shooting in all directions, trying to find the right words to make her loosen up.

A very faint scent of arousal reached his nostrils, hinting that he was on the right track.

Tessa put a hand on his chest and leaned forward. She kissed him lightly, only a feathery touch of her lips on his, then leaned back and looked at her work.

A giggle bubbled up, and she put a hand over her mouth.

"What?"

"You look like a clown. I want to wipe it off." She tried to get up again.

Forgetting about keeping his hands behind his head, Jackson whipped his T-shirt over his head and handed it to her. "Here, use this."

As her eyes landed on his bare chest, the scent of arousal flared, and Tessa swallowed audibly. "You must work out a lot," she breathed.

"Not at all. Unless you count schlepping heavy amplifiers and Gordon's drums to and from our gigs."

She put her small hand back on his chest, the skin-to-skin sensation electrifying. "Are all immortal men naturally muscular?" Using his shirt, Tessa wiped the lipstick off his face with a gentle hand.

"Most are. But not all. Take Vlad for example. The dude is strong like a weightlifter but his muscles are invisible."

Her eyes widened. "He is an immortal too? What about Gordon?"

"Yep."

She wiped the lipstick off her own lips, much less gently than she'd wiped his, then dropped the T-shirt on the floor. "I think it's ruined."

"I don't care. Come back here and kiss me, woman."

Tessa smiled. "I want to do a little touching first." She put both hands on his pectorals and began stroking his chest.

Jackson closed his eyes, willing his dick to behave. But it was no use. Even the thick denim couldn't hide the bulge he'd sprouted.

Tessa's hands kept going down, over his stomach and down to his sides. There was no way she didn't glimpse what was going on south of there.

"Do you mind if I touch you here?" Tessa whispered with her hand hovering over his belt.

He was pretty sure she didn't mean the belt. "You can touch me wherever you want."

Her teeth closed over her lower lip again. "I don't want to cause you pain."

"You're not going to."

"But I can't do more…"

He chuckled nervously. "Don't worry about it. But there is a chance I'll come as soon as you put your hand on me. It's been a while. So if that is something that is going to gross you out or scare you, don't."

She shook her head. "When you're like that, not moving, nothing about you scares me. There is purity in you. I can sense it."

Wrong. But he wasn't going to correct her while he was dying a little with every moment she delayed her touch.

A small smile bloomed on her lips. "The purity I'm talking about has nothing to do with your promiscuous past. It's about your spirit."

"Thank you, but right now I'm all about the body. If you're going to touch me, do it."

As her hand hovered lower, Jackson held his breath, the urge to grab it and force it down so strong it was almost powerful enough to shatter his promise. But then she did it, her touch so light, he could barely feel it through the denim, and yet it was the most erotic thing ever. He groaned, and his head hit the pillow.

Encouraged, Tessa closed her fingers over the contour of his shaft and traced the outline from top to bottom. "You're big."

"Thank you?" He wasn't sure. Normally it would've been a compliment, but maybe not from Tessa. Big could've meant *no way am I ever letting that thing inside me.*

"I guess you're just proportionate all over. You're so tall. Scoot." She motioned for him to make room for her and stretched out on the couch beside him. Her face an inch away from his on the pillow, and her hand still on his crotch, she whispered, "Kiss me, Jackson. I think I'm ready."

CHAPTER 45: TESSA

"*Y*ou want me to kiss you? Like in me kissing you?"

Jackson's eyes were glowing, and when he opened his mouth to talk, she saw what he'd meant about fangs. His canines, which were normally slightly longer than average, had lengthened, making kissing him a bit scary. Maneuvering around these two sharp points posed a challenge she wasn't sure she was up to.

Besides, something had changed inside her. The fear that had always been just below the surface receded, allowing her room to breathe and think without it coloring everything dark.

Perhaps it was the hope of a different future, in which Tessa, the small and weak girl, would become a powerful immortal. Or maybe it was the new look that implied confidence and assertiveness. As with a fake smile, what started as acting might have turned into actually feeling it. Or maybe it was Jackson.

She'd been seeing him for weeks, her trust in him growing with every day. She could let him kiss her and not freak out. In fact, she might even enjoy it.

Tessa had no doubt Jackson was a great kisser.

"Yes." She smiled and cupped his cheek. "I trust you."

With a look of reverence on his beautiful face, Jackson closed the tiny distance between them and pressed his lips to hers in a gentle kiss.

So far so good.

With the very tip of his tongue, he licked at the seam of her lips, and she parted them in invitation.

Here goes.

Tessa tensed as she waited for her fears to kick in as soon as Jackson's tongue penetrated her mouth. But the way he did it, a gentle exploration and a hesitant slide against her tongue, didn't feel like a penetration, it felt like a dance.

She moaned, both in pleasure and relief, her tongue meeting his in the slow dance of courtship. The kiss went on and on, and all through it Jackson's hands remained tucked behind his back, while hers caressed every exposed surface of his muscular upper body. His chest, his abs, his back, his shoulders, his arms.

It felt wonderful.

"Can you hug me?" she asked when they came up for air.

"I thought you'd never ask."

His arms went around her, but he held her loosely, probably afraid of spooking her.

Tessa wanted him to hold her tight against that amazing body of his and kiss her again. "Are you always so gentle and careful with girls?" She suspected he wasn't, but then she couldn't imagine Jackson getting rough either.

"Here, there is only you and me. No one else."

He was right. She needed to rephrase her question. "If I didn't have any hang-ups, how would you kiss me?"

"Do you want me to show you?"

His tone was husky with desire, and suddenly she wanted nothing more than to let him take over and show her how a passionate kiss should be. More than that, she wanted the real Jackson, not a subdued version who tiptoed around her issues.

As her arousal intensified, her eyelids fluttered shut. "Yes."

"Open your eyes, Tessa. You need to see me and know that you're safe."

She forced her lids up. "I'm ready."

In slow motion, still careful not to startle her, Jackson pulled her under him. The difference in heights meant that to kiss her he had to slide his body lower, and his crotch was between her thighs but not touching hers. Braced on his forearms, he looked into her eyes. "Okay?"

She nodded.

He snaked one arm under her, his hand cupping the back of her head. "Still okay?"

"Yes."

Lowering his chest, so he was fully on top of her, he cupped her cheek. "How about now?"

As his weight bore down on her, pressing her into the couch, Tessa had a moment of panic, but looking into the incredible, one-of-a-kind blue of his eyes helped banish it.

This was Jackson, and there was no one else in the world like him. He was unlike any man she'd ever met, and the difference between him and the monsters who'd hurt her was like the difference between a heavenly angel and the darkest demons from hell.

The difference between salvation and destruction.

"It's perfect." Tessa wrapped her arms around him. Holding on tight, she felt his tense muscles relax under her palms.

The kiss started the same as before, tentative and sweet, but as his tongue got bolder and his lips firmer, Tessa felt something she'd never felt before. It started with a tingle, an itch she tried to relieve by rubbing herself against Jackson's hard abs.

Then came wetness. It trickled out of her, moistening her underwear.

Jackson lifted his head and gazed at her with wonder in his glowing eyes. "Oh, Tessa," was all he said before dipping his head and kissing her again.

He knew.

Tightening her arms around him, Tessa felt tears pool in the corners of her eyes. She'd never gotten wet before, using lubricants to make the ordeal of penetration tolerable.

A thing that was so natural for most post-pubescent women was a breakthrough achievement for her at twenty-one.

She was normal.

The monsters hadn't crippled her for life. She was getting better, and for the first time since forever, Tessa believed she could recover enough to have a normal life.

"Thank you," she murmured into Jackson's mouth.

He lifted his head. "No, thank you for giving me your trust. That's the most precious gift anyone has ever given me."

"You deserve so much more."

He smiled, his elongated fangs not detracting from his angelic beauty in the slightest. Her fanged angel, that was what she was going to call him from now on.

"I'm immortal, Tessa, which means that time is not an issue. We can inch our way into it."

"But it must be so hard for you."

He rubbed his nose against hers. "Nothing worth having comes easy. Right?"

CHAPTER 46: NATHALIE

"*R*eady?" Eva asked.

"Just a moment," Nathalie called out from the bedroom. The high-heeled shoes she'd put on made her look slimmer, but they were not practical for the long day of shopping Eva and she had planned.

Phoenix was at Syssi and Kian's, Andrew had agreed to take Fernando to the park, and Nathalie was free to spend the day with her mother, like she'd dreamed of doing for years. Everything was taken care of. She had nothing to worry about.

Checking her reflection in the mirror, she examined her profile critically. Her rounded belly wasn't so bad. It had gone down significantly in the last two weeks, but she still had a long road ahead of her.

Sadly, though, she couldn't hold a candle to her mom no matter what clothes she wore or what shoes were on her feet. Not only was Eva gorgeous, but she was always perfectly dressed and her hair and makeup done as if she'd just stepped out of a salon. Maybe today Nathalie would learn a trick or two from her perfectly put together mother.

For now, she had to do with flip flops, the most stretchy pair of pre-maternity jeans she owned, and a loose T-shirt. The fifteen-pound weight gain made her old wardrobe obsolete. But even if she managed to lose those pounds in the next few months, and the new clothes she was going to buy today wouldn't fit, she'd just call the talented seamstress who'd worked on her wedding gown to take them in.

"Flip flops?" Eva said as soon as Nathalie stepped into the living room, eyeing her choice of footwear with obvious disdain. "We are not going to the beach."

Nathalie kissed her cheek. "I know. But heels would've killed my feet, and I didn't want to wear sneakers. I know you hate those as well."

Eva kissed her back. "We are going to fix that today." She headed for the door and held it open for Nathalie. "As I told you years ago, sneakers are for the gym, flip flops are for the beach, and elegant flats or low-heeled shoes are for a long day of shopping."

As they stepped into the elevator with its mirror-lined walls, there was no escaping looking at their reflection and making comparisons. She pulled her shoulders back and tried to imitate Eva's regal posture. Chin up, a perfectly composed expression, and not a hint of vulnerability.

"How do you do it? Always looking so perfect?"

"A strict mother and years of practice. I couldn't do schlumpy even if I wanted to."

Interesting. Eva hadn't talked much about her mother. "What was your mom like? You've told me very little about her." Since her grandmother had died before Nathalie was born, she'd never gotten used to calling her Grandma. All she had left of the woman were a few old photographs.

The elevator doors opened and they stepped out into the garage level.

"She was a typical mother of her times. Women lived by

different standards then, and she instilled in me the values that were important to her. The main one was to look and act like a lady, and the second to be a good Catholic. Not necessarily in that order. I think in her mind the two were one and the same."

Eva clicked the remote and unlocked her car.

Her mother's Prius was a nice, comfortable car, but Nathalie liked her new minivan better. She felt like the queen of the road, sitting up high and looking down at the sedans passing her by. Not that she'd gotten to do much driving lately. A trip to the local supermarket and back was the extent of it.

She buckled up and looked at Eva. "Where to?"

Lips curving into a smile, Eva turned the engine on. "The mall, where else? I didn't find any boutiques I like yet. Not that I've had much time for shopping. It's been basically nonstop work since I moved to L.A. Even on weekends."

"That's good, right? Better than sitting around and waiting for the phone to ring."

Eva exited the high-rise's parking and eased into traffic. "I'm not complaining. I just wish more of it was local. Too much of my time is wasted on flying to Tampa and back. But most of my clients are there. Andrew promised to talk to his old boss, Turner, about sending some local work my way, but I think he forgot about it."

"I'll remind him."

"Thanks."

They arrived at the mall early, so it wasn't as busy as it was soon going to get. The stores had just opened and salespeople were putting the last finishing touches to the displays.

"Nordstrom is running a big sale today. We should check it out first."

Nathalie cringed. "I've never shopped there. Too pricey, and the salespeople are pushy."

Eva waved a hand. "Leave them to me. And as to the prices, I always say that it's better to buy a few good items than a lot of low-quality ones."

Nathalie sighed. She'd asked for help and therefore shouldn't complain about her mother's choices. Worst-case scenario, they could continue on to Macy's once they were done with Nordstrom. She'd humor Eva and check out her favorite store first.

"Lead the way, Mom. Today I'm your humble apprentice." She bowed. "Teach me, oh wise master."

Eva laughed and leaned to kiss Nathalie's cheek. "You always had a sense of humor."

It turned out Eva had been right. At the end of two intense hours, Nathalie was the proud owner of three new pairs of jeans, which Eva had frowned on but agreed were practical for a stay-at-home-mother, five very nice everyday shirts, one pair of elegant slacks with a matching blouse, two dresses for evenings out, a stretchy short skirt, and three new pairs of shoes, each with a different type of heel. A pair of elegant flats for a day on the town, a platform wedge for casual outings, and a pair of three-inch sling-backs to go with her new dresses.

The price tag hadn't been as bad as she'd expected, but it was much higher than what she was used to spending on clothing. After years of counting every dollar, Nathalie had to remind herself that she could afford it.

But it was enough.

Hefting half of the bags, Nathalie eyed the café adjacent to the department store. "I'm exhausted. Do you want to stop for a cup of coffee?"

Eva grimaced. "Their coffee is terrible, especially after getting used to the fancy brand you serve at your café. Let's eat lunch instead."

I.T. LUCAS

"I'm not hungry, but as long as it's nearby and not on the other side of the mall, I'm game."

Eva transferred all the bags she was carrying to one hand and reached for Nathalie's. "Let me at least carry your bags."

"Na-ah." Nathalie turned sideways and out of Eva's reach. "You're already carrying half of them. What will people think if I let my mother carry everything for me?"

Eva smiled and leaned to whisper in Nathalie's ear. "That I did all the shopping. And you did none. You forget we look the same age."

CHAPTER 47: EVA

*E*ven with a bunch of bags in each hand, there was a bounce to Eva's step that she hadn't felt in ages.

How often had she dreamt about moments like this with Nathalie? How many times had her heart contracted with envy upon seeing a mother and daughter strolling through racks of clothing or sitting in a café?

Too many to count.

She only wished her own mother's words hadn't come out of her mouth now and then. But the shadows they'd cast on Nathalie's fun had been temporary. Her daughter was a naturally upbeat person, and the small jibes that had irritated Eva growing up had bounced off Nathalie effortlessly.

Where did she get it from?

Eva wasn't a cheerful sort and neither was Bhathian. She could blame the shit they had both witnessed for their gloomy dispositions, but she knew it wasn't the case. A person's biochemistry determined their level of happiness and not any external factors. At least that was what the psychology books claimed.

"How about CPK?" Nathalie pointed at the restaurant. "It's the nearest."

"Sounds good to me." Eva wasn't finicky. As long as she didn't have to cook it, she would eat most anything. That was another thing she and Bhathian had in common. The only reason they didn't get fat on all the junk they ate was that Bhathian worked out the calories, while she was mindful of the quantities. With no time for an exercise routine, it was her only option.

"Do you want to sit outside, or inside?" Nathalie asked.

The outside meant open to the mall, not the outdoors, but she still preferred it to the stifling interior with its overwhelming food smells.

"Outside, if you don't mind."

"Not at all. I love watching people."

They got seated next to the fountain. Eva put down the shopping bags and opened the menu. "What do you recommend?"

"Everything is good. What are you in the mood for?"

"Do you want to share a pizza?"

"Sure, and let's add a salad to share as well."

Eva closed the menu and put it on the table. "Perfect."

The waitress took their order and brought them bread to munch on until their food was ready. Nathalie grabbed a piece and dipped it in oil. "I should be watching what I eat if I want to lose the pregnancy weight, but instead I'm eating all the time. Especially bread. It's the worst, I know, but it's the only thing that calms me down. I'm a basket case."

That was news to Eva. Nathalie looked so happy and content in her new role as a mother. "Why are you nervous? Is everything okay between you and Andrew?"

Nathalie rolled her eyes. "You jump straight to the conclusion that it must be his fault. It isn't. Things are great between us. Andrew adores Phoenix and helps as much as he can. In fact, before she started sleeping for longer stretches of time, he wanted to take care of her all night long and let me sleep. I had to insist he get some shuteye before going to work."

"What about the two of you? Being parents and being partners is not the same." Fernando and she had been a great team in raising Nathalie, but not in taking care of their marriage.

Nathalie smirked and leaned closer. "The fun times are back, and we are going at it like a couple of rabbits."

Eva felt herself blush. A rare thing since she didn't get embarrassed easily. But hearing her daughter talk so openly about sex was shocking. "Too much information, Nathalie." She whispered the rest. "I'm your mother."

Nathalie crossed her arms over her chest. "We are both adults. I think we can talk about sex."

Eva sighed. "I'm a product of a different generation, Nathalie. It's difficult for me to adjust to this openness you kids have. I'll try, though. I have no choice." She lowered her voice to a whisper again. "Being immortal means I have to fit in with the current generation."

Nathalie's smile melted, and her brows dipped to form frown lines between her eyes.

"What did I say?"

"I'm worried. I should've transitioned already."

"Didn't Bridget say that it would take time for the levels of your pregnancy hormones to get low enough to allow it?"

"She did and still does, but I had her take a blood sample and check what's going on exactly. The levels are only slightly elevated. I even had her call Annani and ask her if she remembered anything about women in my situation having difficulty transitioning."

"And?"

"Annani said that back then she was too young and preoccupied with other things to notice."

Eva reached over the table and clasped Nathalie's hand. "Don't worry. You will transition. God didn't orchestrate all of these seemingly impossible coincidences just to stop with you."

"But what if God has already achieved his goal? Maybe I was only the vehicle the Fates needed to give Phoenix life?"

For a moment Eva remained mute. What if Nathalie was right?

The possibility terrified her. One of the reasons Eva had run, the reason she was so ashamed of that she'd shared it with no one, was that she couldn't fathom watching her child grow old and die while she remained eternally young.

God couldn't be that cruel, could he?

Of course, he could. For a believer like her, reconciling suffering and injustice with a benevolent God was the hardest part.

"It's possible. I won't lie to you and say it's not. But I don't think it's likely. You're a good person, Nathalie. You've earned it. And I'm going to pray for your safe and easy transition every day until it happens."

"Thank you." Nathalie chuckled. "I'm not a big time believer like you, but for some reason it makes me feel better knowing you're praying for me."

Eva nodded.

Nathalie reached for another piece of bread. "How are things going with Bhathian?"

"We are good."

"Any plans for moving in together?"

Eva shook her head. "I don't see the need. We see each other almost every day anyway."

Nathalie tore a little chunk off the piece of bread and

dipped it in the oil. "It could save time on the drive back and forth."

"Bhathian works in the keep and needs to be there every day. He'll have to drive back and forth anyway."

Nathalie didn't eat the small chunk. Instead, she tore another one. "I think you're scared. That's why you're keeping your distance and cling to your old ways."

It was on the tip of Eva's tongue to deny it and say she was scared of nothing, but it wouldn't be true. Not entirely. She wouldn't call it scared, though. Cautious was a better word.

"I don't want to rush into anything I may regret later. It is much easier to make a clean break when you don't share a home. Trust me, I know. When I divorced Fernando, I walked away with nothing but my clothes."

A sad smile tugged at the corners of Nathalie's lips. "There wasn't much to take."

"That's why I didn't. Luckily, I had my government pension to live on."

Looking down at the piece of bread in her hand, Nathalie nodded. "What happened? Why did you leave? You ran years after the divorce, so that wasn't the reason."

Eva had dreaded the day Nathalie would ask that question again. It had been easier to be elusive about it when Nathalie was a teenager, but now that she was a grown woman with a family of her own, Eva would have to do better.

"Fernando and I weren't a good match. I was not what he needed."

Nathalie pinned her with a hard stare. "How can you say that? He loved you. He still does. In his confused mind, you guys are still married."

Looking into her daughter's big brown eyes, Eva sighed. Nathalie wouldn't let her off the hook until she spilled it.

"If he loved me so much, he wouldn't have cheated on me." And there it was. The cat was out of the bag.

Nathalie nodded. "From the bits and pieces you and he threw around, I gathered that much. But I still find it unbelievable. Let's face it, you're supermodel gorgeous, while Papi is, and was even then, a bald, overweight, average-looking man. Why on earth would he cheat on you? And he loved you. I'm sure of that."

"Looks are not everything, Nathalie, although I'm sure Fernando was so blindsided by it that he failed to notice the other stuff."

"What stuff?"

The conversation halted as the waitress arrived with their order, mother and daughter staring each other down as they waited for the girl to depart.

Eva shifted in her chair. "Fernando had a great personality. He was a happy kind of guy, charming, talkative. He loved people, and they loved him back. I, on the other hand, was the opposite. Still am. People don't change much. I'm gloomy, being around people tires me, and I prefer solitude. He loved to show me off and boast that he'd snagged a pretty wife, but he didn't like spending too much time with me."

The realization was new. If not for that psychology book, Eva would've never thought of that as an issue. But it was spot on. On the scale of happiness, Fernando was a nine while she was a five, maybe even a four, and in that regard, Bhathian and she were much better matched.

Nathalie shook her head. "But he loved you nonetheless. How could he have done it to the woman he loved?"

Eva sighed. "You've worked with him, you've seen how he was with women. Always charming, always flirting. You were too young and too blinded by your adoration of him to realize that it wasn't as innocent as it looked. The conquests stroked his ego, uplifting him whereas I depressed him. I'm not excusing his behavior; God knows how much anger I've carried around throughout the years because of him. But I'm starting to understand why."

Nathalie fiddled with the salad, moving the greens around to coat them with the dressing even though they were thoroughly and uniformly covered. "No wonder you are afraid to take things to the next step with Bhathian. Especially since your history with him wasn't all rainbows and unicorns either."

Eva pulled the salad bowl away from Nathalie and loaded her plate with half of it, then pushed it back. "A smart person learns from past mistakes."

"Still, sometimes you have to take a chance. Bhathian had no choice then but to let you go, just like you had no choice but to run. I was angry at you for leaving me too. It wasn't easy for me, especially when Fernando got sick and I had to step up and take over running the café while taking care of him. But when I understood your reasons, I let it go. What would be the point of having you back in my life and still resenting you? Right? I love you, and I'm happy to have my mom back."

Tears of regret pooled in the corners of Eva's eyes. "I'm so sorry you had to leave college and shoulder all of it alone."

Nathalie shrugged. "No harm done. It made me who I am. I know that I'm strong. I know that I'm capable and that no matter what life throws at me I can handle it. No college could've taught me that."

CHAPTER 48: ANDREW

"Hi, sweetheart." Andrew took the shopping bags from Nathalie. "I see that the hunt was successful." He pretended to weigh the bags hanging from both his hands.

"It was. My mom is a pro. A very opinionated pro, but I can't complain. That's why I asked her to take me shopping. I need some style in my wardrobe."

"Did you eat?"

Nathalie sat in one of the armchairs and propped her legs on the ottoman. "We had lunch. I'm so tired, though. Shopping is exhausting."

Andrew glanced at the bags and frowned. They were all from one store. It didn't seem as if Nathalie and Eva had scoured the mall from one end to another. Or maybe they had but found what they were looking for only in that one store.

"Did you do a lot of walking?"

"Not really. We bought everything at Nordstrom, which by the way put a significant hole in our bank account. But the picking out and the trying on, over and over again, was tiring. The good news is that I'm good for a while. There is a whole new wardrobe in there that Eva deems appropriate. She called my other clothes schmattes."

"What's that?"

"Rags in Yiddish. She used to live in New York. They have a whole lexicon of those."

"Schmattes," Andrew repeated to taste the word on his tongue. "Yeah, it has an oomph to it that rags lack. More contemptuous."

"Right? I thought so too."

Andrew sat on the ottoman, took one of Nathalie's feet in his hands, and started kneading. "It sounds like you had a good time."

"I did. We talked, and I got her to tell me the reason she divorced Fernando. You were right. He cheated on her."

Andrew smirked. "I'm always right, except for when I'm not."

A small smile tugged at Nathalie's lips. "That feels wonderful. You have magic hands." She closed her eyes and let her head drop back on the pillow.

Nathalie didn't seem overly upset about confirming her adoptive father's infidelity. Andrew switched to the other foot and kept kneading. Come to think of it, she rarely referred to him as Papi or Dad anymore. Only when talking to him directly. It made sense though. Whenever she said father, it wasn't clear if she was referring to Fernando or Bhathian.

A moment later her breathing got slower and deeper. Gently, Andrew put her foot down, got up, and snagged the blanket they kept on the couch. He was about to cover her when it occurred to him that she would be more comfortable in bed.

As carefully as he could, Andrew snaked his arms under Nathalie and lifted her up. She muttered something incoherent and snuggled closer, tucking her hands between their bodies.

She felt so soft and so warm that Andrew was torn between letting her rest and undressing her and continuing the massage in a more intimate setting.

Fernando was watching his shows in his room, and Andrew had been hoping for a quickie with his wife before they had to pick up Phoenix from Syssi's.

Maybe he could wake Nathalie up with some kisses?

In their bedroom, he laid her out on the bed and stretched out next to her. She must've been very tired to fall asleep in the chair and then keep on sleeping when he'd picked her up and carried her to their room.

But she was pouting in her sleep, and her lips looked so plump that he couldn't help himself. Just one little kiss and if it didn't wake her up he'd let her sleep and go pick up Phoenix from his sister's.

Slowly, he got closer and touched his lips to Nathalie's.

Andrew frowned. Were they hotter than usual? He kissed her again, this time letting his lips linger. They were definitely hot.

His palm on her forehead confirmed his suspicion. Nathalie was burning up. Panic seizing him, he shook her shoulder. "Nathalie, wake up, baby."

Her eyelids fluttered open. "Is Phoenix crying?"

"No, Phoenix is fine. You're burning hot. I'm worried."

"That's nice." She patted his arm and closed her eyes.

He shook her again. "You need to stay awake."

"Why? If I'm sick, sleep will do me good. Go away." She closed her eyes and pushed at his chest.

He couldn't let her sleep, what if she slipped into unconsciousness? He shook her again. "What if you're transitioning?"

Nathalie's eyes popped open. "I am? Good, it's about time.

I can sleep longer." She closed her eyes again.

The fever was obviously messing with Nathalie's mind. But it seemed that unless he dropped a bucket of ice on her, he wasn't going to keep her awake.

Should he do it?

What if it made things worse for her?

Why was he asking himself questions he should be asking a doctor?

Andrew bolted out of bed and ran to the living room where he left his cell phone. "Bridget," he said as soon as the doctor answered. "Nathalie has a fever, like in burning hot. What do I do? She wants to sleep, and I can't keep her awake."

"I'm on my way."

"Thank you."

He went back to watch over Nathalie and called Syssi from the bedroom.

"What's up, Daddy?" She answered in a cheerful voice that meant she was holding Phoenix.

"I'm afraid you'll have to babysit even longer. Nathalie came back with a fever. Bridget is on her way up."

There was a moment of silence. "Of course, no problem. Do you think it's the transition? Mine started with a fever, also after a shopping trip."

"I think so. Nathalie doesn't get sick often." He frowned. "In fact, I don't remember her ever being sick since I've met her."

"Oh my God, Andrew, it's starting."

"Oh my God, is right." Andrew raked his fingers through his short hair. "What do I do?"

"Hang on. That's the only thing you can do. Don't worry about a thing. I'll stay home with Phoenix and send Okidu to buy more diapers and formula."

"Don't be silly. We have enough to last a month. Send him

over here. The door is never locked." With all the security measures the keep employed there was no need to lock doors.

"Fine." There was another silent moment when neither of them knew what to say but was loath to hang up. Syssi spoke first. "I know it's scary. After watching you unconscious for days I know exactly how it feels. But don't worry. Nathalie is going to be fine. She is strong, inside and out, and she'll fight for you and for Phoenix. She's a survivor."

"Keep your fingers crossed, just not while holding my daughter."

She laughed. "You got it."

"I hear Bridget at the door. I have to go." He strode out of the bedroom with the phone in hand.

"Good luck, Andrew."

"Thanks." He ended the call, shoved the phone in his back pocket, and opened the door for Bridget at the same time.

"Lead the way, Andrew." Bridget was all business.

In the bedroom, she opened her doctor's bag and started taking Nathalie's vitals.

"Hi, Bridget," Nathalie mumbled. "Would you like some tea?"

"No, thank you." Bridget wrapped the blood pressure cuff around Nathalie's arm.

Nathalie kept mumbling nonsense throughout the exam. Had he done the same? Andrew couldn't remember. His memories of the transition were foggy at best.

Bridget finished and returned her tools to her bag. "Same symptoms as you and Syssi and Michael. Except the mumbling, that is. None of you did it."

Andrew smoothed a lock of hair away from Nathalie's face. "Could it be the flu, or a cold?"

Bridget shrugged. "Always possible. The first symptoms are the same. But I don't think it is. Since I've known

Nathalie, she hasn't been sick even once. Pregnancy is not sickness."

"That's what I thought. What do we do now?"

"I'll send Hildegard with the gurney. I trust you can handle the transfer. If she has a comfortable, light nightgown, help her put it on and bring another one in case she sweats through it. People feel better wearing their own clothes rather than a hospital Johnny."

To his shame and utter embarrassment, Andrew got hard imagining his Nathalie in a hospital Johnny, her beautiful ass peeking between the ties. Damn, he needed Bridget to leave. Quickly. "I'll do it right away."

That had done the trick, and Bridget lifted her doctor's bag. "See you both in the clinic." She turned on her heel and left.

Andrew went inside their spacious walk-in-closet and started collecting stuff. Nathalie didn't own any nightgowns. If she slept in anything at all, it was a long T-shirt. He smiled at the designs as he packed them into one of the paper bags he'd emptied. He chose the least childish looking one to put on her. It was blue with white stars and crescent moons printed on it.

For some reason, the design reminded him that he needed to call another babysitter for Fernando. It wasn't night yet, and the guy would need someone to heat up dinner for him and make sure he didn't set the kitchen on fire.

William was the obvious choice since the guy spent so much time with Nathalie's father, but Andrew didn't want to impose. He called Anandur instead.

"No problem. I'll be there in a minute."

The news must've traveled ahead of them, courtesy of Anandur no doubt, because when Andrew wheeled the gurney out of the elevator, there was already a crowd waiting for him and Nathalie in the hallway.

Murmurs of "Good luck" followed him until the door to Bridget's clinic closed behind them.

"Room number one, as always." Bridget pointed to where his transition had happened, and Syssi's before him. From what Andrew had heard, Michael had transitioned so easily, he hadn't even been feverish.

As he lifted Nathalie from the gurney, she opened her eyes again and glanced around. "Why are we in the clinic?"

He laid her down on the hospital bed and covered her with a blanket. "Because you're transitioning, baby. Bridget is going to keep an eye on you."

Nathalie smiled. "About time. Can you get me some water? I'm dying of thirst."

The word dying made him cringe. Not something he wanted to hear while his wife lay in a hospital bed. "Coming right up."

As a veteran of that same room, Andrew knew where everything was. He pulled out a cup and filled it up with water from the tap, which was fine because the keep had its own filtration system and the water coming out of the faucet was top quality. The straw went in next.

He put his foot on the pedal that lifted the bed's back, bringing Nathalie to a semi-reclining position. "Here you go, sweetheart."

Bridget knocked on the open door and walked in. "How are you feeling, Nathalie?"

"Tired, hot, sweaty."

Bridget seemed satisfied with the answer. "I'm glad you're coherent. Let me check your fever again."

The result was the same. A hundred and two.

After Bridget had hooked her up to the monitoring equipment, Nathalie fell asleep again. Bridget told him to nudge her every half an hour or so and see if she responded.

After Nathalie had mumbled the last time Andrew had

done it, telling him to go away and let her sleep, he felt it was safe to leave her by herself for a few minutes and provide an update to everyone in the corridor.

The same routine he had done only seven weeks ago when Phoenix was born.

Andrew was surprised to see Kian standing next to Onegus, waiting to hear the news like everyone else.

"She is sleeping, but conscious." That was all he had to tell them.

Kian approached Andrew and in a rare expression of warmth wrapped an arm around his shoulders. "Don't worry about a thing. Everything is taken care of. I called Bhathian. He and Eva should arrive shortly. Phoenix is doing great, happy as can be with Syssi and Kri making fools of themselves to amuse her. Anandur fed Fernando and is watching a movie with him. Anything else you need done?"

That was Kian, a take-charge kind of guy, and the best brother-in-law a man could hope for. Andrew couldn't have hoped for a better support system.

"Just one thing but it's a big one."

"Anything."

"Is there any chance Annani would come and bless Nathalie the same as she did for me?"

"I'll call and ask her. But you know it will take hours before she can get here."

"I know. But the transition takes time. Syssi was out for twenty-four hours and I was out for days."

Kian clapped him on the back. "Everyone is different. You never know, Nathalie could wake up tomorrow as an immortal."

"From your mouth to God's ear." Andrew shook his head. It wasn't like him to say such things, but as the saying went, there are no atheists in a foxhole.

CHAPTER 49: NATHALIE

*N*athalie had the strangest dream. She was dancing in a lush meadow with Sage a.k.a Mark. They were celebrating, but she didn't know what. It didn't matter, seeing Mark happy was good.

Then it dawned on her. She was actually seeing him, not only hearing his voice in her head. How was it possible? She'd never seen any of her ghosts before…

Panic seized her by the throat and she pulled her hands out of his. "I'm dead, aren't I? My daughter is an orphan and my husband is a widower because I died."

Mark's expression turned into a mask of horror, confirming her suspicion.

"No! No, no! You're not dead, Nathalie. You're still sleeping. I found a way to let you see me, that's all. I'm so sorry that I scared you."

She narrowed her eyes at him. "Are you lying to me? Because it's very bad for a ghost to lie. You will not be allowed to enter heaven."

"Open your eyes, Nathalie. Wake up, girl!" He snapped his fingers in front of her nose. "Wake up! Right now!"

Nathalie's eyes popped open, and she bolted upright. Her heart was racing, and she was sweaty all over, her nightshirt clinging to her body. The room was dark other than the ghostly blue light cast by the monitoring equipment that reminded her where she was.

Next to her, Andrew was sitting on a chair, his body slumped forward and his head resting on his folded arms on her hospital bed, snoring. Nathalie exhaled in relief and lay back down, letting the familiar humming and beeping of the machines soothe her rattled nerves.

How come no one came to check up on her when her heart monitor went wild? Was no one out there? And Andrew, how come he hadn't woken up from the noise?

An absurd thought flitted through her head that she was like Sleeping Beauty but in reverse. Everyone was sleeping, and she was the only one awake. Or maybe this was a dream within a dream, and she just dreamt that she'd woken up and was still sleeping. Like the stupid bathroom dreams when she needed to pee and dreamt of going to the bathroom and then coming back to bed but still needing to pee.

Was Andrew snoring like a broken blender part of the dream? It sounded too real.

One way to find out. "Andrew, honey, wake up." She nudged his arm.

He lifted his head, looking confused. "Did I wake you up with my snoring again?"

That must've been what had done it. "Maybe. Can you pinch me? I don't know if this is real or if I'm dreaming."

"How about a kiss?"

Nathalie smiled. Her Andrew had a one-track mind. "No. A kiss could be part of a dream too."

"As you wish." He snaked a hand under the blanket and pinched her thigh.

"Ouch! That's enough. I'm convinced I'm not dreaming."

A knock sounded on the door, and a moment later Bridget walked in. "I heard you guys talking. Good morning. Can I turn up the lights a bit?"

"Sure." Reflexively, Nathalie tucked the blanket around her exposed thighs.

Bridget turned on a soft light and walked over to her. "How are you feeling?"

Nathalie took a second to assess her body. "Other than the fever, I feel fine. And I don't think it's as bad as it was yesterday."

Bridget whipped out her thermometer and pushed the tip inside Nathalie's ear.

"Ninety-nine point two. The fever went down."

She walked over to the monitors and looked at the history. "I see a spike in heart rate. What happened? A bad dream?"

"You can say that. I thought I was dead."

Andrew gasped. "Don't say things like that."

"I dreamt of Sage, a.k.a Mark. That's why. But he told me to wake up and I did. But with a start."

Bridget looked uncomfortable. "I'm sorry I wasn't here when it happened. I sent Hildegard to get us breakfast, but I had to use the bathroom. It must've happened at that exact time."

"Everything is fine, so no harm done. Are you going to test and see if I transitioned?"

Bridget smiled indulgently. "It's too early. I admit that yours is progressing at a different pace, but if you're still feverish, it means you're not there yet."

"Are you sure? Because I feel different. I can read the letters on that pack of bandages over there." She pointed. "I'm pretty sure I could not have done it before."

Bridget and Andrew both glanced at what she was pointing at, then at one another.

"Those are very small letters," Andrew said.

Bridget nodded. "But if I make a cut and it doesn't heal right away it's going to hurt."

Nathalie lifted her arm. "Do it over here." She pointed at the fleshy part of her upper arm. "This spot is less sensitive than my palm."

"You sure?" Bridget regarded her with a doubtful expression on her face.

"Sure as can be. Cut away, doctor." She held her arm out.

Bridget shook her head. "Give me a moment to collect what I need."

Andrew clasped her hand. "I think it's too early as well. And I don't want you to be disappointed if I'm right."

Nathalie gave his hand a light squeeze. "I'm a big girl, Andrew, and I can handle a little disappointment. But I can't handle not knowing. I'll probably have many more cuts until they all start healing. I don't care. I want to know as soon as possible."

Bridget returned with a small tray with all the things necessary for the test. "Ready?"

Nathalie nodded and offered her arm. Blood and pain didn't scare her, not after going through the difficult recovery from the cesarean.

To Bridget's credit, once the final okay was given, she didn't hesitate, swiftly making the small cut and immediately covering it with a medical gauze pad.

"Take it off," Nathalie commanded. "I want to see."

With a grimace, Bridget dabbed at the wound a couple of times to absorb the blood, then dropped the pad on her tray.

The three of them trained their eyes on the thin red line that was thickening by the second as the wound kept bleeding.

Bridget sighed and tore up another packet of gauze,

pulling out the pad and dabbing at the cut to absorb the new blood. "As I thought. You're not done yet."

Nathalie wasn't ready to give up. "Give it another moment."

"I can't believe it," Andrew whispered. "It's closing. Look, Bridget, the skin is knitting itself up."

"I'll be damned." Bridget shook her head, then offered Nathalie her hand. "Welcome to immortality, Nathalie."

Smiling from ear to ear Nathalie shook the doctor's hand with newfound vigor. "Thank you."

Andrew still looked dazed.

"Come here and kiss me, Andrew. My first kiss as an immortal."

That seemed to shake him out of his stupor and a big grin split his face. "Why do I have a feeling that my bossy wife has gotten even bossier?" He climbed on the bed with her, and Bridget made a hasty retreat, closing the door behind her.

Then her husband kissed her, just as she had demanded.

CHAPTER 50: BHATHIAN

*B*hathian glanced at Eva who was sleeping propped on his shoulder. The waiting room was the same one they'd used while waiting for Phoenix's arrival. The difference was that this time they were alone. Syssi was up in her penthouse looking after the baby, Amanda was at work, and the corridor outside was empty of people anxiously awaiting news of Nathalie's progress.

The reason being that thanks to the merciful Fates, Nathalie had already transitioned. Other than Michael's, her transition had been the easiest. She'd gotten a fever, gone to sleep, and woken up an immortal the next morning.

What a blessing. Last night, driving from Eva's home to the keep, they were both going out of their minds with worry. Whereas delivering a baby was relatively safe, transitioning wasn't; not at Nathalie's age.

The door opened and Andrew stepped out, just like last time but with no baby in his arms. "You guys should go home and get some sleep."

Eva lifted her head off Bhathian's shoulder. "How is she doing, can I see her?"

"If you wish. But she's fallen asleep again. Bridget says it's good for her to sleep as much as possible. The body regenerates best when at rest."

"Then I won't disturb her. When will she be allowed to go home?"

"When the fever is gone. Bridget wants to keep an eye on her until then. Syssi and I were unconscious throughout that stage, and once we woke up, the fever was gone. Nathalie is doing it while conscious."

The door opened again and Bridget stepped out. "Good morning, Mommy and Daddy. Your baby is doing fine. Extraordinarily so. I always knew Nathalie was made of strong stuff."

Andrew rubbed a hand over his stubble-covered jaw. "I feel a little emasculated here."

Bridget laughed and punched his shoulder. "Get over it. Women are tougher than men. That's just a fact you need to learn to live with."

"You've got it, sister." Eva offered her hand in a high five, and Bridget slapped it.

Bhathian was smart enough not to comment. But it got him thinking. Syssi and Andrew had hovered between life and death while transitioning. The situation had been so dire that Annani had flown over to give them her blessing.

This time, when Annani had boarded her plane, it had been all over and Kian had called her to turn around.

"Can I ask you something, Bridget?"

"Sure." She sat in a chair across from Eva and him.

"Michael's easy transition can be explained by his youth, as can Eva's. She was even younger than Michael when she met the immortal male who induced her transition. But Nathalie was older than Syssi and still transitioned just as easily as the other two."

Bridget lifted her hands and shrugged. "I wish I could tell

you why. But I don't know. I guess each person is different and it's not as age dependent as we thought, or not completely. Nathalie is still young. Syssi and Andrew are brother and sister and their genetic makeup is similar, which might explain why both had a hard time."

For a moment he contemplated the possibility that it had been Kalugal's potent immortal genetics that had made Eva's transition easy. His mother was no doubt an immortal that Navuh had kept since the very beginning. Very close to the source. But then Syssi and Andrew had been turned by Kian who was even closer, and Michael was turned by Yamanu who was very old but not that old.

"What if both mother and father are immortals? Will their Dormant child's transition go easier?"

Bridget nodded. "It would make sense. I can ask Annani. She should remember that."

"What about that child's child? Will she or he be considered closer to the source?"

"I have no idea."

"What if a child is born to an immortal female, who wasn't turned at a young age? Will that child have as much difficulty transitioning as an adult as a Dormant who's the product of generations of other Dormants?"

Bridget frowned. "What's going through your head, Bhathian? Where are you leading with these questions?"

He wasn't sure himself. There was a thread of thought he was trying to get a grasp on but it eluded him, and talking it out seemed to help.

"Eva's immortal was Navuh's son."

An audible gasp sounded, and Bridget's intelligent eyes peeled wide. "What? How?"

Bhathian had been sure news about the discovery had traveled throughout the keep. The only ones who'd known about it were Eva and him, Robert, Amanda and Dalhu, Kian and Syssi. That was quite a few. How was it possible none of them had told anyone? Usually, gossip spread through the keep like wildfire.

"I'm surprised you don't know. Apparently some people are not as gossipy as others."

Bridget grimaced. "It's possible everyone knows but me. For some reason, gossip skips over my clinic while it spreads everywhere else. Please tell me how the heck that could've happened."

"I've done some digging, and apparently one of Navuh's sons gave his father the slip during WWII. He and his platoon were presumed dead, when in reality they deserted and are probably hiding somewhere in the U.S. Robert described him to a forensic artist who drew his portrait. Eva recognized him."

Bridget put her elbows on her knees and leaned forward. "That's fascinating information on many levels, but not really relevant to what we are discussing. As a close descendant of the gods, Kalugal's venom was more potent which could explain Eva's easy transition. But Nathalie was turned by Andrew. We have no reason to think he is one too."

Andrew stretched his head. "No offense, doctor, but I'm not sure you're right. While I was battling with my sexual urges during Nathalie's last trimester, I talked with a few of the guys, and it seemed to me that those who are further away from the source have more control. Some are nearly at the level of average human males."

Bridget didn't look happy about Andrew challenging her opinion. "You were also a newly transitioned male. It's like going through puberty again."

Andrew's chest deflated and he sat down next to the doctor. "Yeah, you're right. That could explain it too."

Bridget waved her hand in a circular motion. "Please continue, Bhathian."

"What I'm trying to say is that maybe these Doomers managed to accidentally turn more Dormants. And we might have done so unknowingly as well. Maybe Eva's case is not as isolated as we all thought, and there are more immortal females out there who have no idea what happened to them and are running and hiding just as Eva did. Those women could have Dormant children who transition better as adults."

As the wheels in Bridget's brain processed the information, her eyes began to glow. "If we research Michael and Eva's family trees, we may find an immortal female ancestor."

CHAPTER 51: EVA

"How are you feeling, sweetheart?" Eva tucked an errant lock of hair behind Nathalie's ear.

"Physically, I can barely drag myself to the bathroom. Mentally, I can walk on water. Thank you for praying for me. Apparently your prayer was heard."

Eva smiled and leaned to kiss Nathalie's forehead. "I have a feeling it had more to do with you, my amazing and strong daughter, than any praying I've done."

Nathalie beamed at the compliment. "I'm grateful for how unbelievably easy it went." She pushed more of her long hair behind her ears. "Can you do me a favor and braid my hair? It's all over the place."

A wave of nostalgia washed over Eva. It had been one of her favorite things to do when Nathalie was little. Once in the morning and again at night.

"I would love to. One braid or two?"

"Two. With Bridget insisting on keeping me in bed, it will be more comfortable." Nathalie leaned closer and whispered, "I think it's payback for me snatching Andrew from her. Did

I tell you that they had a thing?" Nathalie parted her hair into two sections.

"Before he met you, I hope."

"He broke up with her for me."

"Ouch," Eva said, finger combing one side. "Do you have a brush I can use?"

"Andrew forgot to bring it."

Eva parted one side into three sections. "I'll remind him to bring it." Andrew had gone to check on his daughter, and Bridget had taken a break to catch a nap, leaving her phone number with Eva in case she was needed back. "Isn't it awkward for you to be treated by Andrew's ex?"

"A little. But she is awesome. I wouldn't trade her for any other doctor. My only problem is my jealousy. It comes in waves, out of the blue. I know it's stupid, and I know Andrew loves me, and still that jealous monster inside my head keeps popping up."

Eva finished one braid and got up to search for rubber bands. "Insecurities will do that to you. They have a way of creeping up unexpectedly."

Nathalie snorted. "You don't have any insecurities."

Eva lifted a brow. "Oh, really?" She found what she was looking for in one of the drawers and returned to Nathalie's side. "You said yourself that I'm afraid of taking things with Bhathian to the next step." She secured the braid and moved to Nathalie's other side.

"That's not the same as having insecurities. You're the most composed woman I know, other than Amanda, that is. And Annani. But then one is a goddess, and the other is her daughter, so of course they are confident."

"But the root of it is the same. Fear is keeping me stuck in one place instead of going forward." Eva finished the second braid and leaned back to look at her work. "You look cute."

Nathalie pouted. "The look I'm going for is sexy, not cute."

"Did someone say cute and sexy in the same sentence?" Andrew walked in with a paper bag in hand. "They must've been talking about my wife." He crossed the room, and as if his mother-in-law wasn't there watching planted a kiss on Nathalie's lips. "I brought the hairbrush, but I see you managed without. You look adorable."

"And sexy?"

"Incredibly."

Eva's heart warmed at the easygoing banter between Andrew and Nathalie. On the scale of innate happiness, they were perfectly matched. Both were upbeat, happy people.

She got up and collected her purse. "I'd better leave you alone." She leaned and kissed Nathalie's cheek.

"You don't have to go, Mom. We are just joking around." There wasn't much conviction in Nathalie's tone. She wanted to be alone with her husband.

"I do. I still have tons of things I need to take care of today, and I'm running out of steam. I only had one hour of sleep last night."

Nathalie caught her hand. "I love you, Mom."

God. How long had it been since she'd heard these words? Too long. She turned back and embraced her daughter. "I love you more than anything in the world, my Nathalie." Eva kissed her again then bolted out of the room to hide the tears she could no longer stop from spilling.

In the corridor, she leaned against the wall, pulled a handkerchief from her purse, and dabbed at her watery eyes. Damn, she wasn't an emotional woman. What was wrong with her?

Heaving a shuddering sigh, she returned the handkerchief to its place and pulled out her phone. "I'm ready to go. Can you take me home?"

"Are you still at the clinic?"

"I just stepped out. I'll wait for you by the car."

"I'll meet you there."

She should've taken a taxi or an Uber instead of bothering Bhathian. He had work to do that she was interrupting. But it had been a knee-jerk reflex to call him.

I'm starting to behave like a wife.

Depending on a man for things she could've easily taken care of herself was a bad sign. It was a slippery slope. Today it was a ride home, tomorrow it would be something more consequential, until one day she couldn't imagine living without him.

Not a good place to be in.

Pressing the elevator button, she pulled out her phone again. "Bhathian, you don't need to take me. I'm going to use an Uber."

"I'm already in the car. Stop talking nonsense." He disconnected, not giving her a chance to argue.

Ugh, stubborn man.

As she got to the car Eva was puffing and huffing, not because she'd run, but because her ire had risen to a boiling point. She pulled the passenger door open and glared at Bhathian. "Don't you ever shut me up like that."

He frowned, both thick brows creating a villainous triangle shape. "What the hell are you talking about?"

"Don't play dumb, Bhathian. You disconnected the call before I could argue with you about this." She waved a hand at his SUV.

If ever a man looked lost for words it was Bhathian at that moment. She almost felt sorry for the guy. Almost.

"I'm sorry. Are you really mad about that? I didn't think it was such a big deal. I want to take you home. I don't want you to take a fucking Uber. Is that such a horrible crime that you're ready to tear me a new ass for it?" His own temper seemed to be gaining momentum, and Eva realized they were both overreacting.

Big time.

Eva climbed up to the passenger seat and closed the door. "No, it's not. I blame lack of sleep and stress."

"Apology accepted."

She turned her head and pinned him with a stare she knew was deadly. "Are you kidding me? That wasn't an apology. That was me acting mature and diffusing the situation."

Bhathian shook his head. "I'd better shut up before I dig a deeper hole for myself." He turned on the engine and eased out of the parking spot.

The silence continued throughout the rest of the ride, turning the air inside the cabin stifling. Eva opened the window and let the cool morning air brush over her face. It had been a stupid fight over nothing, and she'd started it.

It was on her to make it better.

Did she want to, though?

She and Bhathian had reached an impasse, or rather a crossroads. It was time to choose whether she wanted to move forward or part ways. They were both too old for playing the boyfriend-girlfriend game, especially since they had a grown daughter and a granddaughter.

In all honesty, letting go of Bhathian was like self-inflicting a wound for no good reason. There was no upside to it, just downside. The two of them fit well together. The only thing keeping her stuck in neutral was fear.

The fear of failure.

Eva's relationship record wasn't good. She'd tried her best with Fernando, but her best hadn't been good enough. What reason had she to believe it would be better this time?

Neither she nor Bhathian were easy people. How would they make it work?

But there was no other choice. If she didn't want to let him go, she needed to take a chance.

Bhathian parked the car next to her rented house and got out to open the door for her, but she beat him to it. He frowned like he always did when she didn't wait for him, but smartly he said nothing.

"Would you like to come in?" she asked.

"Are you going to yell at me?"

She chuckled. "I'm done. But we need to talk."

CHAPTER 52: BHATHIAN

e need to talk.

Was that it? Was Eva ending things with him because of one little spat over nothing?

She could try, but he wasn't going to let her. Whatever storm was raging in her head, he would calm it down. And if nothing else worked, he would take her to bed. That always seemed to put her in a better mood.

"Where is everyone?" Bhathian looked around the living room where Eva's crew usually hung out in front of the dumb tube.

"It's morning." She headed toward the kitchen. "They are working. Nick is installing listening devices in an office downtown, while Sharon is researching the firm's background. Tessa is in the office." Eva opened the fridge and started pulling things out. Two kinds of bread, several kinds of cheeses, a package of cold cuts, mayo and mustard.

Bhathian poured two tall cups of water from the dispenser and put them on the table, then brought over paper plates, plastic forks and knives, and napkins.

"I'm going to tell Tessa we are here. I'll be back in a

moment." Eva ducked into the small corridor leading to the office.

Bhathian started making a sandwich, first spreading mayo and mustard on the bread slices then adding layers of cold cuts. Cheese wasn't his thing.

Eva came back and sat on the other side of the small kitchen table.

"Can you tell me already what it's all about? I hope it's not over the ride home."

"It's not."

She pushed the left side of her hair behind her ear, then started playing with the curling ends. It wasn't like her. Eva had no nervous ticks. She was starting to worry him.

"I think you should move in with me."

Boom!

As usual, the woman never did what he'd expected her to. Instead of kicking him out for good, she was inviting him to move in?

It got him suspicious. "Where is this coming from? A few days ago you sent me home because you felt crowded. What's changed?"

She shrugged. "I had an interesting talk with Tessa and another one with Nathalie. It was interesting to hear their perspectives on relationships, and they got me thinking."

He arched a brow. Since when was Eva taking advice from anyone, let alone her assistant and her daughter, people she considered her charges?

"We are stuck in neutral. Not your doing, mine. We can either go forward or backward. Forward means taking the next step in our relationship, backward means parting ways."

He'd be lying if he were to say that her words didn't scare the crap out of him.

"I realized that I care too much for you to let you go, and that my life without you would be much worse than with you. Which left only one direction to choose —forward."

It wasn't a declaration of undying love, or even a heartfelt invitation, but it was an invitation nonetheless. Bhathian had promised himself a long time ago that he would take whatever Eva could offer.

He nodded. "Okay."

A sad smile curled Eva's lips. "I watched Andrew and Nathalie today, how easygoing and lighthearted they are with each other, and I truly wished I could be like them. But I can't help who I am. I'm the glass-half-empty kind of person while they're the glass-half-full kind of people. Do you think you can live with that? I don't want to be anyone's downer."

Bhathian got up and walked over to Eva, lifted her up from her chair, then sat back down with her cradled in his arms. "Do I look like the glass-half-full kind of guy to you? I'm not. I'm like you. Or worse. If you can live with my cloudy disposition, then we are all good. Because to me, you're my shining light. Waking up next to you in the morning brings a smile to my face, and coming home to you is the highlight of my day. You lift me up. You can never bring me down."

Eva let out a sigh and put her head on his chest. "You're my rock, and it scares the shit out of me. I don't want to become dependent on you, but I already am. I expect you to come when I call you, and I expect you to be there when I need you."

Bhathian kissed the top of her head. "Then I must be dependent on you too. Because I expect the same. That's what having a life partner means. Someone who'll always have your back."

"I'm not a naive girl, Bhathian. Nothing is for life. Nothing lasts forever."

"This does. Mates are not the same as husband and wife, it is so much more. The bond we forge is unbreakable."

Eva looked up at him with a pair of glowing amber eyes. "Promise?"

He put his hand over his heart. "I'll do better than that. I'll pledge that I'll always be there for you. Like in your human marriage. I vow to love you and honor you, in sickness and in health—although we don't get sick, so that doesn't apply—in good times and in bad, for richer for poorer, until death do us part—which again doesn't apply since we are immortal."

Eva chuckled. "Do immortals have their special marriage vows?"

Bhathian kissed her forehead. "I have no idea. The two marriage ceremonies I've witnessed Annani perform were so different from each other that I think she makes it up on the spot."

Eva closed her eyes and sighed. "I can't wait to meet her."

Bhathian pressed his forehead to hers. "I know of a sure way to do it. She presides over all marriage ceremonies."

"I'm not ready for that."

"I know. But I'm getting you used to the idea. The more I talk about it the better chance I have of you actually saying yes one day."

Eva looked up at him. "Thank you. For your patience and for your determination and for just being you. Day after day, in a thousand little and big ways, you prove to me that my past does not need to equal my future and that you're a better man than I thought possible. You give me hope."

Her words were both a precious gift and an impossible challenge. He wasn't human, but he wasn't a god either, and even they had been far from infallible. There was no way he wasn't going to disappoint her at some point.

"I'm not perfect, Eva, and I'm going to make mistakes, and

you're going to get mad at me for this or that. All I can promise is to always love you and to try my best. But please don't expect me to never disappoint you because I will."

She kissed the hollow of his neck. "I know that. And your honesty and humility prove to me more than anything that I was right to take a chance on you."

CHAPTER 53: RONI

"*A*re you almost done?" Roni's new handler asked.

"Not even close, Barty. Go get yourself a beer and come back in three hours."

The guy didn't like working overtime. Which was fine with Roni. Those were the perfect hours to work his magic on nongovernment private projects. The ones he was getting all kinds of payments for. Not money, that would have been caught right away, but favors. Like Andrew helping smuggle Sylvia in so they could have a few private moments without his handler hovering over them.

Not to mention sex.

Oh, boy, the sex.

Roni didn't have anyone to compare her to, but Sylvia was a goddess. The things she was teaching him. The things she was making him do. Roni shifted in his huge swivel chair and adjusted himself. Easy to do since he was wearing training pants—his everyday attire since he'd started working out.

Sylvia had liked him even when he was scrawny, but she liked him better with some muscles on. And what the lady liked, he was going to deliver—to the extent of his limited abilities as someone who was under indefinite house arrest.

Fifteen years to be exact.

Three served and twelve to go. The thing was, Roni was pretty sure they weren't going to release him even then. They'd find some trumped-up charge to accuse him with and keep him working for the government, paying him the miserly government wages even though his skills were worth millions. Hell, to the right people he was worth billions.

Roni was the best, and it wasn't arrogance. It was the truth. He'd been one of the best when they'd caught him, but he'd improved by leaps and bounds since.

Glancing at the thick glass separating his private kingdom from the rest of the large office, Roni saw Bart leave. The guy wouldn't be gone long. He always returned early to try and catch Roni doing something he wasn't supposed to. It was so ridiculous that he wanted to howl with laughter. As if Bart had any idea what Roni was doing. He could be coding a hack into the President's private computer, and Bart wouldn't have a clue.

Roni only needed a few minutes to load the flash drive with the software Andrew had given him. It turned out Andrew knew a guy who was as good at programming stuff as Roni was at hacking into it.

The guy had the software, Roni had access to enormous data, it was a match made in heaven. He would've loved to meet the guy in person and share notes.

Matching faces on driver's licenses was simple. The sophistication lay in the facial recognition capabilities of what the guy had designed. Supposedly, it was much better than the crude version the government had. More accurate and faster.

Andrew's objective was to identify licenses with the same pictures but different names. Probably to catch terrorists, which was Andrew's job, but Andrew refused to say. It was highly classified information he couldn't share with Roni.

Still, Roni found it odd that the agent had brought in an outside, unapproved software. It was a big no-no. But Andrew had said it was the best and that he needed it to do the job.

Anything to keep the homeland secure.

Roni didn't really care about the why. Once he delivered the matches, Andrew was going to sneak Sylvia into Roni's apartment and let them spend most of the night together, instead of the hour he'd allowed before when he'd needed a favor.

With Andrew's program running in the background, Roni went back to the work he was actually supposed to do.

Bart returned less than an hour later. "When are you going to be done?"

"I still have a lot to do. Get someone to replace you if you need to go home."

Bart hoisted his pants up and planted his fat ass in his chair. "I'll stay. The overtime pay is worth it." He pulled out his cellphone, a set of wireless earphones, put his feet up on the desk, and started watching what must've been a comedy show since he kept bursting into peals of laughter every couple of minutes or so.

Roni shook his head. Having this guy shadow him was such a waste of government resources. He was doing absolutely nothing.

Four hours later Roni decided to call it a day. Bart had fallen asleep with his feet up on his desk and his head hanging back from his neck, snoring loudly enough to cause an earthquake.

How the guy hadn't been fired for sleeping on the job was a mystery. Everything that happened in every room in this building, except the few that were off limits, was under constant surveillance. Didn't anyone see Bart sleep?

Roni shook his head and checked on Andrew's project. He couldn't leave until that was done. As soon as it was, he was going to download the matches to a flash drive and erase all traces of it ever going through the system.

The timer showed twenty more minutes to go.

Curious, Roni decided to check what the software had found so far. Turning his enormous swivel chair around, so the tall back blocked the monitor he was using from the surveillance camera's view, he started scrolling through the results. The program was almost done, and yet there weren't many matches.

Not really paying attention, he kept going until one caught his eye. Roni stopped scrolling and leaned closer to get a better look, then quickly enlarged it as big as it would go.

"Fucking hell!" He slapped a trembling hand over his mouth and leaned even closer to check the dates.

It can't be. No way!

The end... for now...

Eva & Bhathian's story continues in Book 13
DARK GUARDIAN'S MATE
Click here to Find out what happens next!

Dark Guardian's Mate is available on Amazon

Dear reader,

Thank you for joining me on the continuing adventures of the ***Children of the Gods***.

As an independent author, I rely on your support to spread the word. So if you enjoyed the story, please share your experience, and if it isn't too much trouble, I would greatly appreciate a brief review on Amazon.

Click **HERE** to leave a review for Dark Guardian Craved.

Love & happy reading,

Isabell

SERIES READING ORDER

THE CHILDREN OF THE GODS ORIGINS

1

GODDESS'S CHOICE

When gods and immortals still ruled the ancient world, one young goddess risked everything for love.

2

GODDESS'S HOPE

Hungry for power and infatuated with the beautiful Areana, Navuh plots his father's demise. After all, by getting rid of the insane god he would be doing the world a favor. Except, when gods and immortals conspire against each other, humanity pays the price.

But things are not what they seem, and prophecies should not to be trusted...

THE CHILDREN OF THE GODS

1

DARK STRANGER THE DREAM

Syssi's paranormal foresight lands her a job at Dr. Amanda Dokani's neuroscience lab, but it fails to predict the thrilling yet terrifying turn her life will take. Syssi has no clue that her boss is an immortal who'll drag her into a secret, millennia-old battle over humanity's future. Nor does she realize that the professor's imposing brother is the mysterious stranger who's been starring in her dreams.

Since the dawn of human civilization, two warring factions of near-immortals - the descendants of the gods of old - have been secretly shaping its destiny. Leading the clandestine battle from his luxurious L.A. high-rise, Kian is surrounded by his clan, yet alone. Descending from a single goddess, clan members are forbidden to each other. And as the only other immortals are their hated enemies,

Kian and his kin have been long resigned to a lonely existence of fleeting trysts with human partners. That is, until his sister makes a game-changing discovery - a mortal seeress who she believes is a dormant carrier of their genes. Ever the realist, Kian is skeptical and refuses Amanda's plea to attempt Syssi's activation. But when his enemies learn of the Dormant's existence, he's forced to rush her to the safety of his keep. Inexorably drawn to Syssi, Kian wrestles with his conscience as he is tempted to explore her budding interest in the darker shades of sensuality.

2

DARK STRANGER REVEALED

While sheltered in the clan's stronghold, Syssi is unaware that Kian and Amanda are not human, and neither are the supposedly religious fanatics that are after her. She feels a powerful connection to Kian, and as he introduces her to a world of pleasure she never dared imagine, his dominant sexuality is a revelation. Considering that she's completely out of her element, Syssi feels comfortable and safe letting go with him. That is, until she begins to suspect that all is not as it seems. Piecing the puzzle together, she draws a scary, yet wrong conclusion...

3

DARK STRANGER IMMORTAL

When Kian confesses his true nature, Syssi is not as much shocked by the revelation as she is wounded by what she perceives as his callous plans for her.

If she doesn't turn, he'd be forced to erase her memories and let her go. His family's safety demands secrecy – no one in the mortal world is allowed to know that immortals exist.

Resigned to the cruel reality that even if she stays on to never again leave the keep, she'll get old while Kian wouldn't, Syssi is determined to enjoy what little time she has with him, one day at a time.

Could Kian let go of the mortal woman he loves? Would Syssi turn? And if she does, would she survive the dangerous transition?

4

Dark Enemy Taken

Dalhu can't believe his luck when he stumbles upon the beautiful immortal professor. Presented with a once in a lifetime opportunity to grab an immortal female for himself, he kidnaps her and runs. If he ever gets caught, either by her people or his, his life is forfeit. But for a chance of a loving mate and a family of his own, Dalhu is prepared to do everything in his power to win Amanda's heart, and that includes leaving the Doom brotherhood and his old life behind.

Amanda soon discovers that there is more to the handsome Doomer than his dark past and a hulking, sexy body. But succumbing to her enemy's seduction, or worse, developing feelings for a ruthless killer is out of the question. No man is worth life on the run, not even the one and only immortal male she could claim as her own…

Her clan and her research must come first…

5

Dark Enemy Captive

When the rescue team returns with Amanda and the chained Dalhu to the keep, Amanda is not as thrilled to be back as she thought she'd be. Between Kian's contempt for her and Dalhu's imprisonment, Amanda's budding relationship with Dalhu seems doomed. Things start to look up when Annani offers her help, and together with Syssi they resolve to find a way for Amanda to be with Dalhu. But will she still want him when she realizes that he is responsible for her nephew's murder? Could she? Will she take the easy way out and choose Andrew instead?

6

Dark Enemy Redeemed

Amanda suspects that something fishy is going on onboard the Anna. But when her investigation of the peculiar all-female Russian crew fails to uncover anything other than more speculation, she decides it's time to stop playing detective and face her real problem —a man she shouldn't want but can't live without.

6.5

My Dark Amazon

When Michael and Kri fight off a gang of humans, Michael gets stabbed. The injury to his immortal body recovers fast, but the one to his ego takes longer, putting a strain on his relationship with Kri.

7

DARK WARRIOR MINE

When Andrew is forced to retire from active duty, he believes that all he has to look forward to is a boring desk job. His glory days in special ops are over. But as it turns out, his thrill ride has just begun.

Andrew discovers not only that immortals exist and have been manipulating global affairs since antiquity, but that he and his sister are rare possessors of the immortal genes.

Problem is, Andrew might be too old to attempt the activation process. His sister, who is fourteen years his junior, barely makes it through the transition, so the odds of him coming out of it alive, let alone immortal, are slim.

But fate may force his hand.

Helping a friend find his long-lost daughter, Andrew finds a woman who's worth taking the risk for. Nathalie might be a Dormant, but the only way to find out for sure requires fangs and venom.

8

DARK WARRIOR'S PROMISE

Andrew and Nathalie's love flourishes, but the secrets they keep from each other taint their relationship with doubts and suspicions. In the meantime, Sebastian and his men are getting bolder, and the storm that's brewing will shift the balance of power in the millennia-old conflict between Annani's clan and its enemies.

9

DARK WARRIOR'S DESTINY

The new ghost in Nathalie's head remembers who he was in life, providing Andrew and her with indisputable proof that he is real and not a figment of her imagination.

Convinced that she is a Dormant, Andrew decides to go forward with his transition immediately after the rescue mission at the Doomers' HQ.

Fearing for his life, Nathalie pleads with him to reconsider. She'd rather spend the rest of her mortal days with Andrew than risk what they have for the fickle promise of immortality.

While the clan gets ready for battle, Carol gets help from an unlikely ally. Sebastian's second-in-command can no longer ignore the torment she suffers at the hands of his commander and offers to help her, but only if she agrees to his terms.

10

DARK WARRIOR'S LEGACY

Andrew's acclimation to his post-transition body isn't easy. His senses are sharper, he's bigger, stronger, and hungrier. Nathalie fears that the changes in the man she loves are more than physical. Measuring up to this new version of him is going to be a challenge.

Carol and Robert are disillusioned with each other. They are not destined mates, and love is not on the horizon. When Robert's three months are up, he might be left with nothing to show for his sacrifice.

Lana contacts Anandur with disturbing news; the yacht and its human cargo are in Mexico. Kian must find a way to apprehend Alex and rescue the women on board without causing an international incident.

11

DARK GUARDIAN FOUND

What would you do if you stopped aging?

Eva runs. The ex-DEA agent doesn't know what caused her strange mutation, only that if discovered, she'll be dissected like a lab rat. What Eva doesn't know, though, is that she's a descendant of the gods, and that she is not alone. The man who rocked her world in one life-changing encounter over thirty years ago is an immortal as well.

To keep his people's existence secret, Bhathian was forced to turn his back on the only woman who ever captured his heart, but he's never forgotten and never stopped looking for her.

12

DARK GUARDIAN CRAVED

Cautious after a lifetime of disappointments, Eva is mistrustful of Bhathian's professed feelings of love. She accepts him as a lover and a confidant but not as a life partner.

Jackson suspects that Tessa is his true love mate, but unless she overcomes her fears, he might never find out.

Carol gets an offer she can't refuse—a chance to prove that there is more to her than meets the eye. Robert believes she's about to commit a deadly mistake, but when he tries to dissuade her, she tells him to leave.

13

DARK GUARDIAN'S MATE

Prepare for the heart-warming culmination of Eva and Bhathian's story!

14

DARK ANGEL'S OBSESSION

The cold and stoic warrior is an enigma even to those closest to him. His secrets are about to unravel...

15

DARK ANGEL'S SEDUCTION

Brundar is fighting a losing battle. Calypso is slowly chipping away his icy armor from the outside, while his need for her is melting it from the inside.

He can't allow it to happen. Calypso is a human with none of the Dormant indicators. There is no way he can keep her for more than a few weeks.

16

DARK ANGEL'S SURRENDER

Get ready for the heart pounding conclusion to Brundar and

Calypso's story.

Callie still couldn't wrap her head around it, nor could she summon even a smidgen of sorrow or regret. After all, she had some memories with him that weren't horrible. She should've felt something. But there was nothing, not even shock. Not even horror at what had transpired over the last couple of hours.

Maybe it was a typical response for survivors--feeling euphoric for the simple reason that they were alive. Especially when that survival was nothing short of miraculous.

Brundar's cold hand closed around hers, reminding her that they weren't out of the woods yet. Her injuries were superficial, and the most she had to worry about was some scarring. But, despite his and Anandur's reassurances, Brundar might never walk again.

If he ended up crippled because of her, she would never forgive herself for getting him involved in her crap.

"Are you okay, sweetling? Are you in pain?" Brundar asked.

Her injuries were nothing compared to his, and yet he was concerned about her. God, she loved this man. The thing was, if she told him that, he would run off, or crawl away as was the case.

Hey, maybe this was the perfect opportunity to spring it on him.

17

DARK OPERATIVE: A SHADOW OF DEATH

As a brilliant strategist and the only human entrusted with the secret of immortals' existence, Turner is both an asset and a liability to the clan. His request to attempt transition into immortality as an alternative to cancer treatments cannot be denied without risking the clan's exposure. On the other hand, approving it means risking his premature death. In both scenarios, the clan will lose a valuable ally.

When the decision is left to the clan's physician, Turner makes plans to manipulate her by taking advantage of her interest in him.

Will Bridget fall for the cold, calculated operative? Or will Turner fall into his own trap?

Dark Operative: A Glimmer of Hope

As Turner and Bridget's relationship deepens, living together seems like the right move, but to make it work both need to make concessions.

Bridget is realistic and keeps her expectations low. Turner could never be the truelove mate she yearns for, but he is as good as she's going to get. Other than his emotional limitations, he's perfect in every way.

Turner's hard shell is starting to show cracks. He wants immortality, he wants to be part of the clan, and he wants Bridget, but he doesn't want to cause her pain.

His options are either abandon his quest for immortality and give Bridget his few remaining decades, or abandon Bridget by going for the transition and most likely dying. His rational mind dictates that he chooses the former, but his gut pulls him toward the latter. Which one is he going to trust?

19

Dark Operative: The Dawn of Love

Get ready for the exciting finale of Bridget and Turner's story!

20

Dark Survivor Awakened

his was a strange new world she had awakened to.

Her memory loss must have been catastrophic because almost nothing was familiar. The language was foreign to her, with only a few words bearing some similarity to the language she thought in. Still, a full moon cycle had passed since her awakening, and little by little she was gaining basic understanding of it--only a few words and phrases, but she was learning more each day.

A week or so ago, a little girl on the street had tugged on her mother's sleeve and pointed at her. "Look, Mama, Wonder Woman!"

The mother smiled apologetically, saying something in the language these people spoke, then scurried away with the child looking behind her shoulder and grinning.

When it happened again with another child on the same day, it was settled.

Wonder Woman must have been the name of someone important in this strange world she had awoken to, and since both times it had been said with a smile it must have been a good one.

Wonder had a nice ring to it.

She just wished she knew what it meant.

21

Dark Survivor Echoes of Love

Wonder's journey continues in *Dark Survivor Echoes of Love*.

22

Dark Survivor Reunited

The exciting finale of Wonder and Anandur's story.

23

Dark Widow's Secret

Vivian and her daughter share a powerful telepathic connection, so when Ella can't be reached by conventional or psychic means, her mother fears the worst.

Help arrives from an unexpected source when Vivian gets a call from the young doctor she met at a psychic convention. Turns out Julian belongs to a private organization specializing in retrieving missing girls.

As Julian's clan mobilizes its considerable resources to rescue the daughter, Magnus is charged with keeping the gorgeous young mother safe.

Worry for Ella and the secrets Vivian and Magnus keep from each other should be enough to prevent the sparks of attraction from kindling a blaze of desire. Except, these pesky sparks have a mind of their own.

24

Dark Widow's Curse

A simple rescue operation turns into mission impossible when the

Russian mafia gets involved. Bad things are supposed to come in threes, but in Vivian's case, it seems like there is no limit to bad luck. Her family and everyone who gets close to her is affected by her curse.

Will Magnus and his people prove her wrong?

25

Dark Widow's Blessing

The thrilling finale of the Dark Widow trilogy!

FOR EXCLUSIVE PEEKS

JOIN THE CHILDREN OF THE GODS VIP CLUB
AND GAIN ACCESS TO THE VIP PORTAL AT ITLUCAS.COM
CLICK HERE TO JOIN

INCLUDED IN YOUR FREE MEMBERSHIP:

- **FREE** NARRATION OF GODDESS'S CHOICE—BOOK 1 IN THE CHILDREN OF THE GODS ORIGINS SERIES.
- PREVIEW CHAPTERS.
- AND OTHER EXCLUSIVE CONTENT OFFERED ONLY TO MY VIPS.

41244738R00180

Made in the USA
San Bernardino, CA
01 July 2019